As he walked around the side of the house he prayed his hay fever would not make him sneeze. The thumping of his heart could probably be heard in Basingstoke.

Why should creeping around people's houses have to be done by him, rather than some Hunky Regular hero? Before the class and sexism legislation there had been a popular fictional character called Bond. Now *he* would have known how to deal with situations like this. Someone conventionally macho like him would have fitted the bill far better.

Horatio peered in at the kitchen window by the back door. As he put his hand up to the pane he felt a sudden sharp jab in the small of his back.

'Hands up! If you make any sudden movements I'll put a bullet in you!'

His hands shot up.

'I'm a rambler,' said Horatio, proud of the cover he'd concocted for himself, 'and I'm exercising my Right to Roam.' He was about to turn around and explain about the recent Private Property (Ramblers' Rights) Directive 77/107 when the voice – deep, husky, but he thought a woman's – added: 'The slightest false move and you're dead.'

Andrew Roberts took a First in Modern History at Gonville and Caius College, Cambridge. He writes occasional political commentary for the *Daily Mail*, and book reviews for the *Spectator* and *Literary Review*. His two previous books, *'The Holy Fox': A Biography of Lord Halifax* and *Eminent Churchillians*, were published to critical acclaim. He is now at work on the biography of Victorian Prime Minister, the third Marquess of Salisbury. Andrew Roberts is married to a barrister and lives in Chelsea.

For Camilla

The

AACHEN
MEMORANDUM

★ ★ ★

Andrew Roberts

ORION

An Orion paperback
First published in Great Britain by Weidenfeld & Nicolson in 1995
This paperback edition published in 1996 by Orion Books Ltd,
Orion House, 5 Upper St Martin's Lane, London WC2H 9EA

A CIP catalogue record for this book
is available from the British Library.

ISBN: 0 75280 349 2

Printed and bound in Great Britain by
Clays Ltd, St Ives plc

CONTENTS

PART
I

09.22 Sunday, 2nd May 2045

The first thing Horatio saw on entering the drawing room was the Admiral's corpse lying prostrate on the sofa. He dared to hope death had come naturally, but an indefinable something about the room suggested murder.

As in every crisis of his life, Horatio's first instinct was to panic and run as fast and as far as his asthma would let him. This time, however, he sat down on a chair beside the nearby *escritoire* and breathed deeply five or six times. He took a suck on his Salbutamol inhaler as his huge brain kick-started itself into life.

He was tempted just to retrace his steps and leave by the front door. It took something approaching a full minute of cogitation before he leant over to the fone on the desk and dialled 112. If he *was* being set up for this, he reasoned, that at least might work in his favour.

"Hello? Police? Hello. Listen, I've just found a dead body."

"Who's speaking please?"

"Horatio Lestoq." For once there was no snigger at the absurdity of his name. "That's L-E-S-T-O-Q."

"Please switch on your vid." It was a woman's voice. Efficient. In control. Altogether irritating.

"There doesn't seem to be a screen – it's one of those old-fashioned fones."

"Postcode or g-mail address?"

"Sorry?"

"What is the postcode there?"

"Look," he answered, clearly and slowly, trying hard to suppress a sense of mounting hysteria, "I have just found a dead body, I'm not trying to send a sodding parcel!"

"Please be calm. We need to know where you are."

"No idea of the postcode, I don't live here. But it's a rectory in . . ."

Then he saw writing paper standing in a rack on the desk. "Hang on. Yes . . . yes, here it is. RG2 4RW – Hampshire." There was a pause.

"The Rectory, Ibworth, near Basingstoke?"

"Yes, that's it."

"Police and paramedics will arrive soon. Right now, though, I need some more details." Horatio took another long suck from his inhaler. He hoped he'd brought a refill.

"Name of deceased?"

"I'm fairly sure he's Admiral Michael Ratcliffe."

"You're not certain?"

"I've never met him before. But it's his house."

"Spelt?"

"R-A-T-C-L-I-F-F-E."

"Cause of death?"

"Don't know. He's just lying there. Heart attack?" The moment he said it he knew it was not.

"I.D. number?" Her cool, impersonal tone had definitely got on his nerves now. Perhaps it was also the way she kept omitting the definite article.

4

"How should I know? I'm not going anywhere near it, if that's what you're suggesting."

"Not his. Yours."

"Oh, I see. All right, yes, it's 478 A 34QW." She tapped it onto her modem.

"Checking – 478 A 34QW."

"Yes." There was a millisecond's pause.

"How long has deceased been dead?"

"No idea."

"According to this you're a doctor."

"I'm not that kind of doctor."

"What first aid have you administered?"

"None. The man's dead for God's sake!"

"Are you sure?"

Horatio forced himself to look across at the body. White-haired and crumpled, it hadn't moved a millimetre since he entered the room.

"Yes. Pretty much . . . Yes."

"OK. Stay where you are. Touch nothing. Police will be with you momentarily."

The police . . . *In a moment*, thought Horatio. He later prided himself on having been pedantic even in that crisis.

They arrived far sooner than he'd expected, the sirens audible through the half-open French windows almost immediately after he had replaced the receiver. He glanced around the room, trying to avoid the body, but failing. There was no sign of blood. He thanked God for that. As a child *any* sight of it, let alone his own, had always made him retch. Coming face to face with it now would put him off his food for months. And that would never do.

What was it about the room which alerted him to the

5

possibility of murder? There were the floor-to-ceiling book-shelves, the inevitable naval prints, several silver photograph frames on the piano by the French windows. All very twentieth-century decor. The photos were mostly of a much younger man, presumably Ratcliffe himself, in naval uniform on decks, but there were a couple of a small child and one wedding shot. The groom was also wearing naval uniform, but Horatio did not think it was Ratcliffe. They were arranged carefully in rows, with three gaps. Had some been removed?

Try as he might to avoid it, Horatio's gaze kept swivelling back to the body, which was dressed in the sort of clothes someone might have worn a century ago. Tweeds, cavalry twills, an old cardigan, even the frayed end of an M.C.C. tie was visible. One of the sofa cushions lay over and partly covered what Horatio could see was a well-polished pair of vintage, dark brown brogues.

Looking away again, Horatio's eyes rested upon an even stranger anachronism. On the desk there was a sheet of white blotting paper, set in dark green leather. Otherwise virgin, it was stained at the very bottom by some thin ink marks.

Police autos were speeding up the drive around the other side of the house. He could hear gravel flying. On an impulse, unusual in someone who thought of himself as a congenital coward, Horatio tore off the marked piece of blotting paper – about three centimetres by ten – and crossed the room to the large mirror above the mantelpiece to read what was reflected.

"Mrs Robson," he saw, and, underneath, "your roving godfather," and below that, "Michael." The investigative hack in him got the better of the law-abiding citizen. He folded it in half, put it in his mouth and salivated hard.

"Here!" he shouted, chewing, as the police got to the front door, "first on the left!"

Two armed men burst in. Horatio swallowed.

The first — the one pointing the N-series machine gun — showed no gratitude for Horatio's directions. "On the floor!" he yelled. "Face down! Hands and legs apart!"

Horatio did as he was told. The second man came forward to frisk and then handcuff him. In the police auto he was told that by law he was required to speak and that everything he said would be videoed for certain use against him. He was then driven the four miles to Basingstoke police station, where he was asked to hand over all sharp objects. His cash, pager, watch-fone, I.D. card and belt were also taken, after which he was led away to what they termed the "custody suites".

Horatio did not protest. He decided, for the thousandth time in his twenty-nine years, that discretion would probably be the better part of valour.

Once in the cell he lay on the bed, fingers interlaced behind his head. It was his deep-thought mode. Ignoring the camera in the ceiling, the graffiti and Inmates' Charter on the walls, the all-pervasive stench of urine and the likelihood of catching scabies off the filthy mattress, he put to use the one sharp implement the police could not confiscate.

His brain.

He hadn't got a double-starred first in the logic paper of his Finals for nothing, he told himself. He presumed this would not be a case London would let the local force keep. Assuming C.I.D. used the M3 special lane, and allowing for the fact that police autos were not fitted with speed governors, he probably had an hour. In that time he must work out for himself exactly what was going on.

And for *that*, he must go back to the beginning.

09.12 Saturday, 1st May

The moment he opened his eyes that Saturday morning, Horatio wished he hadn't. He was lying on his side facing the wall, curled up in the foetal position against the coming onslaught. The hangover reminded him of the bombardments in old black-and-white films of the First Nationalist War. Constant, rolling, heavy, booming thuds. Here an H.E. shell, there a landmine. Once again he told himself he really could *not* go on drinking like an undergraduate.

The bedroom wall was about two metres away. It kept coming in and out of focus. The print of All Souls had fallen down over a month ago but he still had not got round to putting it back up. It had been a rather unimaginative present from his mother to celebrate his Prize Fellowship seven years ago. Pretty much the only present she had ever given him, he thought self-pityingly. Then there was the empty space where Leila's photo had been. Not filling it was a kind of tribute to her. Stupid, really. The other gap was where his Paul Johnson watercolour had hung. He'd bought it at Sotheby's in the days when he was flush. That had gone to pay last month's Atlantic Gas bill. His life, he thought, was better summed up by what was missing from that wall than what was on it.

The capacity for recall returned only very gradually. He had the kind of hangover they had used to call a "stonker" at Oxford. He was almost proud of it.

It had been May Day Eve. Marty had given the traditional bash at his flat. Horatio must have put away more units last night than the latest Alcohol Consumption Directive prescribed for a month.

Someone had brought along a case of contraband bourbon. He remembered peeling off one of the "Produce of the United States of Europe" labels on the back of a bottle to read "Made in Kentucky" stamped underneath. Had it been the two Excise men? It wouldn't have surprised him. Especially the sort Marty would know.

That was definitely when disaster had struck. One could hardly turn down genuine American whisky when some brave and enterprising soul had gone to all the trouble of smuggling it over for you.

What had happened though, other than the boozing? He'd been very popular, he thought. And he'd been kissed during a power cut.

By whom?

He remembered chatting up two girls, both pretty glamorous. An American blonde and . . .

Horatio suddenly remembered the rest. He turned over.

She was lying on her side. Head resting in her palm. Looking at him. Smiling. Not the Yank. The other one.

He smiled back, fumbling for the name. Unusual. Ancient world. Bathsheba? Aspasia? Some show-offy name like that anyhow.

The first thing he noticed was that she had shaven armpits, in defiance of the prevailing federal fashion. Great. The second was that she was easily the most beautiful woman he had ever seen.

9

Was that just the hangover talking? No. He double-checked. She was pitilessly beautiful.

Mid to late twenties? He was no good at estimating age. Sin-black hair. Aquiline nose. Tanned complexion. The lips were a feature, as well, although he couldn't quite describe them just then. He could devise plans for them though.

"Hello," she said.

Were those tinted contact lenses, or were her eyes really that shade of green? Turquoise, really. Shipping could get lost in them.

"Hello."

"How do you feel?" Definitely a Queen's rather than an Estuary-Grunge accent. That was better news than the armpits; Horatio had long since given up pretending he wasn't a rampant snob.

"Terrible. *Terrible*."

"Same here."

She didn't look it. Too corny to say that though.

"What's the time?" She checked her watch-fone.

"Twenty past."

"Past what?"

"Nine hundred." He groaned.

"What time did it end?"

"It probably hasn't," she answered, "it was still going strong when we left."

"When was that?"

"About oh-three hundred. Maybe a bit later."

"I'm reminded of a line in *Lucky Jim*. Do you know it? By a twentieth-century writer called Kingsley Amis."

"He's banned, isn't he?" Horatio thought quickly.

"Well, more discouraged." Christ, how idiotic of him. She worked with Marty, and was thus probably a spook of some kind. Yet there he was, blithely about to quote from a discouraged writer. Worse still, one who was Dead, White, Anglo-Saxon *and* Male. Better backtrack. "I read him at school, before the Directive. Anyhow it's a funny line, not sexist or ageist or anything-ist."

"I couldn't mind less if it were. Tell me."

They couldn't be contact lenses, she'd only woken up. They really were that colour you only see in seas, and then only in travel brochures on the Caribbean, and *then* only when a tint has been slipped over the camera lens. Her complexion, which last night he'd assumed had been made up, was, on closer inspection, just silky healthiness.

"Well, the hero wakes up with an award-winning hangover and Amis describes him as *'spewed up like a broken spider-crab on the tarry shingle of the morning'*. Then there's something about his mouth having been *'used as a latrine by some small creature of the night, and then as its mausoleum'*." She laughed.

Hallelujah!

Getting into his stride now, Horatio continued: "He also felt like *'he'd somehow been on a cross-country run and then had been expertly beaten up by secret police'*." He was proud of his quoting ability. That particular one was something of a morning-after favourite. Not that he'd had many girls to try it out on. And certainly none like this.

"Well, that's rather what *did* happen, didn't it?" She smiled. "I work in P.I.D., which I suppose means I'm about as close to a secret policeperson as you can get. And although it was nothing masochistic like a cross-country run, we did get quite . . . physical last night."

The way she said "physical" had his guts – and there were plenty of them – trying to leap into his throat. Stay calm, he told himself. This must not be allowed to degenerate into a one-night stand.

Her unexpected forwardness broke any remaining ice. He'd begun to worry that the way they had made love the night before had – so far as he could remember – contravened about six provisions of the Sexual Hygiene Directive. It had been so long since anyone had come back with him that he'd forgotten where he'd put the diggle forms. So she hadn't signed any, which, as it was his flat, was his responsibility. On *both* the Health & Hygiene *and* the Harassment Protection fronts, therefore, he was vulnerable. If this girl – it started with a "C", he remembered: Cassandra? Clytemnestra? – put in an official complaint it could cause him real trouble professionally, even as a freelance.

"I can't remember much about the party," she said, still lying there, looking at him. "What was it like?"

"Dreadful. No wonder I drank so much. Full of H.R.G.s." She looked quizzical. "It's an acronym Marty and I use sometimes. Stands for Hunky-Regular-Guys-At-Ease-With-Their-Own-Bodies. You know the type. The enemy for someone like me. Rugger friends of Marty's."

"But Marty's a bit hunky and regular himself, isn't he?"

"Physically, yes. But in personality he's a million kilometres away from a true one."

"Such as who, then?"

"Oh, I don't know . . . Alex Tallboys, say." The name seemed to register with her.

"The tall blond with the blue eyes?"

"That's it."

"You don't think much of him?"

"No, I don't. Classic H.R.G. material. Did you see him last night? Telling notoriously old anecdotes. I mean some truly

12

ancient chestnuts. So old they should be listed by the Culture Commission. What's worse, he was telling them really badly, and then he started pretending they'd all happened to him. It was cringe-making."

"How do you know him?"

Alex Tallboys was one of those who had bullied and taunted Horatio at Oxford into what Robert Virgil and another doctor had both diagnosed as something approaching a nervous breakdown. He wasn't going to tell her that though.

"University. He was in the year above. God knows why Marty keeps inviting him. Must be because they work together."

"Have you met his wife?"

"No." It was his turn to look puzzled, by the infinitely sad look on her face. "I'm sorry? Are they friends of yours? I suppose you must work with him too. I'm sorry if I've put my foot in it. He might be really nice now for all I know." He was backtracking fast, but could tell it was nothing like fast enough.

"He's not. You're right about him. That's why I'm getting a forty-eight-hour quickie divorce from him next week."

Horatio turned over to bury his face in the pillow. It muffled a heartfelt "Oh shit!". Quite apart from the gaffe itself, he now remembered Tallboys' jealous stares across the room last night. He'd just managed to cuckold a double blue! Rugby and karate, he remembered, with a shudder.

"Don't you remember?" she continued. "You told me that you were surprised I hadn't laughed at your name, and I said I was hardly in a position to, glorying in that of Cleopatra Tallboys." It all raced back. He nodded. He must have been *well* away last night to suffer this sort of memory lapse. Horatio put on his apology voice, the one he'd perfected at prep school. Fringe flopping over spanielly eyes. It never failed.

"I'm *so* sorry. Of course he's not *that* bad. For one thing, he's certainly very" – he racked his brains for something credible – "good-looking."

"Listen," she said, with a flash of irritation, "I'd hardly be here if I loved or respected him, would I? It's all right, we've separated. And as I've already said, you're right about him. So who else was there last night?"

Horatio felt like asking for her maiden name in case he accidentally slandered any other family member. Was that why she had gone home with him? To spite her husband? Or, after years of being married to a Neanderthal, had she wanted an Oxford don out of some kind of intellectual snobbery? Horatio had heard some of the Fellows boast about the phenomenon at High Table. "The Monroe/Miller Syndrome" they called it. The beauty parades the brainbox around to impress her friends, hoping his cleverness might ooze into her through some kind of psychic osmosis. He'd always assumed his colleagues had been teasing him, or just fantasising, but perhaps not.

"Who else was there? Now you're sounding like a police . . . person. Well, there was Peter Riley, the red-headed guy. He was sent down from Magdalen at the end of my first year."

"Really? What for?"

"He proposed the Loyal Toast during some boaty dinner."

"How absurd."

"Well, Oxford always was supposed to be the home of lost causes."

"No, not him. Them. How ludicrous for the college authorities to overreact like that. They ought just to have laughed it off. Sending him down is precisely how to make a

Carlist for life out of him. Sometimes those dons can be pathetically conformist. The Mountbatten-Windsors probably left before Riley was even *born*. Now he's probably toasting The King Over The Water every lunchtime."

She put out her hand to brush back some of his hair which he had made fall over his eyes when he was apologising. "We have to keep tabs on the Carlists at work. Once they were romantic, but with these riots and everything, they're getting far more dangerous. Some of them are still rather sweet though."

The way she said "romantic" made Horatio wish that she would say that about him one day. He again wondered why, despite all the macho Hunky Regulars at the party, this goddess had wound up going back with a hundred-and-ten kilo, one-metre-sixty-something, drunken old hack? He couldn't even remember whether he had been particularly witty or charming last night, although he felt fairly confident he'd been both.

The full-scale bombardment had receded somewhat, but there was still a sustained mortar and small-arms skirmish being fought in the no-man's-land between his forehead and his right temple.

"Any chance of some coffee?" she asked. "Some real stuff?" Horatio grinned. The blatant reference to black market Brazilian surely meant she was no nark.

"You're not sounding very police-ish," he teased.

"I hope I wasn't last night either." Once again that open, easy, natural reference to their love-making. It was so Twenty-First Century Cosmo Modern Womanish.

"When you're engaged in tracking down the enemies of the state, young man," she continued, in a passable Morningside schoolmarm accent, "your boss doesn't much care if your lover's coffee comes from the American Free Trading Area or some industrial processor in Hamburg."

"Lover" made him blush. He blushed deeper when he got out of bed to waddle to the kitchen in search of a coffee cup free of pin mould. He hated her watching his generous buttocks as they disappeared down the corridor. They were like the jowls on a bloodhound. Tallboys' were probably tight, pert and small as a man's clenched fists.

Or had she meant "lovers" in the plural? Everything was so complicated already.

"Mmm . . . this coffee's really federal," she said appreciatively. That ludicrous slang again.

Once safely back in bed he blurted out: "You're really lovely, you know. Just sort of . . . you know, perfect." He felt an idiot the moment he'd said it.

"Thank you," she smiled, looking down in embarrassment.

"God that sounded spas – sorry, I mean pathetic – but you are."

"It didn't and I'm not. I'm really not." She looked at him for just a fraction of a second. As if she meant what she said and was giving him a warning. A last chance.

" '*I always tend to talk crap when I'm nervous.*' That's a line from Martin Amis. *The Rachel Papers*." Another D.W.A.-S. Male writer.

"Quotations from Amis *père et fils*! What a morning." The way she said it, it somehow didn't sound too sarcastic. "Martin was made compulsory at my school at about the same time they 'discouraged' Kingsley," she said. "Oh, and by the way, I think you're lovely too."

At that sublime moment Horatio's bedside vid-fone rang. He flicked it on, regretting it as soon as he had.

"Hi Horrid, it's Roddy. Hey! What have we here?!" Horatio realised Roderick Weaning could see Cleo. He quickly switched off the vid link. Cleo seemed utterly unfazed by the fact that she'd been spotted in Horatio's bed by a total stranger.

"Whatever happened to privacy?" complained Horatio.

"I'm a newsperson. Don't believe in it. More to the point, Horrid, whatever happened to your Aachen piece?" Horatio turned around to Cleo and mouthed "The Boss" to her.

Roderick Weaning was one part joviality, two parts cynicism, one part pure aggression. Deputy editor of *The Times*, he was the man who paid the freelance Horatio's mortgage. And knew it.

"Look, Roddy, can I call you back? As you've seen I'm with someone at the moment. You gave me till Monday. I'll file by noon."

"Sunday night it's due in by. And we're hyping it on the masthead, so it must be. Your first two pieces were really federal. They've set the scene very well, so we want something just as good this time. But that's not why I called. I need you to come round. Now. I need to discuss something important." He put just enough emphasis on "important" for it to sound simultaneously enticing and threatening.

"Can't we talk over the fone?"

"No, sorry."

Horatio looked at Cleo lying naked in his bed. How could he possibly leave her?

"You're a tough hack, Roddy."

"Northcliffe, Rothermere, Beaverbrook, Black, Weaning. That's what they say. Be here by ten-thirty. Oh, and say goodbye to your friend from me!" He clicked off with a laugh.

"Sounds like my time's up," said Cleo. Lying on her back

now, her hands behind her head, she didn't seem to notice that the sheet had fallen back to reveal her breasts. Horatio, as immature sexually as he was sophisticated intellectually, found it took all his self-control not to stare at them, salivate or even make a half-hearted attempt to grab. For once, he told himself, he must play it cool. He must try to act as though women like her, who could model for the front cover of *Chic Alors!*, were the regular occupants of his smelly old scratcher of a bed.

Why did Weaning have to call on this of all days? When would he be in a position to be able to tell people like Roddy where they could go?

He showered and dressed, took Cleo's pager number and told her where the coffee was. She was the first girl he'd left in his flat since Leila, but he instinctively knew it was all right.

An observer of their lingering goodbye kiss might have been forgiven for assuming Horatio was about to cross the Arabian Empty Quarter on foot, rather than just take a tram to the eastern end of the Strand.

The worst thing about being a semi-detached academic, thought Horatio as he made his way down Collingham Place, was having to be at the beck and call of nargs like Weaning in order to earn a living. Prize Fellow of All Souls College, Oxford, sounded grand, but it didn't provide him with much more than a set in college and occasional dining rights. Journalism was how he tried to earn what his bank manager kept telling him, less and less politely, wasn't quite a living any more.

The tram journey from his flat in Brittan Court – Earl's Court before Whitehall had over-zealously interpreted the new Classlessness legislation – took half an hour. Horatio used the time to read his messages and the news off his pager. The usual stuff. Some junk-mail. An invitation to the Brasenose Gaudy. His mother wanting to know if he was coming down for the weekend. Why? Probably for a reconciliation with his stepbrother and stepsister. Marty was asking how he had done with Cleo, couched in his usual uncouth vernacular. An outraged rant from a reader about the first of his *Times* articles on the Aachen Referendum. Why, he wondered, do nutters always use italics, underlinings and multiple exclamation marks? A couple of bills, including a message from the Atlantic Gas people saying that as of 1st July his supply would be cut off and his ration reallocated owing to non-payment. He looked out of the tram window at the bright May morning. Summer was on its way, he shouldn't need Atgas for a while now anyhow. He wondered for a moment whether his aversion to paying them had anything to do with his father's death, but decided it was probably just poverty.

He g-mailed his mother to ask who else would be down next Saturday, and decided to let Marty stew. He would tell that cow Penelope Aldritt "for the last bloody time" *not* to give his private pager number to readers. They could write to his home modem if they had to.

The news was more interesting. He preferred reading the splash headlines on other passengers' tabloid newssheets rather than the *Times* stuff off his own pager. NAT RIOTS IN SHEFFIELD AND DONCASTER. Poor old North England Region. When was there last any good news from up there? SPACE AGENCY SLEAZE: TWELVE INDICTED, announced the *European*. THATCHER ASSASSINATION: NEW EVIDENCE, cried the *Mail*. Yet more indications that it had not been the I.R.A. after all. This was getting to be the twenty-first-century equivalent of J.F.K.. He considered whether the market could take yet another book on the subject. He might be able to get a good advance for himself, but what would they say in college? Did he really care any longer?

The *Sun* led with TENTH MAY GROUP PLOT TO LASER ENTENTE BRIDGE. The other story in all the papers was about how the last of the Cornish trawlers had been arrested by Spanish Region frigates for fishing in the Irish Box. It finally spelt the end of the industry. The *Indy*, which liked to specialise in stories about the ex-Royals, carried the news that King William of New Zealand had finally been granted a visa to visit London over the coming week. U.S.E. AND A-P.E.Z. AGREE ON WILLY'S VISA, ran the headline. The long-running diplomatic row between the United States of Europe and the Asia-Pacific Economic Zone had at last been resolved. It would be the first Royal visit since the Family left in 2017, and all the papers carried speculative pieces about the warmth of the welcome he could expect from the people, if not from the authorities.

Horatio briefly wondered whether the Commission decision to try to beat both the American Free Trading Area and The Asia-Pacific Economic Zone to Mars might be ruined by the amazing degree of corruption at the Euro-Space Agency, extraordinary even by Union standards.

The story he followed up in *The Times*, though, once he found the relevant column in his pager, was the one about the Tenth May Group. The paramilitary wing of the English Resistance Movement had been hitting what they termed "legitimate targets" for over a quarter of a century now. It would be a major departure from their established *modus operandi* to attack a public utility like the Channel Bridge.

How had they got their hands on a laser? That would be a significant advance on their usual terrorist acts. His hack's nose told him that the story was pretty speculative. *The Times'* lack of coverage seemed to confirm that. The E.R.M. had officially denied it, and Horatio suspected the story might have originated in the Information Commission's dirty tricks department. He made a mental note to ask Marty, who always knew about such things.

After about half an hour the tram pulled up outside *The Times* building in Fleet Street. It was rare for Weaning to request a face-to-face meeting. Horatio hoped it was nothing bad.

3

10.25 Saturday, 1st May

The Times building in Printing House Square was a steel and glass cylindrical monstrosity rising high above the rest of Fleet Street. Totally out of sympathy with all the surrounding buildings, it had won many prestigious architectural awards. Horatio loathed it with a passion he normally reserved for structures built in the third quarter of the last century, or the Van der Rohe-style horror which the Berlin-Brussels Bureau had just commissioned for their new headquarters. He was looking forward to the eightieth anniversary of Le Corbusier's death this summer, when he would hold his own private celebration.

The electronic frisker on the door swallowed his I.D. card and returned it instantaneously. Then the security guards waved him through with their N-series, and after two minutes on the travelator he was there. Most employees of the daily paper were away for May Day, but some of those working on the Sunday were around. One of the advantages of having been sacked, he mused, was that he now knew precisely who were his real friends on the paper. And, more importantly, his real enemies.

It was almost a year since the Works Council had held the poll. He later found out from a friend in Optic-Fibres how

22

everyone had voted. As a manager, Weaning had taken no direct part, but he had seemed keen enough to take Horatio off the payroll the moment the vote had gone against.

Just as he was about to enter Weaning's office, Horatio saw Penelope Aldritt, the cow who had spoken against him at the meeting. She was rearranging books. A few of her phrases still rankled. She had told the Works Council that he was "a suspected tobacco-abuser", who "maintained surplus and antisocial weight levels despite every opportunity to work out" and who was thus an increased pension and benefits risk and deserved "constructive redundancy" in order to give him more time to "get in touch with the real him".

His supporters had decried her blatant stoutism, but the alternative forms of words suggested to the meeting were no better. He did not want to be called "generously-proportioned", "over-nutritioned" or "horizontally-challenged", let alone "a person of size". Neither did he have an "alternative body image". He was just fat. He didn't much mind, either, except that it led to his having such little success with women. Until now.

One day, Aldritt, you fully paid-up, card-carrying bitch, he promised himself. One day. . .

Fortunately her legs resembled those of a Shetland pony. They were shorter, fatter and hairier even than Horatio's. That, once allied to a vast nose, rendered her satisfyingly unattractive. She was thirty-six, unmarried, and by all accounts getting desperate.

"Hello, *Ms* Aldritt," he smiled as he passed behind her desk, putting special emphasis on the "Ms". By the time she'd turned round he was already in Weaning's glass office.

"Hello, Horror." Weaning was also thirty-six but he looked fifty. Overweight, jowly and balding, he had never really got over the regionwide smoking ban. "Sorry to get you out of bed."

"Not ever half as sorry as I'll be for the rest of my days for letting you."

"It's important though. We've received a complaint from Commissioner Percival's lawyers that you've been harassing him. He wants the Berlin-Brussels Bureau Media Liaison Unit to vet your next Aachen piece before publication. Of course we've said no, but the Ed wants to know what's going on."

Horatio gave a brief outline of what he'd found in the Federal Records Office the day before. He then played Weaning the pager tape of his conversation with Percival.

"Have you contacted the Admiral?"

"No. Not yet."

"Well, get on with it then. Do it now. Sounds like a great story. Make sure you record the conversation." Horatio raised his eyebrows at this slur on his professionalism. Did Weaning *really* think him such an amateur?

"If I gave you my grandmother's address would you send her a memo on how to suck eggs?" Weaning acknowledged the rebuke.

"Sorry. It just sounds very exciting." It was, but would Weaning stand by him if this all started to go wrong?

"How worried are you about Percival?"

"Very, of course. I'm hardly likely to want to anger the Commission Secretary just for the hell of it. But if it hangs together . . ." Weaning smiled. Always a dangerous sign. "Anyway, we have great faith in you not to do anything that might get our licence revoked."

His look said just the opposite. It said: "Watch out if you want to keep this job which pays your mortgage, you podgy little egghead. The Editor told me to hire you even though I wanted a truly hard-bitten news hack who'd done his time as a reporter on a local paper like me and not some smart-arse academic like you who's just swanned in from Oxbridge where the Editor went but I didn't." Horatio had seen the look a thousand times. Pure, unadulterated chippiness, mixed with a (well-deserved) intellectual inferiority complex. A damn dangerous combination in a boss.

Just as Horatio was about to leave the office, Weaning looked over Horatio's shoulder through the glass partition.

"By the way, do you know Gemma Reegan?"

The name clanged a huge gong. Horatio frowned. Trying to remember anything that morning was not easy.

"OK, be subtle. Take a look behind you at the woman talking to Penelope."

Yes, that was her. The other woman from last night. The Yank. Tall. Power shoulders. Long straight blonde hair. Never-ending legs.

"Yes, I do. She's an American hack. Writes rubbishy books on the Mountbatten-Windsors. Nice girl though. Sexy, as you can see. I spent rather a long time chatting her up last night."

"She wants me to hire her to cover the King's visit. From the historical angle. What do you think?"

"I'm sure she'd do it well. Watch her though, as she's got loads of ludicrous theories."

"Such as?"

"Oh, she's hit on this clever but completely bogus theme that the Mountbatten-Windsors are all illegitimate."

Weaning's frown meant he didn't understand. He rarely did. For all his drive and ambition, Weaning actually *knew* very little. Which was partly why the Editor had demanded they hire Horatio.

"For example, she goes around trying to find the marriage

25

certificates of George IV and Maria Fitzherbert, William IV and Dora Jordan, Edward VII and Lillie Langtry and so on."

Weaning's look of incomprehension told Horatio there was little point in persevering, but he did nonetheless.

"It's all to prove that William isn't the rightful King of the Kiwis. It doesn't stand up for a minute of course, but it goes down very well in A.F.T.A. for some reason. I imagine the Commission approves too. I don't think she commands much academic credibility over here." He thought of the High Table deconstruction of her latest book. "In fact, I know she doesn't. Cracking-looking, though, don't you think?"

"Suppose so, yes. And you chatted her up last night? What a Lothario you're becoming. Who did I see on your vid-fone this morning? Is that why you didn't follow this one up?"

"No, she's got a seven-year-old kid. Too much hassle." Weaning's face fell.

"No wonder this office voted you antisocial. That was a blatantly lone-parentist remark." The tone suggested that he was almost saying it for the record, as if his office was bugged. "Let's just talk about her professionally, *if* you don't mind?" Chastened, Horatio repeated that he didn't think she carried much intellectual credibility.

"Amongst you Oxbridge types, no doubt, but here at the screen-face it's different. She's the sort of person who sells news-space. Send her in. Oh, and let me know about what the Admiral says before you go."

Horatio felt lucky to get away without some chippy lecture about his glaring lack of qualifications from the University of Life. In a way, Weaning was right; had Horatio attended that particular seat of learning, rather than Oxford, the best he could ever have hoped for was a Third. *And* he'd probably have also wound up on Weaning's staircase.

Ever the egotist, Horatio rather hoped that Gemma might show a scintilla of pique at his having gone off with Cleo the night before. To his irritation she didn't. She kissed him twice on each cheek – another new federal fashion Horatio despised – and beamed when he whispered to her that he thought she was about to get hired. As she walked off towards Weaning's office she looked over her shoulder: "Are you ever in the I.H.R.?"

He did half his work in the Institute of Historical Research, but he couldn't remember seeing her there.

"Yes, quite a lot."

"Might see you there sometime?"

"How about Monday? Afternoon-ish?"

"Fine. Yes. Great." Rather pleasingly the conversation had taken place right in front of Penelope too. What a great May Day he was having.

Leaning back on the assistant editor's chair, his feet up on his old desk, Horatio pressed "Record" on his pager and called the Admiral's number. He got straight through, but no image came up on the screen.

"Hello, I wonder if I might speak to Admiral Ratcliffe?"

"This is he." Old but clear. Plus he hadn't taken forever to get to the fone, like some of the nonagenarians he'd interviewed.

"Oh, hello sir. My name's Horatio Lestoq. I write for *The Times*. I'm presently working on a series of articles on the Aachen Referendum and I was wondering if I might ask you a couple of questions?"

"Horatio Lestoq did you say?" Oh dear, not another oh-so-droll remark about his name. Why had he not been christened Simon, George or Reinhard?

"Yes, apparently it's naval. I was named after a nineteenth-century sailor."

"Well, of course I know all about Nelson. I was a naval officer for forty-two years you know," the old boy said testily.

"I *am* sorry, yes of course." This one would have to be handled carefully. "It's just that we were not taught about him at school. He was taken off the syllabus during Depatriation and I rather assumed . . ."

"He was taken off more than that, young man," said the Admiral. "You know Delors Square?"

"Yes, of course." Uh-oh. Was the old boy senile? How could he not know of London's most central location?

"Well, it used to be named after Horatio Nelson's greatest victory. His statue was up where Schuman is now, on the top of the column."

So what? Site-renaming had gone on ever since universities in the 1980s had started calling junior common rooms after Nelson Mandela. Horatio knew that Attali House, the headquarters of the European Bank for Reconstruction and Development at the other end of the Mall, had once been the palace where the Royal Family had lived. The huge Asia-Pacific Economic Zone headquarters on the south side of the Thames used to house London's local government. Everyone knew that the vast gothic Westminster Heritage, Amenity and Leisuredrome had been a palace where the British Parliament had sat. It wasn't too hard to believe that Delors Square had once commemorated a battle against our Union partners and fellow citizens. His mother might even have mentioned it once. Strange, though, that he hadn't been taught it at school.

"I was wondering how long you'd take to get in touch, Horatio," said Ratcliffe. "I'm ninety-one now, so you've left it rather late in the day. But it's good to hear from you at last."

What on earth could he mean? What amazing vanity to assume that, having only been a minor official in the referendum process, he would be on the call list to be interviewed for this piece. Horatio persevered nonetheless.

"Well, if it's all right I'd like to ask you a few questions about your role in the Aachen Referendum."

"Haven't you anything else to tell me before that?"

"I'm sorry, how do you mean?"

"Don't you know who I am?" The vanity again. The classic cry of every pompous sub-Commissioner complaining about his hotel room, or Christian Democrat M.U.P. upbraiding the *maître d'* over a table allocation.

"Yes. You're Admiral Sir Michael Ratcliffe" – the oldies usually liked it when he referred to them by their pre-Classlessness titles, ex-peers especially – "you were Chief Scrutineer for South-West Region."

"And that's *all* I am to you?"

"Yes. As I said, I'm a journalist working for *The Times*. We haven't met before, have we?" Had he ever interviewed Ratcliffe for any piece he had written?

"I know all that. I heard you the first time and you needn't speak slowly. I may be ninety-one but I'm not senile." Horatio was unconvinced.

"What was your mother called?"

"I'm sorry?"

"What was your mother's maiden name?"

"I really can't see what that can possibly have to do with this interview." Horatio was regretting the call. He didn't want to be cruel. He'd just wrap the whole thing up as soon as possible. In the meantime he'd humour the old boy. "Her name was Heather Ellis." Another long pause.

"All right, fire away."

29

"Did you ever meet Commission Secretary Gregory Percival at the time of the Referendum to discuss . . . finance? He was Foreign Commissioner Mackintosh's special advisor at the time." A long silence this time. After about fifteen seconds Horatio feared the Admiral had fainted, or fallen asleep, or simply walked off.

"Hello? Admiral Ratcliffe, sir?"

"Yes, yes, I'm still here. I heard what you said. Look, I think you'd better come down here. There's something I must tell you . . . yes. It's best that you do. There is something you ought to know . . . Something that you of all people *must* know."

"Could you tell me now?"

"No . . . Certainly not. Not like this. Not over the fone. Come down tomorrow. In the morning. Early as you like. In the meantime I'll try to get my thoughts down about . . . everything. How long's it been?"

"What? How long has what been?"

"All the Aachen business."

"Thirty years. My article is to commemorate the anniversary on Tuesday."

"Well, that's quite long enough. It needed something like this to happen. And you're exactly the right person . . . Yes . . . To tell everything to. How extraordinary. I'd like to see you too. Do you drive?"

"No," said Horatio, slightly ashamed of himself. Poverty and malcoordination had combined to make him immobile.

"Listen here then. Take the shuttle from Maastricht Terminus to Basingstoke. Ibworth is three or four miles out of town. Take a taxi from the station. I'm in the Rectory, on the right directly after the Free Fox public house. You go down a drive and you're there." There was another pause. "Oh, and Horatio my boy."

"Yes?"

"Be careful and please tell no one about this. About me."

"I promise."

"I mean it, it really matters."

"I promise." He would try one last time. "Sir? Before you click off. Can you give me any hint at all about what you want to discuss?"

"None at all over the fone, but I'll draw up something for you to take away afterwards. A memorandum. Something to make your and your editor's hair stand on end. I'll do that right now."

Mystified but intrigued, Horatio said goodbye.

Should he bother? He had plenty of other work he needed to do. It was Sunday tomorrow. He might be able to spend the day in bed with Cleo reading the Sunday printouts. Drinking champagne. Making love. It was probably only some semi-senile meandering. But Horatio held the same view of individuals as of other research material. Direct personal contact and hard graft paid. He'd go.

As he tried to switch off his pager, Horatio's podgy forefinger pressed the wrong button, and instead called up "Last Access". Not for the first time the Luddite in him rued the new technology. It never was designed with him in mind. It seemed that whenever Horatio ventured out onto the Information Superhighway he got run over. Just as he was about to jab the "Off" button again something caught his eye.

Last access 03.03 1/5/45.

He couldn't remember using his pager last night. Not that he could remember much about last night. He was drunkenly following Cleo bedwards, after all. But no one had his PIN number except him, his mother and Registry. How could anyone have accessed his pager? Who would have wanted to?

Seeing Gemma had gone, Horatio went next door to play Weaning the tape. He told him he would go down there the next day, and got approval for his paltry travel expenses. Leaving the office, he again passed Penelope Aldritt's desk.

"Very nice material," he said, pointing at her dress with the sweetest of smiles. Just as her face lit up at the compliment he added, "You really ought to have a dress made out of it."

"Lookist," she spat.

"Uglyist in this case, actually," he grinned, "which I don't think is quite illegal yet."

"A case of the pot calling the kettle coloured, isn't it?"

"No, sweetheart, there's a difference. I'm ugly and proud. It just *kills* you."

"No wonder all the wimmin in this office hated you."

"They didn't, only you did. Farewell, sweet maiden. Don't let me take you off your", – he patted the bookshelf "interesting work." He hoped she got the allusion. Probably not. Just to make sure, he tapped the shelf again. "I shouldn't *stay on it* too long though, if I were you."

"Sometimes you can be a right bastard, Lestoq."

"Surely it should be parentally-challenged," he retorted, with exactly that smug smile which he knew would infuriate her most.

08.10 Sunday, 2nd May

London's Maastricht Terminus — which Horatio knew really *had* once been named after a battle against our Union partners and fellow citizens — was unusually busy for a Sunday morning. A holiday group of Belgian tax assessors off Eurostar were chatting excitedly prior to taking the tube to Aldwych. Crossrail passengers from Paddington and Heathrow, weighed down with bags, were busily trying to engage the Polish porters and hail taxis. Drunks, down-and-outs, beggars and ex-farmers were causing their usual mayhem. It was a scene which made Horatio nostalgic for the days before the Noise Pollution Directive, when buskers had played popular tunes in the tunnels.

He made his way over to a ticket dispenser, pulling a fifty-euro note from his pocket. He studied it for a moment to check it wasn't one of the counterfeits which the Chechen mafia had mass-produced in Bradford last year. Apparently one could only tell by looking closely at the width of Edward Heath's huge grin. The note looked genuine. Unlike the grin.

He took the ticket and his change. Then he walked down platform 22 towards *The Flying Dutchperson*. The ads along its side reminded him yet again how grossly unfit he was. "*Come Heli-Diving in Greece*", an almost naked Amazon was cooing.

Sex, sex, sex everywhere, used to sell everything. The next advert told him how "accommodating" everyone was on Club 13–30 holidays in Sardinia, presumably a reference to sex as well. From the moment he woke, every paper, cable channel, EuroNet, pager, modem, tram and poster, until the sky searchlight ads lit up at night, yelled sex sex sex at him. Even the ad for the Mo Mowlam Palace of Popular Culture at Windsor showed a leggy model wearing only the bottom half of a Beefeater's costume. He thought about Cleo.

As he slotted on his seatbelt, Horatio scanned his fellow passengers' papers. More rioting in the North. Halifax, Leeds and Hull now. He was mildly surprised the Information Commissioner allowed such graphic reports of it. Union Jacks were apparently being flown with impunity. COHESION FUND TO BUY SICILY. No surprises there. TALLINN MOB FIRED ON BY EURO-ARMY. He thought of poor Leila. The secessionist movements in the Baltic protectorates were as brave as they were doomed. There was the inevitable royal story in the *Indy*: WILLY TO SPEAK IN HYDE PARK. His pager was full of a joint assault by the Environmental Health Agency and Customs & Excise on a pub in Catford where it was suspected that nicotine cigarettes were being sold. A dealer had died in the shoot-out.

The cream of his university generation had gone into the E.H.A. He'd have probably wound up there himself if he had not won his Fellowship. He hoped it hadn't been anyone he knew. An operation like that would probably have been undertaken by a SWAT team rather than his contemporaries, although since "elitist" Civil Service fast-streaming had been abolished, one never knew.

On the business pages Horatio saw that the Cannabis Sales Division of the Feel-Good Factory Inc. had announced a 2.2

billion-euro pre-tax profit for the year ending 1st April 2044. He was in the wrong business.

He scanned the *Telegraph*. Little of interest apart from a photograph in the Letts Column's "crumpet corner" – as it had been nicknamed before the Sexism Directive – of Lucy Percival, the Commission Secretary's daughter, who had been nominated as one of the "Euro-Women Achievers of the Year" for her work on the Attali House fine art collection.

Horatio failed to stifle a smile at the obituary of the eighty-five-year-old journalist and author Christopher Silvester on the next page. Ever since the Entente Bridge had opened in 2014, rabies had been rampant amongst dogs and foxes. For Silvester to die of it after a bite from his grandson's pet hamster was a fate few would have predicted.

Horatio stared out of the shuttle window as it trundled through the countryside at an energy-efficient 80 kph. The planting of oil seed rape across the whole of Hampshire left the countryside a uniform electric yellow colour. With Surrey and Kent ordered by the Agriculture Commissioner to be set aside until 2048, the Home Counties were a depressing sight.

His fellow passengers did little to raise his spirits. A couple of regulators behind him were arguing over the merits of the Channel Islands sale. It annoyed him more than he could easily explain. The thin, bearded narg with the Easiwriter in his jacket breast pocket was monotoning: "It's got to be a good deal if the P.E. value is nine point five or above. I mean, Barry, what are future earnings likely to be?"

Horatio sympathised entirely with his strange-looking friend, who was arguing that it wasn't solely a financial question: "Paris shouldn't be allowed to buy something which for centuries has been part of South English Region, just because they offer enough. London should never have accepted." This drew nervous glances from around the carriage. It sounded suspiciously like Anglo-patriotism or, even more dangerous, nationalism itself.

The shuttle drew into Basingstoke station not a moment too soon. Horatio got the first taxi on the rank and asked for Ibworth. He discouraged conversation by ostentatiously reading his pager messages. His mother was looking forward to seeing him at the weekend. It would give him a chance to make up after their latest row. It seemed as if their relationship was under constant strain these days. She always seemed to take his half-brother and half-sister's side against him, even when, as over this latest money thing, Dick and Marcia were clearly in the wrong. He assumed there was some textbook psychological syndrome which made her withdraw her love and support for him where her new family were concerned, but that hardly made it any easier to bear.

Or was he perhaps just being paranoid? Vain, egotistical and snobbish he would admit to unhesitatingly, but Horatio was damned if he was going to add paranoia to the list without some more evidence. For his mother to take their side when he could not even pay his Atgas bill, while Dick drove a grade 1 petrol auto and Marcia swanned around in Cordiale and Pagan Dior dresses at two grand a throw, seemed plain wrong.

Settling himself down into a satisfying self-pity mode, Horatio thought next about her attitude towards his potential girlfriends, such as there had been. She had got on very well with Leila, but no one else. She'd positively frozen all the others out with her blatant vetting procedure. Liz had been sat down on their first meeting and virtually interrogated about how much her father earned. He wondered whether, were things to work out with Cleopatra, she might get on with her? They would be poles apart politically, of course. He resolved not to introduce, or even mention, Cleo until he was certain it was safe.

The next message was from Cleo, apologising for not being able to see him tonight. Could he make Monday? Of course he could but . . . damn. Marty was still demanding "all the gory details" from Friday night.

It was still quite early when the taxi reached the outskirts of Ibworth. Horatio asked to be dropped off, deciding, despite his asthma, to walk the last quarter of a kilometre or so to the Rectory. It was a beautifully clear and sunny May day.

Almost as soon as the taxi pulled away, he regretted his decision. It felt like an exceptionally high pollen count. He would walk slowly. Across the fields, Horatio could make out a classically pretty Hampshire village. Church, pub, high street, pond, green, Euro-Lottery booth, the lot. The sign they had passed announced that the village was twinned with Rannoch in Scotland, Obvirsk in Slovakia and La Grenche in Walloonia.

Suddenly an auto swung around the bend ahead.

It was going fast. Well over the Union speed limit.

And it was heading straight at him.

Horatio, never an athlete at the best of times, had time only to fling himself into the hedge. Even as he leapt clear the auto's wing mirror hit his elbow.

The auto shot around the next bend and was gone.

Lying panting on the verge Horatio slowly came back out of shock. His elbow started to hurt. No expert on autos, he thought it was a grade 2. Definitely petrol and he doubted it had speed-governors. He hadn't had time to see the plates or the driver's face.

His elbow throbbing powerfully, he sat up to suck on his

inhaler and feel very sorry for himself. Tears welled up. Horatio hated pain.

The auto had been going far too fast down a narrow country lane. Had anything been coming in the opposite direction there would certainly have been a fatal crash. As it was he was bloody lucky not to have been run down.

Still sitting on the verge, he paged Basingstoke police station with a complaint about a speeding greyish grade 2 petrol having caused him A.B.H. He knew they wouldn't do anything, it just made him feel better. Only when he was well rested several minutes later did he get up, brush the grass and earth stains off his trousers and make his way towards Ibworth, rubbing his aching elbow as he walked.

A short way further on was The Free Fox. He could see it across a field, around the next bend. The name on the sign had been altered, presumably after the Country Sports Directive. Originally it had been The Horse & Hounds. With thousands of foxes gassed, trapped, electrocuted and shot by farmers every year, it was in the days when they were hunted (often rather incompetently) that they had actually been most free. Horatio enjoyed paradoxes like that. Since the ban on the wearing of fur thirty-five years ago, the mink had become so prevalent and destructive of rural wildlife that the Agriculture Commission had even been forced last year to subsidise an industry which turned their pelts into fur coats. For export only, of course.

The Rectory drive was, as the Admiral had said, almost opposite the pub. The house itself was a solid, dark red Queen Anne affair. He walked up the drive, still holding his elbow, past some purple rhododendron bushes on the right. The door had "1708" above it, fashioned in yellow brick. He rang the bell. As he waited for an answer, he took another pull of Salbutamol.

If the old boy didn't have a housekeeper, he thought, a nonagenarian might take some time to get there, so he waited patiently in front of the door, which was ajar. After a minute or so he composed himself and pushed it open. He called "Hello?" inside. Then he waited.

Nothing.

Louder now: "Hello, Admiral Ratcliffe, sir?"

Still nothing.

Next, almost at a shout, he called: "Hello, is there anyone at home? It's Horatio Lestoq here from *The Times*!" Perhaps the old boy had forgotten and gone out?

He pushed the door wider, to reveal a panelled hall. It was quite dark inside. There was an antique bronze naval shellcase with walking sticks and umbrellas standing in it. A muddy pair of green napoleons were standing next door to it. Otherwise the room was empty. A staircase on the right led to a landing. Horatio stepped forward, called again, and decided to walk into the large room first on the left.

As he crossed the threshold he saw the body.

5

10.40 Sunday, 2nd May

The custody suite door opened and a policeman came in to handcuff him and lead him upstairs. From the stares of other police on the way, Horatio assumed they had mistaken him for the contract killer the Macedonian mafia were believed to have hired in Basingstoke. It had been in all the papers last week. Even after an hour in a cell though, Horatio hardly felt he could look like an Albanian hit-man. The rest of the gaol was probably full of the usual collection of muggers, drunks, anglers and petty thieves.

He was left alone in the interview room.

He knew they wouldn't come in immediately, but would let the anxiety and pressure build up. They'd tried the same thing at Paddington Green over Leila. He just wouldn't let it. There was nothing to look at and no window. Just a copy of the Suspects' Charter on the wall behind him.

Eventually three men came in, the first of whom was a large, red-faced officer who introduced himself as Detective Chief Inspector Raymond Snell from the C.I.D. So London *had* taken the case out of Hampshire's hands.

Snell looked as if he wore a wig. Horatio thought he recognised him. Was he the *flic* off Courtroom Channel 44?

He was very routine in his first questions, matter-of-fact

even, but Horatio could tell that he was more interested in the case than he cared to show. He probably thought it would help his cable career to nail the killer of a distinguished sailor.

Horatio told him everything he knew, except for the blotting paper, which would have been construed as withholding evidence. It soon became clear they had already heard his conversations with Commissioner Percival and the Admiral off his pager. Was that legal, he wondered, without a warrant? Horatio explained that he had wanted to interview the Admiral in his capacity as a former Aachen Scrutineer, which Weaning would confirm.

If he was about to commit murder, Horatio pointed out, he would hardly inform his boss that he was going to the scene beforehand. When asked who he thought might have "dunnit", he mentioned the grey grade 2 which he said could well have been the getaway auto. He said he had reported it immediately afterwards. Then he showed them the bruise on his elbow, which was changing to a purply yellow and throbbing painfully. A junior detective left the room to check out details of missing and stolen autos.

"Get some satellite shots of the area," Snell ordered the retreating figure. "Did you do this for the money, Dr Lestoq?" Snell obviously preferred the direct approach. It doubless made better cable.

"What money?"

"The money, a tidy sum I must say" – amazing, thought Horatio, that the police really *do* always speak in clichés, just like in their caricatures – "which the Admiral left you in his will."

"His will? No. You must be mistaken. I'd never met him or spoken to him before yesterday."

"Can you prove that?"

"Listen to my pager."

"We have. By the way, do you usually record your private conversations?"

"When I'm working on a story, always. It'll show you that I've never spoken to him before."

"We've already checked your pager thoroughly, Dr Lestoq," said Snell. "In the conversation Admiral Ratcliffe actually asks you . . ." – he turned to a page in a folder marked "Transcripts" – "'*I was wondering how long you would take to get in touch, Horatio . . . Haven't you anything to tell me before that? . . . Don't you know who I am? . . . And that's all I am to you?*', et cetera, et cetera. So you see, although you do not admit knowing him on the tape, Admiral Ratcliffe certainly thought he knew *you*. It sounds as if he thought you ought to know him too. Plus a cursory initial investigation of the Rectory has already turned up these." He tossed three large red leather scrapbooks across to Horatio, who opened them.

Inside were pasted newspaper cuttings. Almost every article and book review Horatio had ever written. All in chronological order. They started with his *Isis* contributions of ten years ago.

"Still deny knowing him?"

Horatio nodded, dumbfounded.

"You stand to inherit half of everything he had. Until, of course," Snell put on his "nasty cop" voice, "we stick you with this murder."

Horatio's brain turned turtle. He had got so far in his thoughts over the past hour to realise that the Admiral's death on the morning of his visit was no coincidence. Someone knew he would be going there at that time. Either his pager or the Admiral's fone must be tapped. But to be framed as comprehensively as this . . .

"When did you first meet Admiral Ratcliffe?"

"I've never met him. Alive, that is."

"When did you first speak to him?"

"Yesterday morning."

"When did you first know of his existence?"

"The day before that – Friday."

"Friday, the 30th of April," said the Chief Inspector slowly, for the video record.

"Yes. Listen, when was the will dated?" Horatio's mind was clouding over. He must not let it.

"I'm asking the questions." Snell allowed a short silence to show his audience who was in control, then: "Eleventh of April 2016."

Horatio made a quick calculation.

"I was about three months old then. Are you *sure* it hasn't been tampered with?"

"Certain. This is an exact copy of the original, not some printout. You've been a major beneficiary in Admiral Ratcliffe's will for twenty-eight years. It all fits in very nicely. I'm thinking aloud here . . ." Horatio immediately recognised Snell's trademark, his catchphrase from the programme. It was the moment his fans loved and endlessly imitated. He was being interrogated by none other than Inspector "I'm thinking aloud here" Snell of the Yard. "You're, er, financially disadvantaged . . ."

"The word you're groping for is poor. Hard up."

"Since you put it that way, yes. We could tell that from the look of you, even if our investigations hadn't shown you defaulting on your Atlantic Gas bills. Do you deny being in difficulties?"

"No. But that doesn't make me a murderer." Horatio could indulge in cliché catchphrases too: "I demand to see my lawyer." It sounded impressive, even though he hadn't got one. He wondered which of his university contemporaries would do the least bad job of defending him. Or should he should call Dick at Zetland & Dunbar?

"Not under Legal Directive 14/714 you can't. Preliminary police interrogation takes place without notaries being present so long as the full discussions are videoed." The Chief Inspector jerked his thumb behind him and up to the corner of the ceiling. "Say cheese." Horatio glanced up and grimaced at the tiny camera there.

"Why, might I ask, if I committed this crime, did I then call the police. Twice?"

"You heard our sirens. You were covering yourself."

"You mean to say you were on your way already? It was not me who called you first? Who did then?"

"I'm hardly likely to tell you that."

"Can your sirens be heard on the tape of my call?"

"No, just your heavy breathing, which may have been designed to mask them when they were in the distance." A film of blood-red anger descended over Horatio's eyes.

"Look, I'm asthmatic! I'd just walked to the house on foot. I was bloody nearly run over! I get hay fever and it's a high count today. Plus," he was getting angry and was almost out of breath again, "plus I had just discovered a dead body for Christ's sake!"

"Calm down Dr Lestoq. We're running tests on the background noise on the tape right now."

"And I'd already rung you to tell you about the car."

"A diversionary tactic, perhaps, to transfer suspicion onto an imaginary person and waste our time."

"It sounds to me," said Horatio, trying to think logically, "that the murderer called you himself."

"Or herself," said Snell. Yes, thought Horatio, the Chief

Inspector really was playing to his overwhelmingly female Channel 44 audience all right.

"Or herself, knowing me to be on my way there. In order to set me up."

"The call was not from an auto-fone, if you mean the alleged petrol-auto driver."

"What do you mean, 'alleged'? How did I get this 'alleged' bruise, then, I'd like to know?" He was tired. It was aching. He was scared.

"The Admiral might have put up a fight."

"The murderer, if he was trying to frame me, would hardly be likely to call from his auto-fone, would he?" Horatio found it hard to avoid sarcasm when dealing with this man. "He'd have used a watch-fone or a vid-fone with the vid switched off to give you as few tracking possibilities as possible."

"We believe it was a vid-fone with the screen switched off. And we're working on the voice patterns now. We'll have a profile soon." Snell paused for full effect. "Listen" – the Chief Inspector's voice took on a sympathetic tone so bogus Horatio nearly laughed out loud – "are you sure you wouldn't like to confess? The case is open and shut. Motive, opportunity, method. All there. All we need is the murder weapon and you're . . ." he drew his finger across his neck, "*kaputt!* And we think we've got that too. The caller was probably a neighbour who'll come forward once it's announced that you're under arrest. You know you could" – Horatio couldn't believe the Inspector was about to mouth that ultimate police cliché – "save yourself and everyone else a lot of bother if you were to confess now."

At least the idiot had let him know that the caller had been anonymous.

Horatio, never much of an optimist, felt utter despair. To

have been brought from the height of human happiness — waking up with a naked Cleo in his bed yesterday morning — to *this*. It was the very unfairness of it all which made him swear not only to get out of this, but to destroy whoever was behind it all.

The prospect of being tried under the new Legal Directive appalled him. The old English common law had at least provided a duty solicitor, impartial barristers and judges, as well as a jury. Under the Union system, judges were appointed by the Justice Ministry, usually more for obedience or to fill the various gender and minority quotas than for knowledge of the law. Prosecutors were often ambitious politicians out to make names for themselves. Judges put questions themselves and then interpreted the "spirit" of the law rather than sticking to its letter. Justice was a lottery and, as with the Euro-Lottery, the state usually won.

"Thank you, Dr Lestoq. You are going downstairs now. In the next half-hour, assuming Pathology comes back with a report of asphyxiation rather than heart failure . . ."

"He was ninety-one for God's sake!"

"We're quite aware of his age. We're also aware of the fact that someone foned us two minutes before we caught you to say that he was being smothered with a sofa cushion. As I was saying, assuming the lab reports asphyxiation, I'll be charging you with the murder of Admiral Michael Ratcliffe." He rolled the R's, clearly enjoying the theatre of it all. Horatio suspected that the video of the interview would be played at his trial and the Chief Inspector was probably setting himself up for a Courtroom Channel 44 Trial Special. There'd be interviews, in-depth profiles, performance fees. Snell might be able to get his own show out of it, or a lucrative advertising contract: "*Buy this tasteful fawn Detective's Raincoat, as worn by Snell of the Yard.*"

Back in his custody suite, Horatio went over the interview again in his mind, trying to apply some logic to what he'd heard.

What had Snell asked about when first he'd heard of Ratcliffe? *That* was surely the day he ought to have cast his mind back to. Not the events of Saturday at all, but of the day before. Last Friday. May Day Eve. April the 30th.

The day of his discovery.

PART
II

09.35 Friday, 30th April

The tram deposited Horatio outside the Federal Records Office, a series of large, low, pentagonal buildings of beige brick overlooking the Thames at Kew. He estimated it at about eighty years old. Horatio knew the complex well, both from his research for his thesis and from his many journalistic forays there, providing the historical context to current news stories. He was perversely fond of the ugly old info-factory.

It was here that he had won his journalistic spurs back in January 2042. Using the Fifty Year Rule, he had discovered that in December 1991 the then British Foreign Secretary, Douglas Hurd, had struck a clever if cynical deal with Herr Genscher, his German opposite number. Hurd had promised British recognition of Croatia and Slovenia in return for German acquiescence in a British opt-out from the Social Chapter of the Treaty of European Union which they were then negotiating at Maastricht.

Horatio had long suspected that the recognition of the two breakaway Yugoslav republics exactly a month after the Social Chapter opt-out had been no coincidence. He was looking forward to next January, when the 1995 papers might, unless they were very well weeded, reveal that Hurd had assumed all along that the Social Chapter would be gradually infiltrated into British law by the back door anyhow, via the use of the Euro-Court. The same court that freed Myra Hindley.

It had also been whilst he was slogging away at the Records Office's labyrinthine libraries of files, microfilms, CD-Roms and EuroNet computer logs that Horatio had discovered the clues that led to his twin successes – the historic revelations which had made him the toast of Oxford's senior common rooms. As he settled himself in front of the computer terminal on the first floor and began ordering up documents, Horatio indulged himself with the memories of the two great sleuthing triumphs which had brought him his thirty minutes of global fame three years ago.

From a will at Somerset House, Horatio had tracked down a diary in Vienna, from an entry in which he later found a lost property ticket dated November 1919 and stamped "Reading Railway Station". From that clue he discovered in an attic in the French-Algerian quarter of Stratford-upon-Avon the original manuscript of Lawrence of Arabia's *Seven Pillars of Wisdom*.

Far from being stolen, as Lawrence had believed, the manuscript had been conscientiously handed in to the lost property office by an absent-minded old lady who had been sitting next to him before he changed trains. The attendant there had kept it, but had been unable to sell it privately. Fifteen years later his home was blitzed in the Second Nationalist War. The surviving effects had gone to a sister in Warwickshire, from whose grandson's loft Horatio had triumphantly extracted the long-lost typescript.

Horatio's second, even greater, coup came a year later when he worked out from a clue in John Stuart Mill's papers that the housemaid had not after all burnt the first draft of Carlyle's *History of the French Revolution*, as literary tradition had always supposed. In fact Mill, for purely ideological reasons, had attempted to suppress this magisterial denunciation of liberal democracy, and had secretly deposited it in a strongbox in a Dublin bank. From where Horatio – "Demon Document Detective" as the *Mail* had by now dubbed him – retrieved it under the glare of all the major global cable networks' camera lights.

Mill had thought Carlyle incapable of the effort of rewriting the tome, but, as the first draft was to show, the final version was actually far better than the original. Mill's reputation suffered further when Horatio went on to prove that, after Mill had sacked the maid, she had died in penury protesting her innocence. Even the *Sun* had covered the story, albeit under the headline EGGHEAD'S CLEANING OPERATIVE SHAME.

It had been a risk. What a fool he'd have looked if the strongbox had *not* contained the manuscript! Sometimes even now he woke up in the night sweating from the recurring nightmare that he was opening the box only to find it contained waste paper.

What had happened since those heady days, Horatio wondered, to turn the Demon Document Detective into such a disappointed, sad and boozy hack? Instead of making headlines in the world press, as he had at twenty-six, he was just churning out background pieces to fundamentally dull occasions like the thirtieth anniversary of the Aachen Referendum. The relevant papers had all been released back in 2040 under the Twenty-Five Year Rule.

The Referendum had been crucial constitutionally, of course, but there was nothing new to say about it today. Here he was, thrust along by poverty and Weaning, wandering down yet another blind alley in his career.

It was only towards the end of this all-too-typical bout of

self-pity that Horatio, still at the terminal, noticed Alex Tallboys sitting at Table 4, Desk E about fifty metres away. Quite apart from an initial feeling of irritation at his having lost his favourite desk, close to the queue for the files when they were produced, Horatio experienced a sharp pang of panic. Tallboys was nearly two metres tall, a cruel, brutish slab of muscle. He had never missed an opportunity to embarrass or humiliate Horatio. What could he be researching here?

Just as he turned to go downstairs and beg a day's grace from Weaning, Tallboys looked up and smiled at him. At least his eyes narrowed and the ends of his lips elongated momentarily. He then looked back down and carried on reading. It was something of a revelation to Horatio that the savage was capable either of smiling *Or* reading. His Oxford place had been solely the result of social affirmative action, after all. Horatio found a desk as far away as possible – 26Y – and waited for his documents to arrive.

"Sorry love, all yours have already been called up," said Kylie-Terèse from behind the counter when, half an hour later, he had gone over to complain to her about their late delivery.

"What, *exactly* the same ones?" he expostulated. The odds against that must be a thousand to one.

"Yeah, an' they've used override by the looks of things." She looked genuinely sympathetic. The system by which Commission officials could jump the queue for documents was as unpopular with F.R.O. employees as it was with researchers.

The perfect adjective for Kylie-Terèse, thought Horatio, was "blowsy". He had once given her tea in the cafeteria downstairs, listening sympathetically to her complaints about her unfaithful hairdresser boyfriend, all told in her Estuary-Grunge accent.

"How about the others?"

"Nope. Two've been reclassified under the Fifty, one's missing altogether and three are out to another reader."

"Who?"

"I can't say who. You know that."

Almost on a whim Horatio asked: "It isn't 4E by any chance?"

She looked at her screen for a second, smiled and answered quietly, nodding over towards the oblivious Tallboys. "It would be quite improper for me to confirm that that dishy-looking hunk over at 4E seems to have overridden all your requests this morning. And from the looks of things, only about two minutes after you made 'em an' all."

"What can I do about it?"

"Nuffink on those. Got any others? I could do 'em by hand if you like."

"You heroine," said Horatio, slipping a ten-euro note across the counter. He rather hoped she'd tuck it into her bra like in the movies, but no.

"Could we do it without filling in the slips? I'd prefer him not to be able to check what I'd seen." Before she could refuse he handed her his pencil and was calling out file numbers.

"FO 373/10742 and 743, PREM 18/4011, HO 384/44280, T 444/56432. That ought to be enough."

She looked up at him.

"I'll bring 'em to you in the microfilm room. So, anyway, what's up between you two then?"

"No idea, but it can't just be bad luck."

"Well, all I can say from where I'm standing" – she giggled, sneaking another look at Tallboys – "is that if it's over a woman, you're only in with a chance if she prefers brains to brawn. And not many of us girls do!" From anyone else that would have been hurtful, but somehow not from her.

"How's the horny hairdresser?"

"Dumped him. Can you believe it" – she giggled again but didn't even lower her voice – "he was gay!" It was Horatio's turn to be conspiratorial. She must have known that using that word in public could get her the sack under the new Anti-Sexism Directive. Not for the first time he wondered why the cockney working class – as they used to be called before Classlessness – were so much more robust in ignoring the new legislation and Designated Vocab than anyone else.

He wandered back to his desk, collected his pad and pencils, checked the infra-red was in his jacket pocket and made quite a scene of leaving. He looked suitably dejected, waving to Tallboys with a brief open hand movement, like he'd seen motorists give when passing in narrow lanes.

Once out of sight, instead of going downstairs to the exit, Horatio made his way to the microfilm room on the second floor. He chose a seat behind the door and waited. Tallboys had purposefully stymied his research by using the override facility. Out of spite because he'd hated him at university a decade ago. What a jerk.

The bundle of papers, files and printed documents which Kylie-Terèse brought up ten minutes later was about thirty centimetres high. He soon realised they were distinctly second-rate. Horatio had naturally ordered up the most important and interesting files first, but those were all with Tallboys. Nevertheless, as a veteran researcher, he knew that even the most dull dross could yield up gold. He'd discovered the clue to his Carlyle coup in the twelfth and last volume of household accounts kept by Mill's butler's wife.

Three and a half hours passed and Horatio found nothing.

He had worked through the lunch hour in case Tallboys went to the cafeteria. He was bored, hungry, despondent and feeling more than usually sorry for himself.

Despite attempts by archivists to get him to use microfilms or facsimiles of documents in his research, Horatio always insisted on working with the originals. Anything else, he used to tell archivists, was like being asked to make do with photocopies of one's love letters. They would nod at that line, little realising that Horatio's own archive of love letters consisted of one illiterate postcard from Helsinki sent by a spotty exchange student he'd once tried to interfere with at a teenage pyjama party. Fellow hacks found Horatio's demand for original documents highly idiosyncratic, especially as the texts of most official memoranda were available at home on EuroNet at the press of a button. But he was adamant.

So when, through a mixture of tiredness, absent-minded fantasising about Leila, and a wholly typical bout of malcoordination, Horatio knocked his penultimate file onto the floor, the slip of paper which flew out was an original. In order to replace it he had to turn to leaf 248 of T 444/56432, a tremendously tedious Treasury file relating to the Referendum's financing.

As he did so, something written on it caught his eye.

7

13.20 Friday, 30th April

The note was signed G.R.P., which Horatio knew to be the initials of Gregory Percival who back in 2015 had been Special Advisor to the then British Foreign Secretary, James Mackintosh. Now Commission Secretary, he was the most powerful Civil Servant in the entire regional government and a major power in Brussels as well. At fifty-six, Percival had passed compulsory retirement age, but his position seemed impregnable because he was known to have the ear of the Wilhelmstrasse and was widely believed to be a big noise in the Berlin-Brussels Bureau as well.

Horatio had already interviewed him for the first two of his *Times* articles. Despite Percival's eminence it had been relatively easy for him to get in touch as they had often met at All Souls, where Percival was an emeritus Fellow.

Tall, smooth, impeccably dressed, "a fine all-round sports-person in his day, still a keen yachtsperson" (*The Economist*), and speaking with one of those deep, authoritative voices to which people naturally listened, Percival was everything Horatio knew he could never be. He personified the Eurostablishment at its most confident and distinguished. He had also been helpful and charming to the point that even

Horatio, who was instinctively suspicious of all Commission officials, had to confess himself impressed.

The note was merely a slip from Percival's official notepad. Dated 5/5/15, it informed his opposite number at the Treasury of Brussels' approval of the disbursement of seven million euros to help offset some unspecified incidental costs of the Referendum. They'd left it pretty late, thought Horatio, with the poll only having taken place the previous day. They probably wouldn't have been quite so keen to cough up had the result gone the other way!

As he reached for his infra-red from his jacket pocket, Horatio was suddenly flung forward in his chair by a sharp blow to his back.

"Hello old cock!" It was Tallboys, who obviously interpreted it as a friendly slap. "How're you doing?"

"Fine, fine, Alex." Horatio forced a smile. "No ribs broken. How about you?"

"Pretty fit. Mustn't grumble." God, how he hated this hail-fellow-well-met mateyness. Let alone the old-fashioned Home Counties banter. Next he'd be talking about wizard-prangs and jolly-good-shows. What did the dreadful oaf want? Tallboys took a look at Horatio's pad.

"Still sleuthing away then?"

"One does one's best."

"Found anything sexy?"

"No, after three hours' work, absolutely bugger all. Look at my notes." Tallboys had been anyhow. He gesticulated towards a blank pad of paper with only five lines under "*Aachen Referendum*, 4/5/15" written in a shorthand he felt sure Tallboys wouldn't know. "I think everything to be said about Aachen came out five years ago with the Twenty-Five Year Rule. I haven't been able to dig up anything new today." He resisted the temptation to add, "especially as some tosser has called up all the files I requested".

"Bad luck old thing. Must be a bind. Still, tomorrow's another day and everything."

Horatio was surprised at Tallboys' quoting from a Hollywood film. Rather daring for him. It was probably unintentional.

"Not for me, it isn't. I've got to file by Sunday and this place closes for May Day."

"Rotten luck. I enjoyed parts one and two, though they must have rustled some dovecotes among the Powers That Be." Horatio shrugged. He couldn't decide which irritated him more about Tallboys' conversation – the clichés or the mixed metaphors.

"To slightly change the subject," said Tallboys – Horatio decided on split infinitives – "are you going along to Frobisher's party tonight?"

Horatio nodded. "Yes. Are you?"

"Suppose so. The wife wants to, though I don't really click with all those art-tart friends of his. Anyhow, see you there. Keep up the old scribbling!" Then another slap on the back, hardly any less violent than the first.

Once he had gone Horatio wondered why he had failed to summon up the courage to ask Tallboys why he was screwing up his research. Was it to protect Kylie-Terèse? No, he admitted to himself, that consideration hadn't figured in the equation at all. It was just his old funk.

Standing by the small window in the corner of the room, Horatio watched and waited until he saw Tallboys walk outside and get into an auto. It was a light blue grade 4 electric. At least the creep hadn't got the seniority at P.I.D. to rate a decent one. Marty drove a green grade 3 petrol.

With Tallboys safely away, Horatio took out his infra-red

again and returned to Percival's note, which he had managed to cover with his pad during the interview. Squinting through the machine he could just make out what had been written on the same pad of paper immediately before the note to the Treasury, from the slight indentation the pen had made on the paper below. It was a method he often used, indeed which he had almost pioneered. He'd employed it three years ago to catch out the late Lord Hurd, by reading a doodle which was later destroyed but the minute impression of which had remained on the page underneath.

This was written directly over the Treasury message, but Horatio could still just make out the words. Undated, unsigned and handwritten, it read simply:

S/S, Do Not Panic. S-W.C dealt w by F.E. & me this a.m. Also S.W. Dodson squared — 2m. Ratcliffe tougher, but took 5. S. OK. B-B.B. to pay. I'll arrange. N.R.N. if OK. Repeat: Don't Panic. Destroy this.

No point in going through Mackintosh's papers for the original then, thought Horatio.

This note was worth pursuing. Was it the repeated admonition not to panic, the hieroglyphics, or the word "squared"? Or was it the initials of the Berlin-Brussels Bureau? Back in Aachen days the Bureau had been the praetorian guard of the Euro-federalist movement, and today it was still believed to be a power behind the Commission. Housed in Norman Foster's New Reichstag building in Berlin and also in the Mies van der Rohe in Brussels, it was a visceral force in the Eurocratic leviathan. Since regional powers over Commission expenditure had been curtailed in the two decades after Aachen, few had seriously challenged, or even really questioned, the role of this highly secretive organisation.

All Horatio knew for certain was that he wanted to know more.

His first call was on *Who's Who* for 2015. This yielded three Dodsons: the Director-General of the Child Maintenance Agency, a neurosurgeon, and the arms and munitions supplier to the V.A.T. Inspectorate. None looked promising.

Ratcliffes seemed almost as unforthcoming. Horatio remembered a Ratcliffe as a founding member of Chris Patten's Conservative & Christian Democrat Alliance, but it turned out that he had died in 2012. There were five in the 2015 edition. The Chief Prosecutor for the Environmental Health Agency, a retired admiral, the ex-Chair of the British Beef Council – Horatio felt rueful about that one, he'd loved British beef – and a High Court judge. Finally there was a Cambridge don Horatio had never heard of called Dr Jeremiah Ratcliffe, who listed *Shakespeare the Euro-Poet* and *European Scenes from Dickens* among his publications.

The judge was worth looking into. If the Foreign & Commonwealth Office, as it had been called before the Aachen Treaty transferred foreign policy-making to Brussels, had "squared" a judge it could be a major news story. Perhaps the admiral was worth a glance too, although he'd already retired by the time of Aachen. That was clearly when the note was written, as it directly preceded the 5th May 2015 note on Percival's pad. For the first time in three years Horatio felt that after all that sifting there might at last be a nugget somewhere at the bottom of his sieve.

In the library on the floor above he again consulted all the books on the Referendum which he had used for the first two of his *Times* articles. Neither a Dodson nor a Ratcliffe appeared in any of the indexes. Then he sat down to read the

Introduction of the Report of the Chief Scrutineer. That was a historic document in itself, the last report to be laid before the British Parliament prior to it dissolving itself. On the basis of that Report, half a millennium of representative parliamentary government had been wound up in an afternoon.

In the penultimate paragraph Mr Speaker Dorrell had written: "*I should like to place on record my warmest thanks to all those Regional Commissioners, national and local government officials, regional scrutineers, computer and electronic experts and others who helped make the Referendum run so smoothly. In particular I should like to thank . . .*" There followed five pages of names in small print. Dorrell was clearly painstaking. Horatio spotted *Ratcliffe, Admiral Sir Michael*, towards the top. He'd been Chief Scrutineer for the South-West Region. It took longer to find *Dodson, Jacob*. Eventually Horatio spotted him in the Computer and Secretarial section, also for the South-West Region. One of Dorrell's appendices was a facsimile of Ratcliffe's Report, signed and dated 5th May, which stated that the Referendum in the South-West Region had been conducted "fairly, freely and in full accordance with all the regulations".

A return trip downstairs to *Who's Who* yielded two further nuggets. Dodson had never appeared in it, which was not surprising for a minor computer boffin, and Michael Ratcliffe was still alive.

Ratcliffe, Adm. Michael Keppel, KCB (2013–30); DSO (2000); RN (ret'd); Commander-in-Chief, Naval Home Command 2012–14: b 15 March 1954; s of Leslie John Ratcliffe and Agnes Mary Sorenson; m 1978, Joan Catherine Thorpe (d 2011); 1 s (decd). Educ: Pangbourne Coll, Naval College, Dartmouth. Served: Malvinas (Falklands) 1982, Fleet Signals Officer, Home Fleet 1989, Persian Gulf 1990–1,

*Comdr; HMS Ajax 1997; Capt 1999; Capt 2nd Frigate
Squadron 2001; Dir Signals Div; Admiralty 2004–12; Rear-
Admiral 2008; Admiral; 2010 Dep CDS (Systems) 2010–12;
ret'd 2014. Dir: Racal-Philips 2014–20, Aerospace Commu-
nications 2014–29; Consultant; Siemens-Plessey 2021–34.*
Recreations: *cricket, sailing, gardening.* Address: *The
Rectory, Ibworth, Hants RG2 4RW. Fone 011131 47602*
Clubs: *Euro Yacht Squadron, M.C.C.*

No mention of his role in the Referendum, Horatio noted.
And the Classlessness legislation soon abolished both his
knighthood and Pangbourne College.

Horatio's memory wandered back to that extraordinary
period. He had gone up to Westminster School for the
Michaelmas Term of 2030. He was fourteen, tiny and
terrified. After those bizarre first ten weeks, his mother had
told him that the Classlessness Directive meant that for
reasons of social equality the school was to be closed. There
was some talk of his going to the Eton being set up in some
Norman château, but when another Directive announced that
all private education ran contrary to the Euro-citizens' right to
classlessness, that too was abolished. The only thing, apart
from his friendship with Marty, that he took away from
Westminster was his Queen's accent, which had only got him
teased and bullied by the likes of Tallboys later in life.

Horatio packed up and shuffled out of the building to make
some calls in private. There was a very light drizzle, not
enough to get him too wet as he stood under the only tree in
the middle of the deserted autopark, but just enough to
discourage other people from coming out unless they were
going to their autos. He pressed the "Record" button on his
pager.

It took some time to get through to Percival. Was it *The Times* or All Souls which opened the doors?

"I must say Doctor Lestoq, after your first two pieces I am somewhat nervous about speaking to you." Percival sounded not in the least degree nervous.

"Oh really Commissioner, and why's that?"

"To be called a 'smooth operator', and my former master a 'wily Eurocrat', can hardly be described as complimentary." If Percival had *really* minded he could easily have fobbed Horatio off. In fact, he was quite vain enough to enjoy being described as a smooth operator in *The Times*. In Horatio's experience it was often the *éminences grises* who actually secretly enjoyed publicity the most. As for Mackintosh, who had died back in the early Thirties, loyalty to one's deceased former boss could only go so far.

"I do hope I didn't offend you, but on reflection I feel both descriptions are justified. Now, might I ask you a blunt question?"

"Blunt and sharp at the same time, Dr Lestoq. You never fail to impress." Horatio suspected Percival was just amusing himself, playing with him, sparring with an intellectual equal for the sport of it rather than out of any ulterior political motive or sense of professional obligation. Very well, the next question almost asked itself:

"Who were Messrs Dodson and Ratcliffe?"

"I'm sorry?" Pretending not to hear properly or recognise the names. A classic delaying tactic?

"Dodson," enunciated Horatio carefully into the pager, "and Ratcliffe."

"I don't know. A smart shoe shop perhaps? Or one of those small stockbroking firms from the days before community

65

broking?" It was a good performance, but the flippancy betrayed him.

"Jacob Dodson and Admiral Michael Ratcliffe?" persisted Horatio.

"I'm afraid I haven't heard of either of them." Pressing the phone as close to his ear as possible, Horatio thought he could detect, beneath the charming veneer, and albeit to an infinitesimal degree, a tiny note of fear. It was no more than a hint, a *frisson*, if it was there at all. Not guilt. Nor embarrassment. Still less regret – the man could hardly have the capacity for those emotions in his job – but actual fear. Horatio wished he had used a vid-fone and could see whether the same lightning twitch had crossed Percival's face.

"You wrote about them to Mackintosh at the time of the Referendum, might that help?"

"No." The voice was serious now. "As you must know, one writes scores of such notes every day. It was thirty years ago and a very busy period. Now, if you were to g-mail me the text, or better still send the actual thing itself, I might be in a better position to comment on it. What was the reply? That might help jog my appalling old memory." Not wanting Percival to know he didn't have either the note or the reply, if ever there was a reply, and not knowing if Percival knew he hadn't got them, Horatio answered the second question.

"You said no reply was needed if he approved the note." How had Percival known it *was* a note at all, rather than a letter or memo, if he could not remember writing it? "Might Dodson and Ratcliffe have had anything to do with the Referendum in your opinion, sir?"

"Look, I'm not certain I like your tone. As I said, I'm sorry but they really ring no bells at all. Truly they don't. They can't have been very major figures in the whole thing, though, otherwise I'm sure they would. If I were you, Dr Lestoq, I'd concentrate on the major issues raised by the Referendum on the Aachen Treaty. Like you did in your first two rather irritatingly perceptive pieces. This looks like a red herring to me."

Horatio was about to pursue a different line when Percival continued: "Now, as you can imagine with all this New Zealand business, I am tremendously busy at the moment. Indeed, I see I'm already late for a meeting."

"Goodbye, sir. I'm sorry for troubling you and thanks for your help."

"I look forward to seeing you in college sometime. I'll be looking out for your article. Goodbye."

The speed with which he had been dismissed spoke libraries. It convinced Horatio more than anything else that something was definitely up. If Percival had been late for a meeting, why had he accepted Horatio's call?

Returning by the 18.00 tram, Horatio experienced the same sense of exhilaration he had last felt during the Mill/Carlyle affair.

The Demon Document Detective was back in business.

22.10 Friday, 30th April

There was really only one reason why Horatio bothered to go along to Marty Frobisher's May Day Eve party. The women. They could keep the rest of it; the boozing, the networking, the Hunky Regular Guyishness. Not only did great-looking women gravitate towards Marty's third-floor flat in Lower Sloane Street every April 30th, but there were also sometimes a smattering of the slightly quirky ones who had proved in Horatio's limited experience to be the people most liable to fall for him, or the least likely to shy away.

It had been there two years ago that he had met the Estonian Esperanto expert Leila Haapsalu. She had seemed just too lovely to be for real. Sure enough, she wasn't. A member of the Baltic separatist underground movement, she was trying to make contact with the English Resistance Movement. Europol had somehow got onto her and taped everything that went on in his flat. He still sometimes woke up sweating with embarrassment at the thought of it. Thank God Marty had been able to get hold of the vids before Tallboys could give them a public airing around the Political Intelligence Department.

Horatio had never even had a chance to say goodbye to Leila. The first inkling he got that she was anything out of the ordinary came when P.I.D. Special Branch smashed his door down at 03.00 one September night and dragged them both off to Paddington Green.

He'd had no choice but to turn Union evidence at the trial. There wasn't much he could say. The entire proceedings had been held *in camera*. He had testified by vid-link, so he had not had a chance to see her then, either. He later learnt she had been charged with the catch-all "activities prejudicial to the integrity of the Union" offence and sentenced to twenty years in a Finnish detention camp, where she was kept completely incommunicado. He still thought about her.

Right now, though, he had to concentrate on the present. One glance on entering the party and he had categorised everyone in Marty's large drawing room solely in terms of their sexual availability. It was a technique he'd learnt at Oxford from David Fraser, the Conservative Democrat hack. Fraser had told him how within thirty seconds of entering – i.e. in the time it took to cross the room, say hello to the host and get to the drink and pills – he had divided everyone into one of five distinct political categories: safe supporters, probables, dodgy/don't knows, floater/waverers and opposition.

Fraser would then spend the rest of the party steering himself towards the maximum-return groups. He would greet the first – but not waste time actually talking to them – chat up the second and third and virtually salivate over the fourth. He'd always ignore the last. It was cynical, Fraser readily admitted, and it reduced any sort of university social life to a constant stream of hackery, but it paid dividends come election time. Horatio remembered thinking at the time that he had never spoken to Fraser at a party when he hadn't been constantly looking over his shoulder for more important people. This he had hitherto put down to mere social climbing. He found it strangely gratifying to discover that there had been a far more calculating and ambitious reasoning behind Fraser's irritating habit.

Having been President of the Oxford Union and Chairman of the Conservative and Christian Democrat Association, Fraser had gone off to a *stagiaire* internship in Brussels. Today he was a junior spokesman in the Commission Secretariat in Whitehall, the acknowledged first rung on the ladder to a seat at Strasbourg. If he was interested in wielding real power he might even find a job in the Commission itself.

Fraser was at the party, over in a corner standing under one of Marty's huge post-post-modern nude paintings, sucking up to the Deputy Director of South English Region P.I.D., Joachim Bittersich. Old habits die hard. Even from behind, Horatio knew it was Bittersich. His bald, oval head sticking out of his black polo neck and inclined at an angle looked like a rugby ball just before kick-off. Horatio watched Fraser leaning forward with a glass of something doubtless non-contraband and probably non-alcoholic too, nodding sagely and occasionally over-laughing at Bittersich's heavy Teutonic jokes.

Fraser's other piece of advice to Horatio had been to let the seducees do all the talking, as no compliment one could ever pay is half so impressive as being listened to attentively. Fraser looked as though he believed Bittersich to be the most fascinating person at the party, possibly in the world.

Horatio, simply by exchanging women for voters in the formula, trusted in the Fraser method implicitly. Yet he had never had much luck with the opposite sex. He must be the only person in either English region, he told himself, who had more ex-girlfriends in Finnish detention camps than in London.

He avoided the middle of parties if possible. The noise made it harder to shine conversationally. Better to stay at the margin and pick off stragglers. He liked to think of himself as a Russian wolf tracking retreating French soldiers in 1812. Wait until the victim is weak, tired and ideally also drunk. Then pounce. Horatio would love to be able to say it never failed, but with him it almost always did. Every time he went to a party he reminded himself of the basics. It should be second nature by twenty-nine, but he had never got on with Dick or Marcia or their friends when he was young. Whilst his contemporaries were experimenting with flirting, pills, alcohol, party-giving and sex, he was reading Dead White Anglo-Saxon Male literature at home.

So he went over the rules again, just like Marty had told him a thousand times. Identify your victim. Lots of eye-contact. Affect a jokey modesty to put her at her ease. Surreptitiously drop in All Souls if she shows any intellectual interests at all. Flirt mildly and above all talk about her, her, her. "The rules have been the same since the dawn of human communication," Marty had told him, "but it's astonishing how often they're broken."

Well, tonight they weren't going to be.

This party seemed harder than ever though. They looked a real Generation Z crowd. Endless H.R.G.s looking bicepful. The very latest Paris, Milan and Bonn fashions were all on display. And that was just the men. Enslaved to the latest federal fashions, the girls mostly wore little navy blue numbers. Horatio made a mental note to speak German only if there was one present; he was not about to fall for this absurd new fad of speaking it amongst English people.

He estimated about a hundred people had turned up already, all invited by pager at the press of a button last month.

He had to confess himself impressed with the bunch Marty had got along. The flat looked magnificent as usual. How could he afford such a luxurious pad in Central London, let alone all those ludicrous Damien Hirsts on the ceiling? Marty didn't appreciate or value art, but he certainly knew what appreciated in value.

"Horror my man, *very* well done on those Aachen pieces." Mike Hibbert had steered his way towards him from the other side of the room. Tall, cadaverous, ambitious and very clever, Hibbert had always personified for Horatio the old Shakespearian line about Cassius. Hibbert also had a disconcerting habit of taking confidences but never giving any. But Horatio's instinct not to waste any valuable party time talking to other males was easily overcome by his love of praise.

"I'm pleased you liked them."

"You sailed pretty close with some of your remarks, I thought."

"Thanks. I'll take that as a compliment, however it was meant. Might I rate being watched by your lot one day?" Mike worked with Marty.

"Shouldn't imagine so. We know you're a patriot at heart, despite all that Estonian business. I can't quite imagine you spending your weekends putting on a balaclava and burning down German holiday homes in Herefordshire!"

"And what are you up to, Michael?" Hibbert raised one eyebrow. Horatio had always wished he could do that. "I'm sorry, of course you can't say. Stupid question. It's one of the great drawbacks about having friends in P.I.D. that you can't exhibit even a polite and superficial interest in their jobs. It tends to cut out rather a large area of conversation."

"Well, let's keep it on you then," said Hibbert. "When's part three out?"

"Tuesday, to coincide with the thirtieth anniversary."

"Of course. Anything in it to shock us?"

"Guten abend, Herr Doktor, und wie geht's Ihnen?" It was Peter Riley. His ruddy-orange hair, which he always liked to call "auburn" or "russet", was getting quite thin on top now.

"Oh sod off Carrot Top, you're as South English as I am and anyhow it's '*Wie geht's dir?*' Familiar form."

"But I haven't seen you since this party last year."

"Doesn't matter. We know each other, that's what counts in German grammar."

"Does it, Mike?" Riley turned to Hibbert.

"Think so. It's a beastly language, whatever it is."

"Beastly?" said Horatio. "Beastly? Why's everyone speaking in Nineteen-Thirties prep school language all of a sudden? Alex Tallboys was saying 'Golly gosh what a swiz!' to me this morning." Horatio enjoyed exaggerating.

"I think on matters of German grammar," said Mike, ignoring him and nodding towards Fraser, "we ought to ask David over there. Only from the looks of things he's so far up my boss's *Arsch* – that's one German word I *do* know – that only the soles of his shoes are visible."

"Jawohl!" agreed Riley.

A waiter refilled the glasses and offered crisps. Horatio took a handful. He shouldn't have, but he had long ago lost any self-control he might ever have had over matters concerning his weight. Despite his back problems, the sweating when he ran for a tram, the palpitations when he walked up more than two flights of stairs and, worst of all by far, his gross unattractiveness to women, he knew he could do nothing about it any longer. He had never bought Cyril Connolly's old cliché about how inside every fat man there was a thin one trying to get out. Horatio knew that inside *him* was someone obscenely gross struggling to get out. He had played no sports since some rather agricultural hockey at school. Recently he'd considered hiring a tapeworm from Slimfast Inc., but couldn't really justify the 180 euros a month it would cost.

A few weeks before, Horatio had convinced himself he was diabetic. Yes he was always thirsty, yes he did need to go to the unisex lavabo cubicles a lot, yes his hair was starting to recede, and so on. Until it was pointed out by his long-suffering doctor that another major symptom was severe weight loss, Horatio was pleased with his self-diagnosis. Now he appreciated that it was just the same hypochondria which had four months earlier made him rush to the doctor complaining, with no evidence, that his tongue was getting bigger. Over that fantasy, too, he had required a third opinion.

It was largely down to this hypochondria that he didn't pop pills. Unlike everyone else who claimed it was a bad habit they were trying to break, he rather respected those who did it, believing it to be "a cool and sexy thing to do". But he suspected pills destroyed brain cells, however much the Surgeon-General denied it. As his brain was really his sole asset, Horatio knew he simply couldn't risk it.

"God there are some awful people here," said Riley. The malice had already started and Horatio was only on his second glass. Splendid.

"Such as?"

"You see that shy couple over by the door?" Horatio looked over. He despised shyness, rating it alongside frugality and modesty.

"Remember them from university?" asked Riley.

"The Longmans? Yes. Wadham, weren't they?"

"Yup. He's a sound technician or something now, works in the music business. Makes quite a lot apparently. Anyhow, they cornered me just now and insisted on showing me their holiday vid on his pager."

"How awful," said Hibbert. "Where had they been?"

"Aachen!" Mike and Horatio laughed out loud. "This is of me in Treatystrasse, Sally outside the hotel, both of us by the Blair statue, that sort of thing."

"*Quel cauchemar!* It's the old story," said Mike. "At Oxford Jim Longman was a great conversationalist, wasn't he, but since marrying her he's tended to lie doggo. Same rather goes for her in a way. She's Spanish. They got engaged suspiciously soon after the Inter-Regional Marriage Subsidy came into effect." Bitchier and bitchier, thought Horatio, beginning to enjoy himself. It was Riley's turn:

"But neither of them can touch those two City boys over by the window." Mike and Horatio glanced surreptitiously across and looked back. "Both very well off. Must each be getting the Maximum Wage. After the inevitable boring speculation about whether Frankfurt will be sticking up interest rates again next week, they started complaining about having to work there for their hundred thousand or whatever it is a year. They're getting all nostalgic for the Square Mile! I can't tell you how dull it was. All about how wonderful it must have been in the old days when London was a major financial capital, blah blah blah. Made me quite angry, actually. Nostalgia's a form of sedition you know." Said in such a pompous, blimpish way, it rather irritated Horatio, especially when Hibbert added: "It ought to be made an anti-Union activity."

"Oh, come on Mike!" expostulated Horatio, "you can't mean that."

"I do rather. All that sentimental guff about how wonderful it was in the past and how much better off we all were before

Aachen. It's just a subtle way of propagating anti-Union sedition."

This was too much for Horatio. "But what if it's true? I'm a historian, I have to say whether it's true or not."

"Why? Why do you have to shove it down everyone's throats?"

"Shove what?"

"You know. That we're all worse off, that we made a mistake, that we should have stayed independent. Voted no to Aachen. Why do you have to taunt the people with that knowledge?" Riley and Horatio looked at each another in astonishment. Hibbert worked for P.I.D. after all.

After an infinitesimal pause Mike added emphatically. *Too* emphatically: "Not that I believe that myself of course. I mean I really don't!" He quickly looked around and behind him. "I mean for God's sake don't go around ascribing those sorts of views to me. I love the U.S.E. I'm just saying that you lot, you hacks and commentators, cause everyone else a lot of heartache and trouble by making people feel conned and unhappy."

"I thought you said you liked the articles I'd written."

"Yes, well maybe in retrospect they were a tad too revisionist for my taste."

"Well, you're definitely working in the right place if you think that." Hibbert took it as personally as it was intended. The conversation was degenerating fast.

"What do you mean by that?"

"Do you really think that it's quite OK to tamper with historical truth in order to conform to the political mores of the day?"

"Come on, Lestoq, every age has done that. That's why history continues to be written. Don't be so naive."

"It isn't written just to fit in with the propaganda demands of the Political Intelligence Department! Not good history anyway, and certainly not the sort I want to write. I must say, you're making out a good case for just the sort of censorship and pilgering you used to despise at Oxford. Working at P.I.D. obviously changes a person." This stung Hibbert.

"And you're so much better are you? What about quality? You write tripe for the papers. You still haven't published a book, and if you carry on in this anti-Union vein you'll never find a publisher anyhow."

"It's not anti-Union! Are you threatening me?"

"It is and you know it. It's only popular because you titillate your readers with sedition. You probably think you're carrying some sort of flame for your old man. Or for that girl of yours. And although you haven't written anything serious yourself, except some thesis about Logic which no one's interested in and which couldn't find a publisher" – it was all coming out – "God knows you sneer enough at other people's work."

Their voices were raised. People were turning round to stare. Horatio had never guessed how much Mike must secretly hate him. Why?

"Such as, Mister Discerning General Reader?" Horatio looked around theatrically, as though D.H.Lawrence might have gatecrashed the party with Yeats in tow.

"Such as any number of people." Hibbert looked around too. "Well, such as that Yank over there for a start." Hibbert pointed at a tall blonde in a red dress who fortunately had her back to them and was far enough away not to be able to hear. Horatio dropped his voice.

"Who's she then?"

"Gemma Reegan. She wrote *The Secret Family of George V*."

"Oh, for God's sake Mike – or Hibbert, as you seem to

prefer to be on surname terms – that book was complete rot!"
Horatio hadn't read it, but he remembered some of the
reviews. It had been about the supposed offspring of a secret
marriage between George V and May Culme-Seymour in
Malta in 1890. "The whole thing was gone into very
thoroughly when the King sued, successfully by the way, in
1911. It all turned out to be balls."

"Well, they would have said that about the Royal Family in
those days, wouldn't they? And that's not my point. At least
she's written a book, several in this case, rather than just
criticised other people's." Just at that moment the American
turned around. She was striking, thought Horatio, beautiful
even, and much better looking in the flesh than on the dust
jacket of her risible bestseller. Unusual that.

"This conversation's going nowhere," said Horatio to
Hibbert.

Without waiting for an answer he walked off towards the
Yank.

"Excuse me. I hope you don't mind my asking, but are you
Gemma Reegan?"

"Yes, Ah am." The voice was Deep South. She smiled a
wide smile. There was something rather stately about her in
her ankle-length toga-dress. Then he saw it. Give her a
haircut, sandals, torch and horizon-gaze and she'd be a dead
ringer for the Statue of Liberty.

"I just wanted to say how much I enjoyed *The Secret Family of
George V*."

"Why, thank you!" Had her accent been any more Southern
it would have dropped into the Gulf of Mexico. Everything
else looked Southern too. The Texan smile, the shoulder pads,
the long blonde tresses, best of all the plunging *décolletage*, the

most fascinating part of which lay roughly at his nose level. That at least wasn't like the Statue of Liberty.

"I imagine you had to spend some time researching in Malta?"

"Ah sure did, and *boy* did Ah have a great time there. It's a great little place."

"How did you get the visa? I thought the trade war had extended to tourism."

"Ah got it through my university. They can make some exceptions for academics."

"Which one is that? Only, I work at a university myself."

"Do you now?" He found the long, unhurried drawl strangely soothing. On closer inspection her hair looked natural and her eyes were that very light blue he'd only ever seen before in bright, cloudless East Anglian skies in winter. He also took in the full, voluptuous contours. The female form had filled about forty per cent of Horatio's waking thoughts ever since his thirteenth birthday, when puberty had hit him with all the force of an intercity shuttle.

"Ah'm from the University of Texas at Austin. Ah majored in English history. Unlike over here," she smiled a perfect array of bright white teeth, the product, doubtless, of rivet-braces applied during her teens, "we still think of British history as a worthwhile subject." He nodded at the criticism, fully concurring with it. During his time at Brasenose the History Department had been closed in order to direct resources to Victim, Complaint and Grievance Studies. "And which college are you from in Ox-ford?" she asked. The gap between the "Ox" and "ford" was nearly too much, almost like an actress auditioning for the part of Scarlett O'Hara. For further authenticity, he thought, there ought to have been an antebellum Mississippi paddle-steamer called *Southern Belle* tooting "Dixie" on its horn in the distance.

"All Souls."

"The graduate one?"

"Yes."

"How ex-citing. Say, you'll probably know a professor there who goes by the name of Doctor Le Stock?" How excruciatingly flattering. He thought quickly.

"Yes, I do know him. Vaguely. At least we dine together in college every so often. It's pronounced 'Lestock', by the way, as in Leicester. Why?"

"Oh Ah just admire his writing, that's all. Plus Ah'm told he's an interesting person to meet. Plus Ah'm hoping for a job on *The Times* and as he writes for it he might be able to give me some advice."

Horatio whipped off an imaginary cavalier's plumed hat and effected a low bow: "Horatio Lestoq. At your service."

"Why you horn-swagglin' little liar!" She looked around. "Why are all these people staring at us?"

"They're staring at you because you are a very attractive woman, and at me because my extravagant gesture just now probably contravenes some section of our Sexism legislation."

"Why's that?"

"Because opening doors for women, standing up for them when they enter a room, proposing to them on one knee – let alone bowing to them at parties – is thought to imply male domination and is thus discouraged. That's when it's not actually illegal."

"Well, where Ah come from it's called chivalry and Ah like it."

"Thank you."

"What Ah don't like is being lied to by you!" He could tell she was teasing.

"A very gentle ruse to find out anything nasty you might have heard about me."

"Are there nasty things?" Was she flirting with him? He hoped so, but having had so little experience of women he couldn't really tell.

"Plenty, but I doubt the Longmans would know them. How dull for you to be stuck talking to them."

"Not really. Ah'm hoping to cover the King's visit for your newspaper, as well as my own syndicated column back home. Mr Longman is possibly one of the people who'll be organising the sound systems for some of the events. He was real interesting."

"Until he brought his holiday vid out."

She laughed and dropped her voice. "Yessir. Until then! So what will you be doing after your last Referendum article, Dr Lestoq?" she asked, with eyes that seemed genuinely interested in the answer.

"No idea. That's part of the fun of being freelance. I've no plans." It was actually part of the terror of being freelance, but he wanted to look debonair. "And please call me Horatio."

"Thank you, Ah will. An' you call me Gemma, by the way. You know, perhaps we could work together on some project sometime? Ah'd just *love* to do something at Ox-ford. You see, Ah live over here full time now." Horatio was happy to hear it. "And Ah want to write something on how misunderstood my country is over here."

"Yes, yes of course." Horatio had never been particularly pro-A.F.T.A, although he enjoyed their movies and coffee. But he liked the look of Gemma, so this would call for some fancy political footwork. His most firmly held beliefs always went into flux when faced with even a passably pretty girl. And Gemma was a beautiful woman. He crossed his fingers in his pocket:

"You know we really ought – I'm sorry if this sounds like a corny pick-up line but I assure you it's not – we really ought to get together sometime to discuss it. I managed to sell those fairly revisionist pieces to *The Times*. I can't see why you can't get them to run a mildly pro-A.F.T.A. article there too. I'll put you in touch with their deputy editor Roderick Weaning if you like."

"Actually Ah've already got an appointment to see Mr Weaning tomorrow morning." Damn. He should have kicked off with a more impressive namedrop. The editor at least.

"May Day morning. That is keen. All right, how about getting together for tea some afternoon?" That sounded nicely non-threatening and it could always progress.

"Well now, there you go and mention the only time in the day that Ah can't see you. Ah have to pick Oliver up from school at sixteen-thirty."

Alarm bells went off in Horatio's mind. Submarine klaxons. Air-raid sirens.

"Oliver?"

"My seven-year-old."

Damn, damn, DAMN! Why no wedding ring? That's the sort of thing that should be stamped out by Europol, thought Horatio, not nostalgia. There had to be a catch. Time at least for one last extravagant compliment though. He chose one which had the added advantage of being true:

"You really don't look as though you could have a child at all, let alone one aged seven."

She blushed pleasingly: "Why, thank you!"

Horatio then spent the requisite number of minutes

showing an altogether bogus interest in the brat whilst mentally planning his escape. He felt like David Fraser must halfway through a promising talk with a floating voter when he suddenly learns that in fact they're a card-carrying Liberal Democrat. Immediate escape looked difficult though, especially after all that stuff about working on projects together.

It arrived in the most welcome, unexpected and frankly glorious shape of someone even taller, fitter and better-looking than Gemma.

"I do hope I'm not disturbing you?" She was about one metre ninety, jet black hair, greeny-blue eyes and physically pneumatic. Pure "Girl from Ipanema", he thought. Tall and tanned and lovely and the rest of it. A few years younger than Gemma, too, Horatio guessed. She looked as though she worked out in the gym while Gemma was picking her son up from school.

Horatio experienced that familiar panic-pang which came whenever he met a truly attractive, ultramodel-type woman. They made him lose his conversational thread, which in turn led him to say stupid things, which, considering his intelligence was his sole selling point, made him angry with himself, which made the burbling worse. Then, just as he grappled his way back and was doing all right, some H.R.G. would come in and whisk her off.

He noticed Riley and Hibbert, who were still talking together in the corner, staring at the two women with unfeigned admiration. He felt a definite *frisson* of pride and pleasure that Gemma and the other girl were both taking such a strong interest in him. Horatio noticed Marty, Fraser and Bittersich all glancing over. Tallboys, too, later on, with a particularly vicious expression on his face. Only James

Longman failed to take any notice of Cleo at all, probably because Olivia was watching him so closely.

She introduced herself as Cleo something, he didn't hear the surname in the hubbub. No wedding ring, he noted. She was wearing a white silk dress roughly the same size as his breast pocket handkerchief. It left just enough to the imagination to have most heterosexuals in the room – even those talking to their fiancées – exhibiting severe Tennis Spectator Neck Syndrome.

And she knew it.

"I'm so sorry for interrupting," she said, "but are you Horatio Lestoq, the writer?" It was for moments like this he had left Oxford. You didn't get this sort of attention in Brasenose senior common room.

"Writer sounds rather grand, doesn't it?" He'd attempt modesty, however bad he was at it: "I'm more of a hack really. Unlike Gemma Reegan here, who's a proper author. I think that sounds best of all." Cleo shook Gemma's hand in a perfunctory, dismissive way, with an unmistakeable now-why-don't-you-toddle-off-little-girl smile. Horatio caught it and yelped inwardly. In his limited experience, women who didn't like other women tended to like men. A lot.

Then all the lights went out.

It was happening more and more, as the Union tried to conserve post-North Sea energy. The cuts were usually well announced and only lasted a few seconds and nowadays people rarely bothered to mention them. It was almost considered unpatriotic to notice, let alone complain. In those particular few seconds, however, something happened. One of the women landed a silent kiss straight onto Horatio's lips. Either could have done it from where she was standing, merely by leaning forward.

The lights came back on.

"Well *that's* something we don't get States-side," said Gemma.

"What?"

"Blackouts. If we ever get round to writing that article, we must mention them."

"We'll be sure to." Neither woman betrayed the minutest indication of having done it. Close examination of their lipstick didn't betray a smudge.

On the stroke of midnight, Marty put on a disc of "Workers of Europe" and, holding hands, everyone sang the four traditional May Day verses lustily.

Across the next room Riley was being pushed quite aggressively by Hibbert. Marty and Brian Watchorn quickly waded over to break it up, Brian being famous for his moderating skills.

"That's strange," said Horatio, perplexed. "Peter Riley is the gentlest of souls. Mike Hibbert almost picked a fight with me earlier, too. I wonder what's up?"

Gemma, her journalist's instincts, or natural nosiness, aroused, went over to find out. She had been on the receiving end of quite enough glacial glances from Cleo. Once she'd left, Horatio nearly asked Cleo if she'd kissed him, but realised immediately how stupid that would have been if it had been Gemma.

Cleo was clearly fascinated by him and he wanted to savour the experience. He was also savouring some of the contraband Kentucky bourbon that was being passed around quite openly. Cleo pointed to a sofa in Marty's cable room next door. Taking Horatio firmly by the hand she said, "Come over here. We can talk properly now that Yankswank's gone."

She switched on the charm. Full beam. It hit him with all

the force of the military laser the Tenth May Group were supposed to have captured. She was vivacious, funny, clever and far sexier, Horatio soon appreciated, than even Europa, the new Channel 88 soft-porn actress who'd been ordered to change her name. He was on form, too, and for once not burbling.

Eventually Gemma returned. She said that the fight had been caused by a snide remark of Riley's about the hypocrisy of singing about workers' rights and opportunities when there were seven million unemployed in the two English regions. Hibbert had apparently threatened to thump him. Not, it turned out, because of Riley's cynicism, but because he had used the demeaning word "unemployed" rather than "involuntarily leisured" or "socially excluded". Yet it was Riley, not Hibbert, who was jobless. One more indication, thought Horatio, that this Designated Vocab thing was getting out of hand.

Gemma, with nowhere to sit, soon felt herself socially excluded by Cleo's sub-zero gamma rays. After a short, rather desultory conversation about modem passwords, in which Cleo revealed that she unimaginatively used her mother's maiden name and her date of birth in exactly the way you're told not to, Gemma left them to it. She later remarked to Marty that it was like leaving a guinea pig wrapped up snugly in the coils of an anaconda. In America, she said, the phenomena was called "acquaintance/date reverse-rape".

Not long afterwards, Cleo checked her watch and said to Horatio: "It's gone oh-three hundred. Looks like bedtime. Coming?"

9

13.20 Sunday, 2nd May

The custody suite door opened and Horatio was escorted upstairs again, except this time he was not handcuffed.

"Please let go of my elbow. It's still very sore."

"Sorry," said the policeperson, not sounding it. Instead of turning right to the interview room again, he was led straight to the front desk and given back his watch-fone, pager – which he checked had been accessed three times in the last five hours – and other belongings.

A door opened behind Horatio and Chief Inspector Snell emerged. He was white with fury. Unable to look Horatio fully in the face, he spoke slowly through clenched teeth with studied self-control. He was quivering with rage.

"You can tell your young friend in the autopark that I do not care if this *is* political. In my opinion, especially as the lab have now confirmed asphyxiation, you're a killer. We've checked Central Records and know all about your links with Baltic separatists. We've got easily enough to slam you up. I mean to take this to the highest authorities right now. You can also tell your Mr High-and-Mighty from Political that I've put in an official complaint with the Interior Commissioner himself. In my opinion you'll be back in custody within twenty-four hours. Now piss off."

Horatio was too stunned by the news to make any snide remark about not wanting to spoil the Chief Inspector's chances of becoming a cable celebrity. He briefly considered telling him to keep his hair on, but if it turned out Snell *was* wearing a wig he might have been charged with offensiveness towards a minority, in this case the follicularly-challenged. The very last thing he needed now was a two-day Holding Order being taken out. Neither did he think there was much point in arguing the toss about Leila. So he just walked out of the tinted glass sliding doors to freedom.

It took a couple of seconds for Horatio's eyes to get accustomed from the darkness of the cell to the bright light of the sunny May afternoon. Once they were, he was able to make out the smiling face of his saviour, standing by the open door of a petrol-auto rather cockily parked on the pavement outside the station.

13.23 Sunday, 2nd May

"**I** hope you realise I'm putting my balls on the block for you over this," Marty said as soon as Horatio got in. He'd always prided himself on his felicitous turn of phrase. "What the hell's going on?" He started the car and drove out of the police compound. Making his way through Basingstoke city centre, Marty sailed through red lights, ignoring cyclists and pedestrians and generally driving in a way only those immune from prosecution can.

"You tell me. God knows, except that I'm clearly being set up for murder. How did you fix this?"

"I've told the C.I.D. jerk, Snell, that it's political and therefore out of their hands. P.I.D. can do things like that every so often. But not very often and certainly not again in this case. Now what have you got yourself mixed up in?"

They pulled into Basingstoke's Megamarket Autopark so that Marty could hear every inflection of the conversations with Percival and Ratcliffe off Horatio's pager. "Let's have that last bit again," he said as they listened first to the Admiral. Horatio pressed "Rewind" for half a second.

"*None at all over the phone, but I'll draw up a memorandum for you to take away afterwards. Something to make you and your editor's hair stand on end. I'll do that right now.*"

Marty was concentrating. Horatio just felt nauseous. He listened to the dead man's voice – all trusting and confidential.

"*Be careful and please will you tell no one about this. About me.*"

"*I promise.*"

"*I mean it, it really matters.*"

And it had mattered. It had mattered to death. Yet he had told Weaning about Ratcliffe, and as good as told Percival as well. Then he'd left his jacket on the back of a chair at the party for anyone to pick up. He'd betrayed the old man just as surely as if he'd denounced him publicly.

Horatio's gorge rose. He had to get out of the auto. He didn't have long. It could have been the revolting prison lunch, the pollen count, the heat, but Horatio knew it was actually guilt and shame. And fear.

His mouth was filling with saliva. He dashed over to the bottlebank, pushed a child away and vomited into the hole. The mother stared in disgust and yanked the kid away. Afterwards Horatio walked shamefacedly back to the car, wiping his mouth with the back of his hand. Marty looked worried.

"Are you OK?" Horatio wasn't, but he nodded.

"Now listen to the conversation I had with Commission Secretary Percival just before Ratcliffe." He pressed "Rewind". Then "Play".

Nothing.

He rewound for another five seconds and pressed "Play" again. Still nothing.

"It's been wiped!"

"How do you mean?"

"That bastard at the police station has erased my talk with Percival!"

Marty was sympathetic but unsurprised.

"This is very serious, Horror. Are you certain you want to be mixed up in it, whatever it is?" Marty, a far braver man, was clearly rattled.

"Let's get away from here."

It was no answer, but Horatio was trying to think. Marty drove off. "How did you know I was there?"

"We hear everything. I was told this morning that the department has been shadowing you since the first Aachen article in *The Times*. It was a touch too salty for Bittersich's taste. I pleaded your case, pointed out that the Leila business was all just a giant misunderstanding and generally tried to dampen it all down. He wanted to reopen your case."

"Those articles could hardly be described as subversive."

"You don't know the sort of paranoiacs and hysterics I have to work with. Anyhow, someone was detailed to keep an eye on you."

"Who?"

"You know I can't tell you that."

"Fine, don't say. But could you find out if Alex Tallboys" – Marty smiled – "has access to a grey petrol-auto which he was driving near Ibworth this morning." He explained what had happened. Marty nodded.

"Fine, I can look into this. What registration?"

"Don't know. I was too busy not getting run over to note it down."

"OK. What grade then?"

"Don't know that either."

"You can't tell me what grade? You really are useless!"

"They all look alike to me. I don't like autos. I think a 2."

"This is a 2. Does it look like this?"

"Sort of. Except it was grey. Anyhow, it tried to run me down this morning as I was walking towards the Admiral's house. There might be a bump where the wing mirror smashed into my elbow." It was still very sore.

Horatio realised Marty had been ignoring the signs to London. In fact he was driving in the opposite direction.

"Where are we going?"

"You'll see." Half a minute later Horatio saw the sign *"Twinned with Rannoch . . . Obvirsk . . . La Grenche . . ."*

"Why are you taking me back here?!"

They stopped in the Free Fox autopark. Marty turned to him.

"We are not doing anything. *You* are. Work it out for yourself Doctor Logic. Wait until tonight. Set your pager alarm for about oh-three hundred. Then put on these" – Marty handed Horatio a pair of black plastic surgical gloves – "and using this" – a heavy black torch – "go straight back into the Rectory to find whatever it was the Admiral was intending to give you. This memorandum he was talking about on the tape. Obviously Snell hasn't got it, otherwise he'd have told me. If you find the murder weapon for God's sake leave it well alone. They're doing checks on the sofa cushions. Our newest equipment can pick up any D.N.A. traces, right down to shed skin microbes, so be sure to wash tonight. But do turn the bloody place upside down if you have to. Whatever the Admiral was trying to pass on to you is obviously the key to this whole shambazz."

The logic was as impeccable as the implications were horrendous. Horatio would be breaking into and entering a house where a murder had recently taken place.

"What do I do if . . ."

"When."

". . . when I find whatever it is?"

"Whatever you think best. I suggest you contact me right

away. But not at the office. At home. I expect my releasing you is going to be pretty controversial back at Thames House. I had E's initial approval, but that might not be for long. He hadn't cleared it properly with Brussels by the time I got onto Snell. And they hate taking any independent action. 'E' only agreed to it because I said I thought you'd been framed in a Tenth May plot to punish Aachen Referendum scrutineers. It doesn't really hold any water though, does it? I also said that there were no fingerprints on anything but the door handles and fone, but they couldn't have heard about you being mentioned in the will by the time I got here. It came as a shock when Snell told me, although of course I pretended I already knew. It'll put the wind up the office though. What the hell was all that about?"

"God knows. I assume it's all part of the frame-up. Will you get me a copy?"

"I'll do my best." There was a pause. It became uncomfortable. Marty was staring at Horatio intently. "Horror? . . ." Marty seemed embarrassed.

"Yes?"

"You *didn't* do it, did you?" He wasn't joking.

"Sod you Marty!"

Horatio got out of the car and slammed the door behind him. A couple of lunchtime drinkers sitting on benches outside the pub looked up from their half-litres. Without turning round to say goodbye, Horatio marched inside, shoving the torch and gloves into his jacket pockets as he went. He heard the auto drive off behind him.

Five minutes later Horatio was sitting alone in the Free Fox snug nursing an aching elbow, a half-litre of Brunswick Bitter and a gigantic sulk. Marty came in.

"Sorry."

"So you bloody well should be. How *dare* you not trust me, however bad it may look." Marty sat down.

"I know. I thought that as soon as I'd said it. I'm sorry, truly I am."

There was a pause. Marty continued: "I've just thought of something."

"What?" said Horatio gruffly.

"How are you getting back to London tomorrow?"

"Hadn't thought." He dropped his voice. "I haven't even decided to go along with your lunatic burglary scheme."

"That's a given and you know it. But afterwards what? You can hardly use public transport if you're wanted by then. Your I.D. will give you away, or the cameras at the stations."

Horatio clicked.

"You're going to have to take me, aren't you?" Marty nodded unhappily. Horatio dropped his voice to a whisper again: "Which also means you're going to have to help me break into the Rectory tonight."

"Not necessarily."

"Of course it does. You've probably done it before in your line of work. Burgling places, installing bugs, that kind of thing."

"Do keep your voice down, Horrid. I'm a pro, an executive. All that Action Person stuff is done by the neanderthals. Only Alex Tallboys actually volunteers for it. And I can hardly get him or one of our other boneheads in on something as very . . . *al fresco* as this."

"You know you have to come with me then." Horatio was elated. "Sorry, Marty, I'm so accident-prone I'd be bound to make a mess of it, or miss something crucial. Remember when we tried to gatecrash the Oriel Commem?" Horatio had broken his ankle and Marty had had to take him to hospital. He suspected it was this malcoordination, rather than any great concern for his travel arrangements, which had brought Marty back. "I was trying to persuade myself that you were up to the job, but just outside Ibworth I thought about it. Someone who could recite Macaulay at eight but couldn't tie up his shoelaces by fourteen was probably not the right bloke for this kind of op. You'd probably break your neck going up and down the stairs in the dark."

As Marty got up to buy himself a drink, Horatio asked if he could borrow his I.D. to make a few calls.

"Why not use your own?"

"I hardly want the police to know I went straight back to the scene, do I?"

"Who are you calling?"

"My mother, *The Times* and the divine Cleopatra." Marty snatched the card back.

"Only if you promise to tell me all about Friday night."

Horatio had some trouble getting to the pub vid-fone for all the young children playing tag in the bar area. How he loathed the Kiddies' Charter.

"Hi!" His mother looked grey. Dark, greying hair and grey-faced. Almost Major-grey.

"Hello Horace, I've been sitting here for hours trying to get hold of you and all I get is your home module." She knew perfectly well it was called a modem. Horatio suspected she played up her technological illiteracy on purpose. He decided not to tell her what had happened. He could explain it all if things worked out. If they didn't, he would have plenty of time to tell her everything.

"Why should Admiral Michael Ratcliffe have left me half his fortune in his will?"

Heather Lestoq looked surprised. "What are you doing

with him, of all people?" Her eyes narrowed. "Where are you?" He could see her shifting in her seat trying to get a better view of the bar behind him, looking for a clue. He blocked her.

"Tell me. It's an emergency."

"Well, he was Flora's father-in-law." It was one of the very few times he had ever heard her mention her sister. "She married James Ratcliffe, the Admiral's son. I'd no idea he wanted to leave you anything. I'd have been nicer to him if I'd known!"

"Why haven't you spoken to me about him?"

"Your father and I didn't like him. He'd adjudicated the Aachen Referendum, you see. Is that how you've come across him?" Still sharp. "Super articles in *The Times* by the way darling. I'm really proud of you." It wasn't often she said that. "How is the old traitor?"

"I'll tell you all about him when I see you."

"I'm glad you're coming down this weekend."

"Who else will be there?"

"Marcia said she'd pop in with the children."

"I think I might be busy actually."

"Horace!" Why of all his many nicknames – Horror, Horrid, Horrific, Horrible, Horseface and so on – did she call him the only one he couldn't stand?

"We'd only row."

"It takes two to row."

"Fine, there'd be two of us."

"Well, it's a shame. And how can you make up if you don't meet or talk?"

"Sorry."

"All right, we'll arrange a different day. I'll probably be coming up to London for the rally this Saturday anyway. Will I see you there?"

"What rally?"

"What do you mean, what rally! You're supposed to be a journalist! The King's giving a speech in Hyde Park. The Commission have said it can go ahead, the fools. Isn't that exciting?"

It was his turn to tease her.

"I thought you'd given up all that boring political stuff."

"I have, but one can still keep one's beliefs. Everyone from here's going up. It'd be disloyal not to. There'll be thousands of us. Tens of thousands. It'll be a historic event. You should be there. It'll be the first time the King . . ."

"Of New Zealand."

"Of more than that and you know it, has set foot . . ."

"Mum, this vid could easily be tapped. Marty Frobisher says Cheltenham have machines now that can listen to one hundred thousand lines simultaneously. They trigger on tapes if certain words are said. You can bet your bottom euro that the word you've just used to denote the first citizen of a certain Pacific island is one of them. So for goodness' sake . . ."

She held up her hands in surrender. "All right! All right! Stop nagging. You know what I mean."

"I do. And no, I won't be there. It's just for you fogies who live in the past, all that kind of thing. How about the weekend after? I could come down then. Or will Dick be there?"

"As a matter of fact he will. But I think you should show your face."

While Horatio considered it she continued, "How funny that old Admiral Ratpoison should remember you in his will. Is there much cash, do you know? I seem to remember he was rolling in it."

"No idea. Possibly. It's a nice house."

"I'm glad our family will be able to get something out of that dreadful old quisling at last."

"There you go again. You can't say the q-word over the vid either."

"Well, you know about such things."

"Yes I do. Remember Leila? Now, I want you to think back to when you knew him. Is there anything you think he might have wanted to give to me? Anything at all? I had a talk with him yesterday and he said he had something he had to hand me." He played her back the Admiral's conversation. He watched her concentrating, her forehead wrinkled in thought. She was only fifty-five but she was starting to chalk up all the telltale signs of late-middle to old age.

"You're talking about him in the past tense. Is he dead?" Horatio nodded. "Well, he must have been ninety at least, I can't say I'm going to mourn. We never liked him."

"What do you make of the tape?"

"I don't know. Is it something to do with Aachen do you think?" She leant forward and whispered, "If it's anything damaging to the Commission do let me have a copy. I'd be able to find a good home for it."

"That's enough!" he barked. People turned on their barstools to stare at him. "Do *not* talk like that over the vid! I wish you'd learn how these things work. And dropping your voice makes no difference either."

"Well, you're on a public fone and it's been so long since I've been involved in politics I doubt they're still interested in me. It would be a nice compliment if they still were! Anyway, you know perfectly well what I meant."

"I do and I'd better go before you say anything indictable. Might see you Saturday week."

"I'll give your love to Dick and Marcia."

"Don't."

"Have you thought what you are going to do with the Admiral's bequest?"

"No. But at least I can pay my Atgas bill now!" As soon as the words left his tongue he knew his terrible *faux pas*. His mother's face fell. "I'm sorry Mummy."

"Goodbye." She clicked off. Not angry, just sad. How bloody stupid and insensitive of him to mention that of all things.

Should he have contacted his half-brother when he was arrested? Dick's legal firm had friends in high places. Not as high as he was making enemies though, and he didn't really want to be under any obligation to him. Not after the way Dick and Marcia had reacted to the Leila thing. He thought of the ads Zetland & Dunbar put out. Horatio privately thought they summed up everything that was wrong with the new legal system:

"Have you been verbally criticised, ridiculed, even insulted?" — went one he particularly despised — *"Has anyone said anything to you in the past seven years that left you upset, or capable of persuading a judge that you were? Then call Zetland & Dunbar on 01171 493 8000 in London or 010 322 222 6000 in Brussels. We're faster on the draw than Hess & Oman and pay sexier rates than Cosworth & Blackwood. Remember, there's nothing to pay if we take on your case; we just take a modest and negotiable percentage of your possibly VAST WINNINGS! A happy client of ours recently won 50,000 EUROS for having been called a right old cow. So call us now."* Then came their famous jingle: *"Sticks and stones may break your bones but words can make you RICH!"*

Although it wouldn't make him rich, Horatio's next call should result in a serious pay hike. Weaning would be delighted with this story. It had Snell of the Yard, a war hero, politics, murder, on-the-spot reporting – everything a news hack could ever ask for. He got through immediately on the vid-fone.

"Roddy, I've got something very special for you." Weaning looked aggressive and angry. He jabbed a finger at him.

"You're off the case."

"I mean something very big. Murder. Could be political too."

"I couldn't give a toss if you've got genocide. You're off the case."

What was he talking about? He'd very soon be eating his words. So Horatio persisted.

"I've spent half a day in gaol for this story."

"Don't care. I've already discussed it with the editor. The decision's final."

"This could be of national importance, Roddy."

"Don't you use that word at me, it's not one I recognise or allow in this office. These are taped fones for Christ's sake! The word's 'regional'. You're turning into a real liability, Lestoq. And this time at last the editor agrees. You academic types are all the same. I was right all along. You just can't be trusted to behave professionally. How long have you been on the last Aachen article?"

"How do you mean?"

"How many hours have you put into it?" Horatio totted them up.

"Well, I've been working pretty much all out over the last five days. You know that, you told me to. Roddy, you have to hear me out. I've been in gaol today. It's an amazing tale. The Admiral . . ."

"I don't want to hear it and I don't care if you've been to

Kazakhstan. You've contravened the Working Time Directive. You *know* you can only put in thirty-two hours a week and you're already doing far more than that. And on May Day. Sunday's double time, too. From the look of the work you've already submitted the Directive was contravened on the first two articles as well. Plus, I'm unhappy about your expenses. And your offensively lookist behaviour towards Ms Aldritt. You're fired."

"It was you who told me to come in yesterday. And to come down here today. God knows I didn't want to." He thought of Cleo.

"Well, you don't need to go anywhere for us from now on. Sorry, Lestoq, you're an out-take. You could get this news-agency's licence revoked. As it is, your own is not worth the microchip it's being wiped off. You broke your contract by not revealing that you'd had sexual relations with a terrorist whilst an employee here two years ago. That sort of thing brings organisations like ours into disrepute. Plus your working hours run completely contrary" – Horatio realised that Weaning was talking unnaturally slowly now, in an on-the-record sort of way – "to the Social Action Programme and the Working Time Directive 97/678. As a result *Times* News-agencies have no alternative but to sever your engagement with us forthwith. Under your freelance contract you have no pension rights or indeed anything so much as a copper handshake. See you at the Tribunal. Goodbye."

The screen went blank.

That was the authentic voice and look of a scared man, Horatio decided. Someone who'd been got at.

How had Weaning found out about Leila? He'd been promised complete secrecy as well as immunity if he told P.I.D. all he knew. His name had been covered by an 'E' notice and he'd testified to the court by one-way vid and voice alterer. How could Weaning know?

If even the mention of a political murder scoop hadn't pricked up his hack's ears, Weaning was acting for political, not managerial motives. Like every hack worth his salt, Weaning regularly contravened the Working Time Directive himself. But if he and the editor were being leant on so effectively, what chance was there of getting an article published elsewhere? No one but the underground press would touch it. And what credibility did they have?

The remark about licences being revoked was revealing, too. No one needed to tell Horatio how subservient the press had become after the Media Privacy Directives. Adopting French-style libel laws had meant that unless he virtually got a signed confession out of whoever was behind this, no one would dare print the story. What did he have anyhow? What actual evidence had he got? Nothing.

Once again he heard the distant barking of a black dog. He hadn't taken any Pluszac for three days now. He *must* have one tonight. All he needed in this crisis was another turn like the one in the Hilary Term of his final year.

Cleo wasn't at the office. He got her at home. She was working at her desk. She looked great. He decided not to mention anything. No point in scaring her unnecessarily or talking over the vid. He could ask her advice when they met.

"What are you doing for dinner tomorrow night?"

"I'm going to *The Last Days of Pompeii* with a girlfriend."

"Could you blow her out?"

"But I want to see it, it's in Total Reality. Apparently you can actually *feel* the heat and ash and smell the lava and the fumes."

"You'd rather smell lava and fumes than have dinner with me, is that it?" He was smiling but . . .

"Well, what's on offer?"

"Anything you like, of course. If you want to see *Pompeii* we could do that. Or there's a little place in Soho where they're putting on private showings of Dustin Hoffman movies." He regretted it as soon as he'd said it.

"Please try to remember sometimes what I do for a living, Horatio. How would it look if the place was raided and it turned out I'd been watching Hollywood films? Haven't you read the Cultural Defence Directive 67/908? I ought to be demanding the name and address of this place." Chastened, he quickly changed the subject.

"Do you like Macao food? We could go to Gerrard Street. Have you been to the new place, Memories of 1996?"

"No, is it safe?" There had been two triad killings in Chinatown that month. The last one in a restaurant across the road from Memories.

"Yes, I think so." She should know. She was the cop. "I love Macao food and I haven't been there yet. Twenty-thirty?"

"Fine. Tell no one at P.I.D. though."

"Very cloak-and-dagger. Why?"

"I can't say just now. Will you just promise?" Her eyes suddenly narrowed in suspicion. She put down her pen.

"Are you in some kind of trouble Horatio? What's going on? Please tell me, I might be able to help. What's wrong?"

He took a deep breath. His initial resolve not to burden her dissipated. If Marty had known immediately at P.I.D. she'd find out soon enough.

"Are you alone?"

"Well, you never really are with vids, but otherwise yes."

"I've been arrested. For a murder I didn't commit."

"Is this some sort of sick joke? Because if so . . ."

"No joke. I'm going to need your advice tomorrow night. By then I might have cleared one or two things up. Will you be there?"

"What about tonight?"

"Can't do that. Or any earlier. But tomorrow night's OK."

"Of course. See you there. Don't tell me any more over the vid."

"I'll tell you everything tomorrow."

"I'll have found out by then."

"See you then."

What a woman! She hadn't flinched, let alone demanded details. He danced a little victory jig in the bar, whooping inwardly. He might have lost his job and was soon to be a wanted man, but he was going to splash a couple of hundred or so on a slap-up with Cleo tomorrow night and the knowledge made him happy.

Back in the snug he told Marty about Weaning. He'd have to find another job. All Souls merely provided him with a room in college. If he moved back to Oxford he'd be able to save his London rent at least. Yet *another* career reversal. His mother had only his father's naval pension, and he'd sponged off her long enough. He certainly couldn't expect anything from Dick or Marcia.

The legacy had to come through. Which, Marty pointed out helpfully, it wouldn't if he was found guilty of the Admiral's murder. Marty offered him a couple of grand to tide him over until he got other work, adding, even more helpfully, that if tonight went badly there was a good chance that he'd be in for many years of completely free accommodation.

Realising how gloomy that sounded, Marty tried to cheer Horatio up by cross-questioning him about his extraordinary success with Cleo on Friday night. After a couple of feints it became clear that he would not be fobbed off.

"She's a cracking-looking girl of course, a superbabe. I won't pretend I'm not flailingly jealous, Horror. I've fancied her like crazy ever since she came to P.I.D. But do watch out." Horatio was fully expecting to be warned about Tallboys, but Marty continued: "I work with her and I know. She's tough. Bloody tough. And unscrupulous. And dangerous. She's not like normal people. She puts everything into her job. And she didn't get it through affirmative action either, like some people there. There's no question of any gender quota with her, it was pure ability. When are you seeing her next?"

"Tomorrow night." Marty nodded.

"Let me put it this way, she's one of our most zealous operatives."

"All of which serves merely to enhance my fascination, of course."

"Of course. You also ought to know she has a husband whose favourite hobbies are pulling off doves' wings and breaking the vertebrae of small children."

But Horatio was only half-listening. He was already thinking about tomorrow night and trying to remember a D.W.A-S.M. quotation: "*Age cannot wither her, nor custom stale / Her infinite variety; other women cloy the appetites they feed, but she makes hungry/ Where most she satisfies..*"

"Come again?"

"From *Antony and Cleopatra*. By William Shakespeare, Europe's greatest poet, you ignorant git."

"And proud of it."

Horatio changed the subject onto something the famously philistine Marty could be expected to know something about.

"Were the E.R.M. really planning to blow up the Channel Bridge, as I read yesterday in my soaraway *Sun*?"

"Off the record?"

"Of course."

"We reckon it could be true. They're taking the armed struggle up a notch. We think they're looking for softer targets now. Why? What's your interest? Thinking of a career in terrorism?"

"Just that when I take Cleo on a quiet, romantic holiday to Sarajevo this summer I don't want anything out of the ordinary to happen." Marty gave him a strange look.

"I'd steer well clear of that lady if I were you. I mean it."

Upstairs in one of the pub's tiny bedrooms, Horatio considered his options. They were pathetically few. Only one avenue seemed worth exploring. The one with rhododendrons up it. Rewinding his pager interview, Horatio again heard the promise that the old man had made to draw up a memorandum for him. If he had done that, and the murderer had taken it, he was lost. But if it was still somewhere in the house, it might just provide the proof he needed, the sort that could be printed.

For all his instinctive cowardice, terror of the dark and fear of being caught by the police – or, even worse, the killer – Horatio could see no alternative to returning to the Rectory that night. At least he would have Marty, who would presumably be armed. If his release was rescinded tomorrow, he would soon be back in jail. He desperately needed any evidence he could find. He'd have years in prison to regret it if he missed this opportunity. So he set the alarm for 03.00 and slept the sleep of the innocent he was.

03.00 Monday, 3rd May

The pager bleeped him awake. 03.00. Christ! What would this adventure do to his body clock?

03.00. The time his pager had been accessed after Marty's party.

He remembered being told how, after the Food & Health Directive had made the public sale and consumption of fried fish and chips illegal and there had been riots in London and Liverpool, the Environmental Health Special Branch had hit the suspected rioters' homes at 03.00.

It had been at 03.00 when Special Branch smashed his door down and dragged Leila away, naked and terrified.

Now he was going to enter a house which was by right probably his already, armed only with a torch. "ALL SOULS FELLOW TURNED BURGLAR." The title of his autobiography, or the splash in tomorrow's *Times*?

He twitched the curtains apart. A half-moon. It was enough. He got dressed quickly and silently. Tiptoeing down the pub's creaky main staircase as quietly as his bulk allowed, he put on his shoes outside the front door. It was cold and quiet and Marty was late.

Marty always was. As Horatio blew on his hands and then warmed them under his armpits, he remembered how Marty had been late on the very first occasion they had met. It had been at house roll call at Westminster. "Frobisher!" the housemaster had called for the third and final time, and a loud "Present!" was heard from the back of the hall as Marty scampered in and sat cross-legged on the floor next to Horatio with an improbable tale about an escaped parakeet. By the end of term his excuses for lateness were legendary.

Just as Horatio was about to give up and go back inside, the door opened. Marty also had a torch and gloves.

Silently they made their way across the pub autopark to the Rectory drive. They took care to walk on the grass verge rather than the gravel, despite occasionally being swiped across the face by stray rhododendron branches.

Horatio was reminded of a line in P. G. Wodehouse – another favourite D.W.A-S.M. author placed on the "discouraged" list after the Classlessness Directive – which argued that one cannot altogether despair of a country which produces lots of burglars, as it takes guts to prowl around strange houses at the dead of night looking for safes behind pictures.

The front door was locked and sealed. Thick yellow plastic tapes, reading "EUROPOL: DO NOT ENTER", criss-crossed it. Making their way carefully around the back of the house they reached the French windows of the drawing room. Preparing to smash a pane of glass with the torch to let themselves in, first Marty, then Horatio, flashed a torch beam inside. Horatio half expected to see the outline of the body taped across the sofa, as in old movies. But instead the silver shaft presented a very different sight.

The entire room had been wrecked.

The first thing he noticed was that the carpet had been torn up and sliced into one-metre squares. Every book from the shelves had been taken down, rifled through, their spines ripped off and flung on the floor. The bibliophile in Horatio wanted to cry "Sacrilege!" at the top of his voice.

The desk he had phoned from, the mirror, and every single picture, print, photo and other article of furniture in the room had been systematically smashed to pieces. Then the pieces had been broken into smaller pieces.

Horatio and Marty exchanged glances in the gloom. Neither had to say it. This was not the work of normal burglars. Or of Snell's men. Or even of abnormally gifted vandals. This was the real thing. They edged their way around the outside of the house and peered into what Horatio imagined had once been the dining room.

Every chair had been tipped upside down and the stuffing ripped out. The sideboards and cupboards were on the floor, hacked into small bits. The paintings had been taken down, turned back to front and slashed. The dining table itself, a strong, solid, Victorian mahogany affair, was upside down in pieces. This had not just been done by the most thorough operators, thought Horatio, but by sadistic, philistine professionals.

They had *enjoyed* it.

It reminded Horatio of that dark September morning when he finally returned from Paddington Green to discover what P.I.D. Special Branch had done to his flat in their search for evidence about Leila.

"Look," he whispered to Marty around the corner, grabbing his elbow, "either they found whatever the Admiral had meant to give me or they didn't. Either way we should go. There's no way we could do a better job!"

Marty, who by this time was surveying a similarly devastated kitchen, nodded reluctantly. They made their way across the lawn, back towards the pub.

Their torches picked out evidence that the garden had been subjected to much the same treatment. There were clods of earth on the lawn where strategic areas had been dug up. A smashed sundial. Even the dovecote was lying on its side on the ground in halves.

Back inside Marty's car and driving away from Ibworth, Horatio tried to think logically. There was no point in involving Marty any further in this. He had got into enough trouble on his account. Marty said that if P.I.D. discovered that Snell had told him about the will it could well be a sackable offence to have released Horatio without having sought further permission from "E". From now on, Horatio decided, he was on his own.

"Horror, old man," said Marty as they approached the Chiswick toll booths, "what are you going to do?"

"What do you suggest?"

"I'd just try to forget about everything. Get away. I'd probably skip the Union to Norway or somewhere. From the look of that place you're obviously up against some very serious people. It was textbook Ultimate Search Procedure. I'm speaking purely as a friend now. Why don't you just chuck it and get the hell out? Something's obviously going on here, but trying to find out what could get you badly hurt." Horatio nodded. "If you need any help in making yourself scarce, I've got some friends in the Emigration Commission who owe me. Let me know what you decide." Horatio nodded again and murmured his thanks.

It was good advice from someone who'd always had his best interests at heart. But he had to ignore it. He promised Marty that if he wanted to bolt, or if the Admiral's memorandum somehow fell into his hands, he'd contact him immediately. But in the drive along the M3, at the exhilarating speed

Marty's ungoverned auto could do in the special lane, a plan had developed in Horatio's mind. More a series of alternating, interlocking moves based on differing scenarios. They were complex and would have impressed the reigning Oxford University chess champion, if it had not been him.

But on a far less cerebral level, Horatio realised just how badly he wanted revenge.

09.00 Monday, 3rd May

Horatio was first into the Institute of Historical Research when the doors opened on the dot of 09.00. It was situated in a high white tower built early last century in Malet Street, Bloomsbury. Formerly the Senate House of the University of London, Horatio remembered reading somewhere that it had also housed the Ministry of Information during the Second Nationalist War. Then it had been concerned with directing, censoring, massaging and witholding information. Today, he hoped it would divulge a lot.

He wished he could have gone to the new South English Library at St Pancras for his information, but it was not due to open until 2051. He wondered whether the billion euros spent strengthening the 1990s structure, which had itself of course never been occupied, would prove worthwhile? He doubted it.

As his I.D. card passed through the sensor he prayed silently that Snell had not put an alert on it since Sunday afternoon. He held his breath. From the totally impassive face of the security guard sitting behind the screen he saw he hadn't.

For the first time Horatio started to think of his I.D. as a potential enemy, rather than, as the Commission ads put it, "your empowering friend". With his photo, thumbprint, citizen number, identifying marks, D.N.A. "fingerprint", biorhythm chart, blood type and signature printed on it, the card was believed to be impossible to forge.

Just as well, because that single magnetised plastic strip with its microchip on the back held his bank account details, property registration, Frankfurt and regional bank credit rating (such as it was), dental and medical records, cash movements record, V.A.T. number, hotel and restaurant customer loyalty points, council tax rating, museum entry pass, Euro-Lottery number, passport and visas, next-of-kin details, emergency services information, organ donor exemption statement, Regional Insurance number, F.R.O. reader's ticket, *Times* office entry pass (doubtless now revoked), health insurance, pension book, flat key, Bodleian, London and Brompton Libraries card, vid-fone card and (post-Leila) Europol record. If he had been a driver it would also have had his auto key, vehicle registration document, auto insurance, driver's licence, Euro-Auto Club breakdown policy, moterway toll charger, depot voltage counter and parking meter points as well. Instead of sending him to prison, he thought, they could always just confiscate his card, thereby condemning him to a life on the streets.

Sooner or later, when buying something, travelling somewhere or making a call from a public box, the card would betray his whereabouts to the police. He knew that. It was how everyone was caught. It was simply a matter of time.

The knowledge had him quickly at the EuroNet terminal on the first floor, in the West Mercia room. His I.D. accessed it successfully. To allow himself total concentration he switched his pager and watch-fone onto "Hold". The blotting paper had mentioned a "Mrs Robson". Allowing for the smudginess, could he assume that this actually referred to Mrs Dodson –

perhaps Jacob's wife, daughter, sister or mother? Where was she? And where was Jacob?

Also "your roving godfather"? Who were Ratcliffe's godchildren? How could he find out?

Calling up the South-West Region telephone directory he found no Jacob Dodson but about seventy Mrs Dodsons. He hadn't the time to call them all. He then checked newsagency obituaries. Nothing. Why should there be anything for a minor electronics expert? After that, old vid-directories, going back year by year. No Jacob Dodson for the Forties, Thirties or Twenties. Then census returns for 2041, 2031 and 2021. Again, nothing. After ninety minutes' search, EuroNet finally turned up a Dodson, Jacob in the vid-fone directory for 2019. He lived in Lymington on the South Coast. He quickly called up news stories involving Dodsons for all the papers local to Lymington for 2019. He prayed there'd be no power cut now. That would ruin everything.

He didn't have long to wait. The computer came up with something immediately, for the very second day of the year. The front-page headline of the *Bournemouth Evening News and Mail* for 2nd January 2019 read "LYMINGTON MAN DIES IN ROADS CHAOS".

Dodson, it seemed, had been one of the first of dozens to be killed that month when the five former British regions adopted right-hand drive, in accordance with the Road Traffic Standardisation Directive. At the Coroner's Court inquest a fortnight later it was reported that Dodson had been driving on an otherwise deserted road in the New Forest when an Atlantic Gas pantechnicon wrote off his auto in a head-on collision. Francis Anthony Evans, 26, the driver, testified that Dodson had been on the left-hand side of the road. The article dwelt on the explosion that might have taken place if the Atgas had caught alight, but Horatio was more interested in the name of Dodson's widow.

From the 2044 vid-directory he discovered Jean Dodson's present address:

Number 4, The High Street, Ibworth, Hampshire, RG2 5SX.

He then started to order up all the Ph.D. theses relating to the background of the Aachen Conference, Treaty and Referendum. Reading the Aachen Ph.D. research work was, he supposed, something he ought to have done earlier for his articles. There were the usual detailed analyses of obscure topics such as late twentieth-century dentistry and studies on the history of post-Cold War hairdressing. How could anyone spend three years writing eighty thousand words on a subject as esoteric as the politics behind Gerry Adams' Nobel Peace Prize, he wondered?

He only wished he had more time. One day he would come back and make time to read *The Rolling Disestablishment of the Church of England, 1998–2020, The Partition of the Middle East Between the Great Powers 2031–2, A-P.E.Z: Free, Independent Nation States co-operating Economically: De Gaulle's European Vision Successfully Applied to Asia and the Pacific Rim 2007–10* and finally *A.F.T.A: Genuine Free Trade Area or American Economic Imperialism?* Right now, though, there was only time to look into works relevant to Aachen.

There were three: *The Aachen Referendum and the Creation of the European Superstate*, by an academic from Oxford Brookes University called Summerskill, *The Aachen Referendum: A Regional Analysis of British Voting Patterns* by Dr Manfred Klaushofer of Vienna University, and finally *Maastricht, The I.G.Cs., The Single Currency, Aachen: Political Opposition to European Unification 1990–2020*. This last had been written by none other than Peter Riley, who after being sent down from Oxford for monarchism had finally found a place at Carl-Friedrichs University in Berlin.

He started with the Summerskill. He could tell by the tone of the introduction that it was very federationist. Syrupy prose, too, for a serious academic thesis.

"The beautiful and ancient town of Aachen, just on the German side of the pre-Schengen border with Belgium, was the ideal place for the Conference which, in March 2015, at last produced agreement for the complete, final and irrevocable political and constitutional unification of the European Continent into the United States of Europe. Over twelve centuries before, in Rome on Christmas Day 800, Charlemagne — Carolus Magnus or Charles the Great — had been crowned Emperor of the West by Pope Leo III. He was the first ruler France and Germany ever had in common. The territory of the original Six of 1957 covered almost exactly the same area as his Carolingian Empire.

The greatest of all the Frankish Kings, born only twenty kilometres from Maastricht, Charlemagne chose Aachen for his imperial capital. It was there he built his great palace. The shade of the Second Great Unifier of Europe was doubtless present when the Treaty was signed there by all the heads of European governments on 1st April 2015. They created the first superpower in history ever to be brought into being at the stroke of a pen rather than by bloodshed: the United States of Europe.

"Only one hurdle remained; to obtain ratification from the peoples of Europe for what their political masters had wrought. This was to come in the form of national referenda, all of which were held on Thursday 4th May 2015. The results were by no means a foregone conclusion . . ."

Horatio doubted he'd learn much from this one. The

regional voting thesis looked impossibly long and dull, so he moved straight on to Riley's.

In the Acknowledgements Peter had recorded his *"thanks to the redoubtable octogenarian Mrs Biddy Cash for allowing me access to her late husband Bill's extensive and invaluable archives relating to the ratification of the Maastricht Treaty of European Union. Also to Messrs Hywel Williams and Iain Duncan-Smith for allowing me to interview them such a short time after their release from house arrest. That they spoke so freely is a tribute to their courage and dedication to the anti-federal cause."*

Small wonder, thought Horatio, that after making such a clearly biased statement, Riley had been denied his doctorate. For over the first page of the thesis was stamped: "FAILED UNDER PROVISIONS 7, 8 AND 14 OF THE POLITICAL ENLIGHT-ENMENT & NOMENCLATURE DIRECTIVE."

Horatio thought it remarkable that the thesis was even made available for researchers at all. Possibly another example of what Riley later described as "the twin unconscious brakes on Euro-tyranny – corruption and inefficiency". Then a surname further down the Acknowledgements page caught his eye.

His own.

"My thanks must also go to Mrs Heather Lestoq, widow of Commander Robert Lestoq." So his mother had helped too. He might have guessed. She wouldn't have been able to resist. Why had she not mentioned it though?

Despite its heavy use of irony and somewhat wooden prose, the Riley thesis made fascinating reading. It took Horatio chronologically through the whole story. The chapter headings said it all: "Maastricht and National Self-Delusion", "The Schengen Agreement and the Abolition of Frontiers", "The 1996 Inter-Governmental Conference: Further Faltering

Steps", "The Millennium: Six Go Down the Fast Lane" (sounds like the title of a book by the discouraged author Enid Blyton, thought Horatio), "Britain Forced to Follow On", "Convergence Pains", "Economic & Monetary Union: The Soft Euro Gets Hard", "Aachen: A Megastate is Born", "Gibraltar; Ulster and the Falklands: Great Britain Disintegrates", "Scottish and Welsh Independence", "Subversion or Insurrection?: The Doomed Revolt of Spring 2016", "Charles III Quits the Scene", "Depatriation", and so on.

There were long and learned appendices such as "Denmark Under Martial Law" and on Brussels' hilariously disastrous attempt in 2022 to outlaw certain American words and phrases. Riley had obviously spent a long time in all the relevant archives researching this. As a veteran of a number of them himself – the Federal Records Office, the Hurd diaries, Commission Records, the Colindale Newspaper Library and so on – Horatio appreciated how much work must have gone into this.

Riley had dug up a few nuggets which brought wry smiles to Horatio's face. Edward Heath's July 1971 White Paper on British Entry into the Common Market, for example, had promised that "*decisions are only made if all members agree*". He laughed out loud when he saw it had also stated that "*There is no question of Britain losing essential national sovereignty.*" That was true enough in a way, there *had* been no question at all. It was inevitable.

Then there was the policy paper, pregnant with threat, put out by the ruling C.S.U./C.D.U. coalition in Germany back in September 1994. "*If European integration were not to progress,*" went "Reflections on European Policy", "*Germany might be called upon, or tempted by its own security constraints, to try to effect the stabilisation of Eastern Europe on its own and in the traditional manner.*" The Chancellor at the time, Helmut Kohl, went on record to describe Maastricht as "*an interim step, albeit an important one, on the road to European Union. The parts of the Treaty dealing with political union are just as important as those concerning economic and monetary union.*"

As Riley pointed out, Europe had been warned. Like Snell had said of him and Ratcliffe's murder, in taking over the *de facto* running of the United States of Europe, Germany had the motive, opportunity and method.

Alex Tallboys appeared in the doorway.

His dark green loden coat, which Marty had told Horatio was the standard uniform of P.I.D. operatives, cloaked nearly two metres of broad-shouldered Aryan viciousness. How had he known where to find him? Probably the I.D. card swipe at the door. Clenching and unclenching his fists, Tallboys stalked over. Horatio glanced around the room. He was relieved to see a number of people at their terminals. Even with people's tendency to look the other way during violence nowadays, Tallboys would surely not try on anything physical here.

"Hello," Horatio said, with as much *bonhomie* as he could muster. But unlike Tallboys' visit to the Federal Records Office on Friday, this was clearly more than a routine snoop.

"Shut up you disgusting, fat" – he searched around for a rude enough noun – "*intellectual*. I know what you're up to. I'm still married to Cleopatra you know, which gives me the perfect legal right to smash your piggy little snout straight down your throat." Horatio made no comment on this novel interpretation of family law. "I know you've got plans to see her."

"I'm not seeing her."

"Oh yes you are. I know you are. I know everything about you. But if you pollute her perfection by laying so much as one of your podgy trotters on her, you die. You can talk all that clever-clever stuff to amuse her over the fone, be all *sophisticated*" – he spat the word – "but that's it. I mean, you're hardly a threat in the sex department, and a short period of seeing you might bring her back to her senses. It will only be short because there's bound to be a warrant reissued for you any moment and when it is I'll be there to serve it. In the meantime watch it. And I'll be watching you. I might even send Cleo the tapes we have of you and that Estonian slut. That'd put her off. Remember" – Tallboys leant forward so close that Horatio could see the hatred in his clear cornflower-blue eyes and smell his garlic-enhanced halitosis – "if you ever touch her I'll find out. And then" – he thrust his huge thumbs straight in front of Horatio's face and hissed – "I will take enormous pleasure in poking out your piggy little eyeballs. I'll squeeze them till they splatter all over my hands like hard-boiled eggs. I'm not saying I'll be *forced* to, mind you. Or that I'll *have* to. I'm saying I'll *enjoy* it."

Then he was gone.

It took some minutes before the spasms and involuntary shaking subsided. It was the last part, about enjoying it, which completely authenticated the threat. That and what Marty had said about Tallboys volunteering for the nastiest jobs. What would he do? Blow Cleo out for dinner tonight, of course. Was that cowardice speaking, or just a man who valued his eyesight? Right now time was running out. Logic told him he must force himself to concentrate on Riley's thesis.

Checking the index he turned to page 231, halfway through chapter ten, and found the reference he had been anticipating when he ordered it up in the first place. Part of him did not want to see it at all. Yet he was compelled to read on. Why? Filial loyalty? Historical interest? Secret nat sympathies? Pride?

"The Anti-Union movement suffered another severe blow three days later, on 6th April 2016, with the death of Commander Robert Lestoq in a gas explosion at his home in Ebury Street, London. Lestoq had recently returned from Azania to join, and perhaps even take up the de facto leadership of, the opposition to the Aachen settlement. He had made his name by leading the near-mutiny of the previous summer after the word 'Royal' was removed from the Navy's title. His posting to southern Africa was widely considered to have been a political move of the Defence Commission to sideline this charismatic patriot."

Merely calling it an Insurrection, when the Political Nomenclature Directive 77/765 had long ago decreed that the troubles of spring 2016 should be described as "the Nationalist Subversion Period", would have been enough to have had Riley sent down from Carl-Friedrichs. Horatio wondered whether anyone had ever actually read the thesis, other than himself and Riley's supervisor. He turned to the back page where previous readers had to sign in.

One of half a dozen names immediately stood out: "M. K. C. Ratcliffe, Archer College, Cambridge. 2/6/36".

He turned back to the thesis itself. After half an hour he had learnt a number of things that his teachers had never mentioned either at school or university. Instead of "empathy modules" and "de-contextualised analysis", he thought, he should have been taught what history was *really* all about: what happened next. The army mutiny, which took place at roughly the same time as the "Fish and Chips" Riots (largely as a result of the British troops' refusal to fire on the crowds) had clearly been the crucial moment. The march of London's street tradesmen, whose livelihoods had been destroyed by Euro-legislation, had provided the spark. Although the ice-cream, hot-dog and chestnut vendors led the way, every other social group harmed by the Aachen result joined in the march on

Commission Headquarters in the old Foreign Office building in Whitehall. It had soon turned into a full-scale popular rebellion. Had the "twinning" of British regiments with larger and stronger Euro-corps not been sedulously advanced for years beforehand, to counter just such an eventuality, the German, Austrian and French units stationed in Knightsbridge, Chelsea and Wellington barracks and pouring through the Channel Tunnel might not have been able to disarm the by then tiny British Army and "restore order".

Horatio read about the Carlist rallies after the Mountbatten-Windsors' decision to leave. They were not banished at all, it seemed, but left of their own accord. The decision was taken on a number of grounds, but principally it was due to their lack of a role in the new continental post-Commonwealth republic. King Charles feared their presence might provide a rallying point for nats and thus lead to unnecessary bloodshed.

The Information Commission had, of course, always presented Charles' departure as being the result of pique at the removal of his head from the stamps, coins and banknotes, and because of death duties and the 95 per cent Euro-supertax which the Family now faced. They had done him a grave disservice, but the myth lived on. Certainly that was what Horatio had always been taught.

With Australia a republic and Canada a founder member of the American Free Trading Area, Charles III decided to accept New Zealand's offer of sanctuary. He settled in Auckland and tried to keep what was left of the Commonwealth together, without ever officially abdicating the British Crown.

Much of this was new to Horatio, as his mother never referred to that climacteric period and few others discussed it even privately. His mother had told him that all his father's papers had been lost when the flat was destroyed, and her memories of that time were altogether too painful for her to disinter. Yet now it seemed she had spoken to Peter Riley nine years ago.

In Riley's opinion the Insurrection had been too sporadic and disorganised to stand much hope of success. It finally collapsed in late May 2016. As he explained:

"Too many individuals had done too well out of the system, regardless of its overall cost to the country. Neither they nor Brussels were prepared to see Great Britain slipping back into becoming a unified, independent, globally-trading nation once again. Unbeknownst to the nats, Brussels had over the years been infiltrating pro-federalist 'agents of influence' into the top echelons of British public life. These people proved a highly effective fifth column during the Insurrection period. The revolt was betrayed from the start, with feds informing Europol of the times and places of secret nat meetings and rallies.

"At the last meeting of the Anti-Federalist Movement, on 3rd April 2016, in Bonchurch Road, off Ladbroke Grove, Special Branch arrested six nat leaders. These were Matthew d'Ancona, the former Editor of The Times, *two former Cabinet ministers, Hywel Williams and Iain Duncan-Smith, the cable-don and broadcaster Dr Niall Ferguson, Michael Gove of the European Broadcasting Corporation and Fred Heffer. Only Robert Lestoq and the Group Secretary Ella Gurdon escaped the round-up, having been under such close supervision by the security services that their attendance was thought too risky.*

"The Bonchurch Six, as they were subsequently dubbed, were charged with Anglo-patriotism and 'activities prejudicial to the integrity of the Union'. They pleaded guilty and were convicted. Four years later they refused to admit to 'grave and culpable political

deviation', as demanded by the Depatriation Directive of August 2020."

That meant that even when Riley went to interview them in the early Forties, some had only recently emerged from prison. Knowing how widespread fone, pager and modem-tapping by the Security Services had become by then, it astounded Horatio that Riley had been allowed even to research, let alone to deliver, a thesis on this controversial and unattractive aspect of the European integration story.

Klaushofer's thesis, despite its fantastically dull title, proved compelling reading. Horatio had known how close the Referendum's "Yes" vote had been – 51.86 per cent to 48.14 per cent, on an 84 per cent voter turnout – but he had never before seen a regional breakdown of how it was reached. Official Commission histories never seemed to refer to it. Horatio had always hitherto assumed the "Yes" vote had been evenly distributed across the country.

"Voter turnout" was, of course, as much a misnomer back in 2015 as it would be today, he thought, as even in those days people did not actually physically turn out to vote, but merely pressed the Yes or No button on their home modems. The binary voting system precluded spoilt ballots and Don't Knows, so only Yes or No counted. The votes were then electronically transmitted to the sixteen regional offices to give area figures, and at 22.00 on Referendum Day they were transmitted to London for the final, nationwide result.

What was remarkable, recorded Klaushofer in his precise, dry, Teutonic prose, was that apart from Greater London and the Home County areas – Southern, South-Western and South-West Central – virtually the entire British Isles had recorded anti-Aachen majorities. The North-East had voted 56 to 44 against, Ulster 59 to 41 and the Highlands & Islands a thumping 63 to 37. But their smaller populations could not outweigh what the German academic called the "M25 beltway" pro-Aachen majorities of southern England.

In some of these areas – particularly the South-West, which had voted 59 per cent to 41 per cent in favour – Klaushofer concluded that "*Stockbroker-belt Britons had considered that the financial advantages to them in joining the superstate outweighed the importance of outdated sentimental concepts such as national sovereignty and independence.*"

During the Government's well-funded "Yes" campaign, it was often pointed out that fragmentation of the United Kingdom would mean substantial tax cuts for those English who put financial wellbeing above anachronistic considerations of nationhood. Much was made of the superior financial responsibility of the Central Bank, which would be run on Bundesbank low inflation principles.

Horatio thought wryly how in fact having to shoulder the burden of the Cohesion Fund, Social Chapters Mark IV and V, the Berlin-Brussels Bureau, the new Eastern Members, the M.U.P.s in Strasbourg, the Common Fisheries Policy, the Social Fund, the Regional Fund, Mediterranean fraud, the occupation of the Baltic Protectorates, the Social Action Directives *and* the New Common Agricultural Policy, meant that the top Euro-tax rates of 95 per cent for 2045 were likely to be increased yet again when Brussels announced the figures for 2046. Stockbrokers' belts would have to be tightened again this year.

Horatio found it incredible that any Britons could have contemplated voting "No" at all. Throughout the campaign the leaderships of the Conservative and Christian Democrats, Liberal Democrats and New Labour had all called for a "Yes" vote. All the major press and cable groups urged it too.

Leading industrialists and business figures such as the Chairs of I.C.I. and the Stock Exchange went on cable to predict mass unemployment in the event of a "No" victory. (Although Horatio noted they did not predict the levels it subsequently reached after Britain voted "Yes".) The chattering classes endorsed the "Yes" campaign *en masse* and the only people left campaigning against were a motley bunch of nat mavericks and political outsiders.

Then there was the heavily loaded wording of the Referendum question itself: *"Do you support Great Britain acceding to the Treaty of Complete Union as negotiated at Aachen by His Majesty's Government, thereby escaping the risk of exclusion from our principal markets?"*

"The overall majority for Aachen," concluded Klaushofer, *"was the result of the large pro-Treaty votes from the three populous southern English regions. The South-West alone accounted for the anti-Treaty majorities in Ulster and Scotland combined."*

Horatio reread the last sentence. Then he read it again. The implications slowly sank in. He remembered the relevant passage of Percival's note and congratulated himself for the twentieth time since leaving Basingstoke police station on not putting that down on his pager too. For it connected Percival personally to the paying off of Ratcliffe and Dodson.

Think logically, Horatio told himself. Stay calm and think it through.

South-West Region had virtually swung the Referendum for the feds. Both its Chief Scrutineer and electronics expert later died in mysterious circumstances. After having been paid by the Bureau via Commission Secretary Percival himself.

This went to the very heart of Europe – if it had one.

It was at that point that Horatio realised that he could be

sitting on nothing less than the greatest scoop – and the greatest scandal – of the twenty-first century.

13

15.08 Monday, 3rd May

Sweating slightly, and trembling with the enormity of what he was increasingly certain he had uncovered, Horatio returned to his task. He called up Admiral Ratcliffe's Last Will and Testament. Sure enough, EuroNet had automatically filed it on the same day as the announcement of death. Snell had been right. It was signed and dated 11th April 2016.

It was short and to the point. Twenty-nine years ago the Admiral divided everything he had – which amounted to over seven million euros, as well as the Rectory – between Horatio Lestoq, only child of the late Commander Robert Lestoq E.N., to be managed by his mother, Ms Heather Lestoq, until he reached the age of twenty-one, and . . .

Horatio could not believe what he saw. Up on the screen was the very last name he could have expected.

"*. . . My granddaughter, Martina Keppel Cleopatra Ratcliffe, only daughter of my son the late Commander James Ratcliffe and his wife the late Flora Ratcliffe.*"

Cleopatra? Cleo!

Using his Freedom of Information rights, he then called up the tax returns for both Ratcliffe and Dodson between 2015 and 2020. He hadn't really expected to discover much, but there it was in green and white. In the return for the year ending 1st April 2016. Listed under income – but subject of course to 100 per cent tax relief – were five million euros paid to Ratcliffe and two million to Dodson.

Horatio had to admire whoever had thought up the payment method. They had won the top two Euro-Lottery Mega-Bumper Jackpots for December 2015. Horatio was prepared to bet they'd both ticked their "no-publicity" boxes. It was probably the only lottery ticket the Admiral had ever bought in his life.

Shaking with excitement, tinged with a certain sense of dread, Horatio took out his pager. His first call must be to Marty for advice on how to deal with Cleo. Realising it would be better for him to be able to watch her reactions when they talked, he walked down to the basement where the vid-fones were situated under the stairwell. He entered the penultimate booth.

"I'm afraid Mr Frobisher is on paternity leave, sir."

"What do you mean? He hasn't got a wife, let alone children."

"Under the provisions of the Social Chapter Mark V one cannot discriminate between parents and non-parents over the statutory three months compulsory paternity leave."

"But that's absurd!"

"Might I warn you that is a sexist and antisocial remark," came the receptionist's singsong voice. "Can anyone else help?"

"Yes, may I speak to Cleopatra Ratcliffe?"

"That was her single name, she's married now. She exercises her right to take on her husband's name. She's called Cleopatra Tallboys now. I'll put you through." A moment later: "I'm afraid Ms Tallboys is not at her work-station either.

In fact from her I.D. card-swipe record I can see that she isn't in the building."

Marty was not at home and could not be raised on his watch or vid. It did not augur well. Horatio left a message on his modem.

Then he called Cleo at home. She had just got out of the shower and was only wearing a small towel. She dried herself as they talked.

"Horatio! Where are you?"

"Never mind that, what's happened to Marty?"

"He's on enforced leave of absence for professional incompetence. For letting you out. The warrant for your arrest is probably not going to be issued immediately. They're watching you though. I've been trying to contact you. I can't talk safely on this but I badly need to see you. Where are you? Can I call you back?"

"Yes . . . No! Oh I don't know. Cleo, I'm horribly confused."

"Same here. Can we meet? There's so much I need to tell you." She continued to dry herself, flicking the towel across her broad shoulders and her fine, muscle-toned back, her breasts fully exposed to his view. And that of anyone else who happened to walk past the hallway vid-fone and glance in. He remembered with a start that Tallboys was still in the building somewhere, probably flexing his thumbs.

"The man you are accused of killing . . ."

"Was your grandfather. Yes I know. I didn't do it, Cleo. You of all people have to believe me."

"Of course I believe you. You're no murderer. I think I can help you, too. But only *I* can. Marty can't any more. Don't try to contact him, I'm not sure you can trust him."

She had absent-mindedly wrapped the towel around her

hair and was reaching for some moisturiser, which she began dabbing on her eyelid. She was standing completely naked and even more completely unconcerned. Her exposed breasts were round and firm and stood up pertly on their own, like a teenager's. He felt a strong stirring. He *must* concentrate. Cleo was seemingly oblivious to the effect she was having. He was at the same time perturbed and turned on by her unconscious immodesty. Or was it exhibitionism?

"Where shall we meet? Speak in code."

"Why are you willing to take these risks?"

"Because I know you'd never kill anyone, especially not for money. And I want to get to whoever did kill him." There was a pause – she looked straight into the vid – "and anyway I think I'm falling in love with you." It was what he wanted, what he *needed* to hear. Standing there naked to the world like a Plazotta bronze, she was peerless.

"Will they have listened to our conversation yesterday afternoon?"

"I doubt it. But this one, possibly."

"OK. Let's meet where we were going to anyway. And at the same time."

"Good." After one last long lingering look at her magnificent physique he clicked off.

Walking back up the stairs towards the West Mercia Room, Horatio saw Gemma Reegan coming down.

Of course! He'd half arranged to meet her here today. He'd entirely forgotten.

"Hi! Ah was wondering whether you'd show." She smiled broadly. "You were right, Mr Weaning did ask me to cover the visit. In fact Ah'm going down to your southern coast tomorrow. To South Hampton."

"Good, I'm glad. Congratulations. It's always heartening to

see the historical background to a story dealt with properly."
Although she was a distinctly third-rate historian whose
theories about the Mountbatten-Windsors were tripe, it
didn't reduce her attraction. Take the Russian girl in the Amis
novel, he thought, it was perfectly possible to be both a
delightful person *and* a crappy writer.

At that moment, looking down the stairwell, Horatio saw
Tallboys coming up.

Had he been there when he had called Cleo? When they'd
arranged to meet again? Had he been viewing into their
conversation? If so, he'd have seen her showing her nakedness
to him. Horatio's eyes suddenly felt very vulnerable.

Tallboys was striding up the stairs. Two steps at a time.

"Were you leaving?" Horatio said quietly.

"Yes, Ah'm off to pick up Oliver."

"Can I come too?"

"Yes, if you like. Ah don't think you'll find it too interesting
though. He's taking his weekly test." Tallboys turned the first
corner. All he needed to do now was look up.

"Great, I'd love to." Horatio steered her towards the exit.
He got them both out of sight just as Tallboys turned the
corner and carried on up the stairs, oblivious.

Just as he was getting into Gemma's bright yellow grade 4
electric outside, Horatio looked up at the windows of the
West Mercia Room. There was Tallboys, gawping down at
him. Horatio pointed proprietorially through the auto roof at
Gemma in the driver's seat. She couldn't see the gesture. Then
he pointed at himself, trying to send Tallboys the message that
he was interested in the American, not in Cleo at all.

Tallboys dashed away from the window and off towards the
stairs. Horatio hopped into the auto.

"And where's Oliver at school?" Horatio asked, trying to

sound natural and praying Gemma would speed up. They drove, horribly slowly, towards the exit and Russell Square.

"Chester Row. It's kinda smart. They take them up to fourteen. They give them a good thorough grounding in history, geography and maths."

"I thought you Yanks called it math."

"Some do, some don't."

Horatio spotted Tallboys in the wing mirror. He was running towards them.

"Would you mind driving a little faster? There's someone following us whom I'd like to lose."

"Wow! Cloak-and-dagger or what?!"

"Gemma, please. I'm serious." She looked across at him and saw his fear.

"OK, Ah get the picture." Very suddenly, after indicating left, she swung right into the Square and off down Montague Street. In the rear-view mirror, Horatio saw Tallboys stop in his tracks, stare after them and then run across to his green grade 3. Within seconds he was after them.

"Is he behind us?" Gemma asked, as she sped down the left side of the South English Museum.

"Yes."

"Right." Pushing the electric to near its top speed of 70 kph, Gemma swung down Russell Street, took a sudden left straight across an oncoming taxi and shot off into Museum Street. She went straight through a red light, narrowly missing an old man on a pedestrian crossing.

Was this was more dangerous than just confronting Tallboys, Horatio wondered? Then he remembered the boiled eggs.

At the end of Museum Street, Gemma turned a sharp right into Bloomsbury Way, through another set of lights. Just as

Tallboys was coming up behind her she pulled a handbrake U-turn at the very last moment and zoomed down St Giles Street, wheels screeching.

Horatio was terrified, exhilarated and proud. Mostly terrified.

Tallboys slammed straight on, and by the time he had been able to stop, reverse and give chase again, they had got down High Holborn and were emerging into Shaftesbury Avenue. By Piccadilly Circus he was nowhere to be seen. Like Horatio's breath.

In between hard sucks on his inhaler he cried, "That was *great*! Better than the Indy 500!" Gemma looked blank as she negotiated her way round Delors Square, past the Regional Gallery, the Sainsbury Wing, the A.F.T.A. Consulate, through Admiralty Arch and down towards Attali House. Halfway down the Mall she asked, "So. Who was he? Ah kinda recognised him from somewhere."

"He's called Alex Tallboys."

"Any relation to that woman who bust up our chat on Friday?"

"Husband."

"Uh-huh. Jealous husband, you mean. Ah see!"

She slammed on the brakes. The auto came to a juddering halt on the Mall, beside the St James's Park gates.

She stared across with a comprehending look. It made Horatio feel very uncomfortable. Autos hooted them as they passed.

"He was at the party. Uh-huh. Ah get it. Ah see. Ah have just violated enough traffic regulations to get me deported and all because you want to carry on your disgusting lounge-lizardry with a married woman! Go on" – she pointed at the door – "get out and walk! Ah'm not getting mixed up in other people's marital problems, Ah've had quite enough of my own. Now git!"

He thought fast. All he could come up with were clichés.

"No! It's not like that at all. This is political. *Please* drive on. I'll explain." He looked nervously behind him. No sign of Tallboys. Yet. But were he to find them, Horatio knew he would last no time at all on foot in the Park.

"Uh-huh."

"I'll explain everything. Only don't boot me out now. It could be a matter of life and death." That much at least was true. "Please take me to . . ." What was the brat's name? Orson? Orlando? ". . . Oliver's school. I'll explain everything as we go. Trust me."

She looked into his eyes and, recognising genuine terror, drove on into Eaton Square. Horatio meanwhile made up a transparently ludicrous story about why he was on the run from P.I.D. It had to do with being an A.F.T.A. spy. He was sworn to secrecy. He dropped codenames of imaginary contacts at Grosvenor Square. Using a combination of friends' first names and Metro terminals, he constructed a cast of spooks who were fighting with him to preserve international peace. He could see she hadn't fallen for Pete Cockfoster, though, let alone Michael Upminster. Thank God it didn't have to last long.

Gemma was able to park almost directly outside the school. She got out, put a ten-euro piece into her headlight-meter and went to lock the auto door.

"Please let me come in. It's not just because of that ape. You see, I'd really like to meet Oliver." She thought for a moment.

"You're lying, but all right. He's taking his weekly Civics and Lifestyle Studies test. It's all Education Commission bullshit of course, which is why they encourage parents to attend Ah suppose. But however bad it gets it won't be half as stupid as what you've been spouting for the last five minutes Doctor Horatio Lothario."

It might be a colossal waste of his ever more precious time, but what else was there to do? It would keep him away from the street cameras for an hour. Even if Tallboys tracked him down here somehow, he probably wouldn't disturb the whole school to drag him out. There seemed little alternative. It would at least give him some time to think about the latest developments over the driver called Evans, the role of the Atgas Corporation, and the Euro-Lottery.

And about Cleo. His cousin.

They found the class on the third floor. Horatio was wheezing heavily by the time they reached it. About thirty children were being tested by an attractive young woman teacher, with a dozen parents squeezed uncomfortably at the back. Roughly half the children wore the blue uniform and gold scarf of the Youth Euro-League. Horatio took one look at the chair designed for a ten-year-old and decided to sit on the table at the rear of the class instead.

When she walked in, Gemma blew a Texan-sized kiss to a sandy-haired boy in the front row, who reddened perceptibly. Horatio felt for him, recalling all those times at prep school when his mother used to approach him in the chapel queue in front of the entire school and publicly give him pots of Nivea cream for his chapped lips. On one sickening occasion he was even given a bottle of Johnson's Baby Shampoo. The teasing had gone on for weeks. It was one of the many tribulations arising from his not having had a father who could have told her the form.

It was a typical classroom, with maps and drawings and nursery rhymes stuck on the walls. Horatio hadn't yet seen any of the new de-monarchised nursery rhymes and carols which had gone down so badly with parents last year. Here they all were though. "The President was in his counting-house, counting out his money. His wife was in the parlour eating bread and honey", went one. "Good Mr Wenceslaus looked out . . ." read another. "Citizen-Commissioner Cole was a very merry soul" was pretty sad, he thought, and as for "The Grand Twilighter of York", surely any self-respecting kid would be bound to ask why just any Yorkshireperson was able to get ten thousand people to march up and down hills in the first place?

"They don't like elitism here," Gemma whispered to Horatio. "It's a mixed ability class." So it soon proved.

"Now, children," said the pretty, auburn-haired teacher whose little *retroussé* nose and fit young figure made the wasted time go easier for Horatio, "who can tell me what Devon is famous for?" She wore a starched, white, traditional school-mistress uniform which Horatio was having little difficulty imagining her not wearing. Only three hands went up.

"Yes, Klaus?"

"Soya, Ms!"

"Correct. Very good. One star." She pressed a button on her desk modem and next to the name "Klaus" on the screen behind her there appeared a third star. Horatio noticed that Oliver also had three, a boy called Timothy had three as well, but no one else had any at all. Anti-elitism seemed to consist of sitting back and watching the cleverest boys answer all the questions.

From the barely-concealed smirks on the faces of the couple sitting across the other side of the table from him, Horatio surmised Klaus' parents were ultra-competitive for their son, and scenting victory.

"What is a carrot?" Both Oliver and Klaus had their hands up this time.

"Oliver."

"A vegetable, Ms."

"No. Klaus?"

"It's a fruit, Ms."

"Correct. Another star." Horatio started rooting for Oliver. Gemma leant over and whispered in his ear, "That was a trick question. I've a mind to . . ."

"Who can name the seven deadly sins?" A number of hands went up this time. "Hans?"

"Jealousy, Anger, Unfairness, Ambition, Nationalism, Avarice and . . ." He was counting them up on his fingers, "is Envy one, Ms?"

"No. Of course it isn't. Envy is *good*. It's important because it is only by envying people happier and better off than ourselves that we can make sure that we all grow up to live in a fair and equal society. Now, who can tell me the last one?"

"Sloth?" asked Klaus.

"No, Klaus, not Sloth either. How can Sloth be a sin when so many people are socially-excluded? Come on now!"

"Lust, Ms?"

"Well done, Oliver. One star." Gemma beamed.

"What is lust, Ms?" asked Oliver. Her smile fell.

"You'll be learning all about that when you're ten. Now then, who can name me the Eight Great Unifiers?"

When Oliver put his hand up, a fraction of a second after Klaus, Horatio noticed that both Gemma and Klaus' parents had their fingers crossed. From the look of insane concentration on her face it was as though Gemma was trying telepathically to tell her son the answers. Horatio started rooting for Oliver, his own problems taking second place to this clash.

"Oliver."

"Please, Ms – Julius Caesar, Charlemagne, Philip the Second, Louis the Fourteenth, Adolf Hitler, Jacques Delors and . . ." There was an agonising few seconds as Oliver tried to remember a seventh: ". . . Helmut Kohl!" he cried triumphantly. Gemma almost hopped out of her seat.

"Well done, one star. Now then, which brilliant brainbox can name me the fifth Great Unifier? Klaus?" He shook his head. "Anyone?"

"Please, Ms," said another little boy, "was it Napoleon Bonaparte?"

"It was. Well done, Arthur! Now, which region of the Union did he come from?"

"Corsica, Ms," ventured Oliver.

"No." Horatio's eyebrows shot up.

"Was it France, Ms?"

"Yes. One point to Timothy." Horatio looked across at Gemma and raised his eyes heavenwards at the teacher's ignorance, but Gemma hadn't noticed anything wrong. Well done Oliver, anyhow. Horatio couldn't remember his own school tests consisting of quite such blatantly federationist propaganda.

A bell rang outside the door and the teacher looked at her watch. "Young Euro-Leaguers can go off to room seven now," she called. "And afterwards Mr Cameron will be taking Flexible Geometry in the Anderson building." There was a great scraping of chairs against floorboards as half the class, all those wearing the blue and gold uniform, left.

"Settle down now the rest of you. We're going on with the test." She turned around to look at the screen. "Oliver is on five stars, Klaus and Timmy four. Come on the rest of you. Now, who can tell me when Switzerland joined the Union?"

"Joined, my arse," Horatio whispered into Gemma's ear, "it was forced in." Gemma nodded.

"Oliver?"

"2036, Ms."

"Well done. One star." Klaus' hand stayed up. "Yes, Klaus?"

"It was actually on 19th April 2036, the hundredth birthday of Founding Father Wilfred Martens, Ms."

"Well, that really *is* impressive. Well done. You can have an extra star." Just as Oliver was about to build up a lead, thought Horatio, whose own troubles had almost been put out of his mind. Klaus' mother looked nervously across at Horatio. She was squeezing her husband's hand, sitting on the edge of her seat. Horatio smiled and gave a nonchalant grin.

"Now children, last question of the test. For two stars," said the teacher, who had turned the large map of the Union in the corner of the room back to front and had come round to sit on the edge of the table, which to Horatio's lecherous delight caused her skirt to ride up her black-stockinged thighs about twenty glorious centimetres. "I want you to put all the regions of the Union onto my modem in alphabetical order. Whoever makes it bleep first gets two points. But remember, you have to get all thirty-six and stars will be deducted for bad spelling."

There followed about two minutes of silence. As the children tapped frantically into their modems, Horatio studied the wall charts and the teacher's fine ankles and calves. The bleeper went.

"Well done . . . Klaus!" Gemma visibly deflated, and the German couple could not forbear looking across at her and Horatio in triumph. "Do you want to call them out to everyone?" The crop-haired child stood up and read out, in a voice Horatio found irritatingly smug:

"Albania, Austria, Bulgaria, Byelorussia, Catalonia, Central Italy, Czechlands, Denmark, Eastern Poland, Estonian Protectorate, Finland, Flemishlands, France, Greater Serbia, Greece, Grossdeutschland, Holland, Hungary, Iceland, Island of Ireland, Latvian Protectorate, Lithuanian Protectorate, Luxembourg, North England, North Italy, Portugal, Scotregion, Serb Macedonia, Slovenia, Slovakia, South England, South Italy, Sweden, Switzerland, Wales and Walloonia."

"Very well done. And with seven stars you come top of the test again this week. Bad luck to Oliver who came second with six. Timmy got four. Shame on the rest of you. Next week you must all pull your stockings up." The mention of stockings made Horatio redden, as coincidentally he had been fantasising about hers.

The teacher returned to the other side of her desk and pressed a button. The opening strains of Beethoven's Ninth filled the small room and the class got up to sing the Union Anthem. Horatio heaved himself to his feet and sang alongside Gemma:

"Peoples of Europe, arise as one!
From centuries of mistrust and hate.
Let us march forward towards the sun,
Partners embracing one common fate!

Our Founding Fathers led the way,
And we arose at such a rate
That thirty-six peoples now can say,
'Europe is here! Not one moment too late!'

We're forging together a common land,

141

Protected, equal, unified, free,
Unbreakable bonds by which we stand,
An Eden on earth for you and for me!"

It lost much in translation from the German, thought Horatio, but at least it rhymed, almost scanned and went with the music. He wondered whether the seven million socially-excluded Britons thought of the Union as "an Eden on earth". From the scale of the demonstrations taking place in the North English Region earlier that week, he doubted it. As the last bars died away, Oliver ran over and jumped up on Gemma, kissing her.

"Hello Mutti!"

"Ah'm trying to get him to practise his German," she explained. "Hello my darling, so what happened in the test?"

"Oh, it was Klaus's turn."

"What do you mean?"

"We take it in turns." His accent was not so pronouncedly American as hers. Gemma had told Horatio at the party that Oliver's father had been a German publisher living in New York.

"Does Ms know?"

"I think so. She doesn't mind. If you win too often yourself you get told off for being too competitive, so he gets two weeks, then it's my turn. Sometimes we let Timmy or Rachel win too."

"Shake hands with Dr Lestoq, Oliver. Ah'll expect he'll tell you it was very different in his day. It sure was in mine."

"Hello, Oliver. Do call me Horatio. It was, actually." They shook hands. "Listen, Oliver, I don't suppose by any chance there's a back way out of here? There could be someone in the street outside from whom I want to escape."

"Yessir!" The boy looked excited by the idea. "Follow me." He turned to his mother. "You can't come, I'm afraid."

"You said you were going down to Southampton tomorrow," Horatio asked Gemma. "Are you driving? Only . . . I'd love to have a lift to Basingstoke if there's any way you could drop me off? It's on the way."

"Fine, yes, Ah'd like that. Is an oh-nine hundred start OK for you? Shall Ah pick you up?" Horatio thought quickly. With luck he'd be with Cleo tonight.

"No, I'll come round to you. Where do you live?"

"Thirty-one Moore Street, Chelsea."

"See you then." They kissed four times.

"Now then young man," said Horatio avuncularly, "I suspect I know where you're taking me."

"Hurry back, honey," Gemma called out. Oliver winced at being called that in front of the other children and Horatio felt for him. He'd have a word with Gemma about prep school etiquette one day. They set off down two flights of steps and off towards the changing rooms at the rear of the building.

They were full of boys and girls changing into Euro-Youth League uniforms, scarves and toggles everywhere. With some help from Oliver, Horatio squeezed himself through the lavabo window at the back. He dropped feet first onto the playground, almost winding himself. He took a suck of Salbutamol, crossed the tarmac quickly and emerged out onto the street.

He was free.

20.25 Monday, 3rd May

Memories of 1996 could easily have been a disastrous choice of restaurant for a first date, even a post-coital one. Macao food came second only to spaghetti for making Horatio look unattractive to women. He was as incompetent with chopsticks as he was insistent on using them. Worst of all, whenever he got excited, which was often, morsels of crispy duck or fried rice would flick out of his mouth. He also asked for all the leftovers of dishes to be packed into doggy-bags. He had no dog but he loved eating the food cold the next morning, while lying in the bath. Despising mineral water, he invariably ordered wine, beer and *sake* by the bucketful, which went down to apparently nil effect. Until he stood up.

He liked to think he patronised Macao restaurants because of what had happened to their people thirty years before, but Portugal's Chinese had not suffered as the former British Chinese had, so it was probably really primarily the cuisine. The Macaoan Chinese had all been awarded European passports by Lisbon, which meant that under Maastricht's freedom of movement Article 101 many came to live in Hackney, Soho and Brent. In parts of Stepney the Macaoans were now said to outnumber even the French Moroccans. Of course it was both racist and nationalist to keep any figures, so no one could ever know for sure how many had come over.

"Table for two, sir? What name?"

"Ellis." He'd booked it in his mother's maiden name just in case.

"Toking or non-toking, sir?" He did not suppose Cleo would take pills at the table, but he again wanted to be on the safe side.

"Toking, please."

"Breast-feeding or non breast-feeding?"

"Definitely non," said Horatio, in a tone that a Sexism Tribunal might easily have construed as unacceptable. He was led to a table in a quiet corner of the second room. Just what he wanted. He took the seat with its back to the wall. That way he could keep his eye on anyone coming in. He was also near enough to the lavabos to try the same gambit as before should Tallboys suddenly turn up.

When Cleo walked in five minutes later, with the stalking, confident pace of a jungle big cat, Horatio felt a gargantuan thrill of physical need. She seemed to suck all the oxygen out of the room. She wore a neck-to-ankle, figure-hugging dark green silk Hong dress, slit to mid-thigh. As at the party, every single male in the room gazed across at her in admiration. The women stared in unfeigned jealousy. He stood up as she approached, breaking yet another provision of the Anti-Sexism Directive. She didn't seem to mind.

He stood on tiptoe to kiss her once on the lips. That kiss alone was almost enough to justify his decision to defy Tallboys' threat. He also knew, logically, that he needed her information. Their kiss went directly against the advice contained in the recent Intimacy-Transmitted Disease Directive put out by the Commission after the "Killer Kissing Bug" scare. Then he pulled out her chair for her and once they had sat down he poured out glasses of white wine and *sake* for them both.

A waiter came over to ask, *sotto voce*, whether they could please obey the law with regard to the recent Sexism Directive 43/629, as he did not want the restaurant to get a reputation as sexist. Cleo surreptitiously slipped her P.I.D. card from her handbag and showed it to him at table height. One look and he bowed and withdrew.

She was strong, fit and wholly at ease with her pulsating sexual allure. She looked at him coolly and levelly for a short while before asking him how he was. "Obsessed with you, you unbelievable beauty", would have been the true answer, but he confined himself to saying, "Fine, considering I'm risking being blinded in order to be here tonight." He explained. She was sympathetic but hardly comforting.

"I'd love to be able to tell you it's all hot air, darling, but I can't. He really is a brute." At least "darling" made it somehow easier to bear. "Anyhow, your eyes aren't piggy, they're . . ." She searched for the right word. ". . . idealistic. They're what attracted me to you in the first place."

And then they talked. They quickly established from the will, a copy of which Cleo had obtained from P.I.D., and what Horatio's mother had told him, that they were cousins. Catching and punishing her grandfather's murderer had become an obsession. The way she talked about it, Horatio got the impression that Cleo was not thinking in terms of the traditional Europol progression of detection, arrest, trial, conviction and eventual imprisonment. She had a far more direct course of retribution in mind.

She told him about being brought up as an orphan by the Admiral. He told her about growing up without a father. She had no idea, beyond a vague suspicion that it might somehow be political, why anyone should want to murder the old man. As they were the only beneficiaries of his will it couldn't have been for the money. She also couldn't say why Ratcliffe had so much, and Horatio was not about to tarnish her happy memories of him by saying. He told her all about the conversation with Percival, though, and how Snell had wiped it. Without mentioning Marty, who was in quite enough trouble already, he told her about the destroyed furniture in the Rectory. This made her yet more furious. She had grown up there.

For the rest of dinner they just talked like people who are falling in love, whilst he ate as carefully as possible. They had much in common. They were the same age, born within a week of one another. They both found it absurd that cheddar cheese could now only be obtained in Sicily. They laughed about their childhood membership of the Youth Anti-Alcohol & Nicotine League. They both thought that the traditional blue plastic awning around the Albert Memorial, under which they both remembered crawling as children and which had been there now for over half a century, should at last be removed.

Prince Albert was a good role model for European cohesion, she thought, despite having been royal. She couldn't talk in any detail about her job, of course, but there was nothing of the sea-green incorruptible fanatic Marty had warned him about. The only thing sea-like about her were those extraordinary turquoise eyes. He dived into them, swam in them, wallowed in them.

Paying the bill, Horatio spotted the time on the receipt: 01.35. They had been talking for five hours! All the other diners had left. The waiters were clearing up around them and stacking chairs on tables. He feared initiating the next stage —

always assuming there would be one – and prayed she would take charge as decisively as she had on Friday night. He suggested nervously that they go on to a nightclub. The Ministry of Fear in Brixton, perhaps, or the Kulturkampf in Belgrave Square, where they could dance to some of the latest Hamburg hits? Much to his relief – at twenty kilos overweight and asthmatic, dancing was hardly his *forte* – she suggested, straight out and without any prompting, that they go back to his flat.

Neither, once there, did she tease him with the will-she-won't-she games that so many women had played in the past, before invariably plumping for the won't. Her superb, sleek self-assurance was far too great for that. After a genuine Russian vodka nightcap which she slipped from her handbag – the imported Government variety, he noticed – she stood up, smoothed her open palms down her dress, over the magnificent contours of her breasts, hips and upper thighs, and said, in an almost matter-of-fact tone, "So, are we going next door?"

"We are," Horatio croaked, entranced. He heaved himself to his feet and tottered off after her into the bedroom.

Unlike him, Cleo had all the legal precursors organised. The diggles – or Pre-Penetration Permission Certificates, as they were officially called – were in her bag, already completed, timed and even date-stamped. They only required signatures to make the next stage legal. Horatio noticed that his handwriting looked distinctly shaky. Permission from the Health Commission was faxed back within minutes – she had a friend there, she explained. As he put the initialled counter-foils for her Harassment Protection (Liability Exemption P12 E) forms into his wallet, she bent down to his height. "And unlike last night, Horatio," she whispered, between long, excruciating kisses, in that combination of purr and demand he found so intoxicating, "you will allow me to enjoy you as much as you are about to enjoy me."

"It's all right to do this if we're cousins, isn't it?" She just looked at him and smiled.

Horatio had only made love to six women in his life, three of whom had required payment. He'd lost his virginity at nineteen. About to make a call from a pimp-sponsored vid-fone booth in St Pancras, one of the ads had caught his eye. She did not look too bad on the vid either, and the pro-tel was only two hundred yards away, in one of the local authority's Toleration Zones. Any excitement, naughtiness or erotic content the occasion might have had was more than dissipated by the Health Commission nurse's check-ups on him before, virtually during and after that singularly unfulfilling half-hour.

His fourth foray had been an undiluted disaster, setting back his sexual confidence and development half a decade. Liz used to laugh at him at the most vital moments. Number five had been Leila, and *coitus* had never been more comprehensively interrupted than at 03.00 on Monday, 9th September 2043 when Special Branch had smashed his flat door down and dragged them both off to Paddington Green anti-terrorist nick. They had been bugging the place, and had specially chosen the most embarrassing time to burst in.

Leila's successor only lasted a fortnight before she went off with some Hunky Regular Guy. She had said she wanted brainpower, but in the end she went for the pecs of a Sportschannel 19 fitness instructor. Horatio was therefore quite content for Cleo to take control. Which she did, expertly. For once in his life he would be making love to a woman who would not be constantly shooting surreptitious glances at the vid-fone clock, wondering when it would be over.

Cleo was extrovert, experienced, inventive, a master of timing and – as he soon discovered – very, very uninhibited. It took all his self-control to hold himself back. He was terrified of her reaction if he failed. So he tried to concentrate on his grandmother's moustache, his Atgas bill, his mortgage and the documentary he'd once seen on operations without anaesthetic in Somalia. He even wound up trying to debate the pros and cons of the Pope's opposition to Turkey's membership of the Union.

It wasn't working.

He tried declining some of the more obscure German irregular verbs. He asked himself why there was no past tense of the Italian verb meaning "to itch"? The vision of Alex Tallboys' thumbs moving closer and closer towards his unprotected eyeballs also helped take his mind off the wonderful thing that she was doing to him so expertly and, more amazingly, with every appearance of relish.

The Sexual Equality Directive had been quite specific. Women were to be on top for at least fifty per cent of the time. On this, if nothing else, Cleo was clearly a conformist. Eyes closed, lips just slightly apart, breathing deep but regular, she was the personification of erotic womanhood. Most men only get to experience lovemaking like this once or twice in their lives, Horatio thought, so he must make every second count. There couldn't be many more, so he must etch each one on to his memory so as to be able to give himself pleasure and pride until the day he died. Which might very well be quite soon if her husband found out.

After another period of ecstasy, which actually lasted only a few minutes but seemed to him to take as long as the decline and fall of the Roman Empire, he warned her that he could stand it no longer. He called out "Cleo!", thinking how appropriate it was that Clio should be the historian's muse, and it was all over.

A great tiredness suddenly descended, but he had read too many articles in *Chic Alors!* not to know that he could not just turn over and fall asleep, however much he might want to. This was the time for the T.L.C. part. Taking a packet of Marlboro nicotine cigarettes from her handbag – how on earth did she get hold of such things? What other smuggled goodies were in there? A Clint Eastwood video, perhaps, or a Sony Walkperson? – Cleo looked at him with a fully satisfied smile.

"If I do go to prison for a terrible crime that I didn't commit," he told her, truthfully, "I will at least now for ever know that I have experienced true perfection."

"Night-night, Horatio."

★ 15 ★

07.00 Tuesday, 4th May

Horatio woke. The watch-fone bleeper said 07.00. He couldn't remember setting it.

Cleo wasn't there.

Rolling himself out of bed he saw her note on the floor in the middle of the room.

"*Had to go darling. Didn't want to wake you. Last night was wonderful.*

Call me. All love C.

P.S. Be v.v. careful, my fone is probably tapped and location-monitored now. Use scramble & talk quickly. 40 secs max each call. Use code if poss. Destroy this."

He slipped it into his jacket pocket and went next door to wash.

As he was getting dressed the "Urgent" bleeper on his desk modem went off in the next-door room. Ear-piercingly demanding, it got louder and louder. He waddled over half-naked to the modem, tapped in his password and read: "*GET OUT NOW! SWAT TEAM ON ITS WAY! NOW! LEAVE!*"

For a split second he hesitated. Should he let them take him? No. He had not got the evidence he needed yet. It would mean a lifetime in prison. Always wondering . . .

He grabbed his clothes and ran to the kitchen window. He tried to fling it open. It was stuck. Or locked.

Where did he keep the key? He had no time for this.

He shocked himself with his determination when he picked up the kitchen chair and threw it feet first straight through the window. He dressed hurriedly.

Then he climbed up onto the sink and squeezed himself through the shattered glass, hoping he wouldn't cut himself. Scrambling onto the fire escape, he was about to run down. Then he thought again. They'd be covering the back. So instead he climbed up and onto the roof.

He could hear sirens. Sucking hard on his inhaler, Horatio forced himself over the two roofs adjoining his. The sirens were getting louder and louder, closer and closer. Then he heard a loud, violent, swooping sound. Looking back he saw a chopper, its nose tipped down so that only the rotating blades showed, heading straight towards him from the Gloucester Road only about half a kilometre to the west. He grabbed the next fire escape down, trying to stay out of sight.

Gasping badly by the time he got to the end of the fire escape, he was feeling dizzy. The steps ended. There was a drop to the bottom of about eight metres. Where was the bloody ladder?

Nowhere.

Lying underneath him was a large pile of cardboard boxes. He'd once read somewhere that stuntmen used boxes as the ideal stopping agent in jumps. But what if these were full of smuggled Japanese white goods or something? He'd break his back. Be paralysed.

The din of the chopper and auto sirens on the other side of the house made his choice for him. He took another pull at his inhaler and held it tight in his fist. "Oh God! Oh God!" He clenched his teeth. Closed his eyes. And jumped. The boxes were empty. The stuntmen were right.

Picking himself up quickly he scampered off down the alleyway around the back of the Swallow Hotel, praying the chopper would not come over his side of the block until he was under the archway and out of sight. When five seconds later it did he was away. As he emerged safely onto the Director's Court Road he could not help glancing the three hundred metres back down Director's Court Gardens towards his front door.

Five police petrol autos were parked at angles in the road. Armed men in navy blue flak jackets wearing heavy helmets and carrying N-series automatic weapons – one, he thought, held what looked like a bazooka – were taking up positions behind the autos.

"Horatio Lestoq!" came a voice from a loudhailer. The words were clearly audible even though he was hundreds of metres away. "This is Europol! You are surrounded! . . ."

The chopper was hovering over the roof like a vast, furious hornet. Marksmen were leaning out of it. Horatio showed as much interest as might any busy man who was late for work, making his way through the crowd which was forming in the street to watch the excitement. After a few seconds he waddled off in the opposite direction towards the Old Brompton Road tram stop. Even in that short walk four more police autos zoomed past him towards Collingham Place.

The tram journey allowed him to get his breath back and stop sweating quite so profusely. He changed trams in the Fulham Road and alighted at the corner of Walton Street and Ovington Square.

The walk to Moore Street was nerve-wracking. He was now officially on the run. What if it had been on the news?

What if Gemma had seen it and contacted Europol? He could now be done for resisting arrest. It would count badly against him when it got to court.

Horatio was basting in anxiety as he made his way down Lennox Gardens. Everything was quiet. Was it *too* quiet for 08.55 on a Tuesday?

Tuesday!

Today was the thirtieth anniversary of Aachen, the day his third *Times* article was due to have appeared. Damn Weaning. Damn Percival. Damn Tallboys. Damn them all.

Doubts descended like his depression used to before he started on Pluszac. Suddenly, overpoweringly, without warning. Should he have just ignored Percival's note? Forgotten all about it? The Admiral would probably be alive today if he had. Horatio's most serious worries would be reserved for his Atgas bill. Not for his life.

He scanned the rooftops for snipers. Was the old boy selling frankfurters at the end of Clabon Mews in fact a policeperson ready to pounce? What about the lad cleaning the windows of the ivy-covered pub? (And since when had it changed its name? It had been called The Australian for centuries. Now it was The Austrian. The sign of the grinning ocker Aussie with corks dangling from his hat had been replaced by some jerk in *lederhosen*.)

He had no alternative. He had to get back to Ibworth, and a private auto was the only way. Even if he had an auto, the satellite "eye-in-the-sky" would have spotted his roof number in seconds. Public transport was out of the question. Gemma was his only hope. The logic was his sole comfort as he knocked on her door at 09.00.

"Hi, Horatio, you're prompt." Four quick pecks on the cheek. Perfectly natural. "Ah've just got a couple of things to do and then Ah'll be right with you. Come on in." He was relieved to be able to get off the street. She disappeared next door, calling, "Go on into the drawing room and watch the cable if you like. Ah've almost finished packing. I think the news should be on soon." He walked in and came face to face with himself on the screen.

"*Doctor Horatio Lestoq, an Oxford don, is being sought for questioning relating to the murder of the ninety-one-year-old former Admiral Michael . . .*" Where was the clicker to switch the bloody thing off? No sign of it. Maybe it was voice-controlled. "Off!" he barked at it, and then tried it again in an American accent. No luck. ". . . *Ratcliffe at his home near Basingstoke on Sunday. The search . . .*" He leapt forward to try to find a wall plug he could pull. But it was one of the new beam ones.

Gemma walked in. Just as she crossed the threshold the screen suddenly went blank.

"Oh God, not another power cut! This really is a Third World continent." It was racist, but he was not about to comment.

"Oh I don't know." Horatio smiled. "I rather enjoy them." Absolutely no response. Perhaps it had been Cleo who'd kissed him. He must get her away before the power returned.

"Well, you're probably conditioned to them by now. Anything interesting on the news?" He shook his head. He could hardly trust himself to open his mouth.

"So tell me, did you manage to evade your pursuer yesterday? The guy you tried to tell me was an agent of a foreign power?" She grinned. "Now what was his name again, Michael Ongar was it? Or Peter High-Barnet? Or . . ."

"Yes, yes I lost him, thank God. And all thanks to that genius of a son of yours."

"Great." She left the room again.

The photograph of him on the cable had been taken two years ago. By Marty, he seemed to remember, at a party a few years back. Grinning, and perhaps drunk, his face looked incredibly callous and vicious when placed above the "Have You Seen This Person?" caption. How had the police got hold of it? Had Marty given them it? Where *was* he?

"Right," said Gemma, reappearing with two travelling bags, "that should be about the lot. Ah'm ready."

"Where's Oliver?"

"He's staying with some friends of mine at the Embassy till Sunday. Would you mind giving me a hand putting this in the boot? Here's the card. It's in Cadogan Street. Look right when you get to the Moore Arms. Ah'm just going to set the alarm."

Horatio heaved the canvas bag up onto his shoulder and stepped outside, half expecting to be cut down by laser beam as soon as he opened the door. There was hardly anyone on the street. With the bag covering the left side of his face and his arm the other he was virtually unrecognisable.

As he walked down the street he surreptitiously read Gemma's I.D. card.

JEMIMA LOUISE REEGAN. A.F.T.A. citizen. I.D. No: 592X 382W Sex: F (Het). Partner Status: Div (one s – Oliver Jefferson Reegan). Address: 31, Moore Street, London SW3 2RS, South England Region, U.S.E. Occup: Author/ Academic. Modem no. 673987 Pager no: 01171 824 6226. Blood Gp: A.B. Auto reg: F765 055. Insurance: Full. D.o.B: 7/7/2015

Coming up for her thirtieth birthday. Not bad. She didn't look it. A divorced foreign authoress in her late twenties, who clearly liked him. Interesting. If Cleo didn't work out . . .

When he reached Cadogan Street he looked right and

spotted her auto. He put the card in the auto boot lock, opened it, shoved the bag inside and shut it quickly. Then he went round to sit in the front passenger seat and buried his face in the electronic A–Z Journeyfinder, working out the best way to Basingstoke and hoping no passer-by would recognise him. An agonising half-minute later, Gemma got in.

He directed her down Moore Street, back through Lennox Gardens and Ovington Square and left out onto the Brompton Road. They joined the Cromwell Road, passing the Victoria and Albert Anglo-German Friendship Museum and the Natural History Museum on their way out west.

"Do you want the radio on?" she asked. The last thing he wanted was for her to hear the news.

"No, let's talk."

In the two hours it took her electric to reach the Basingstoke turnoff they managed to cover just about every subject under the ozone layer. Nothing and nobody was exempt from her attractive, eager, questing brain. Except perhaps sequential thought, for it was something of a grasshopper mind which left a subject the moment she tired of it and hopped onto something more appealing and often unrelated. Horatio soon got over his initial irritation at this.

"How can you say that you've abolished nationalism in the U.S.E. when your soccer matches still turn into pitched battles?"

"Because in a state where there's no other possible outlet for patriotic, partisan sentiment – politics, economics, culture and so on – sports competitions become a kind of war by other means. It's soon going to be dealt with though. Regional teams will no longer be allowed to play each other after 2048, so you won't get the violence you probably saw on the news after the Northern England v. Grossdeutschland Union Cup final in

Copenhagen last month. It'll all be between local teams next season."

"Those people were animals, complete maniacs, those German fans. Did you hear what they were chanting? 'Britons for ever, ever, ever *will* be slaves' and so on. The sheer blatant nationalism of it. Ah can't tell you, it was horrific!"

"I feel rather guilty about admitting this, Gemma, but in a sneaking sort of way I have to say I'm rather proud of our own football hooligans. Did you know the Danish Commission had to deploy more riot police at that match than at the height of their recent anti-Aachen riots? Brain-dead those fans might be, but they're also often incredibly brave. They'll cheerfully attack forces five or six times their number. They just weren't going to take all that German provocation lying down. I sometimes wonder whether it is only amongst the working classes that the spirit of aggressive patriotism . . ."

"Nationalism, you mean."

"Yes, all right, if you like, nationalism, lives on. The social and intellectual elites are all conforming to the new cosmopolitanism like crazy, talking German, naming opera houses after Jacques Delors and so on, but ordinary working people and their families are still sticking up Union Jacks and pictures of William Windsor in their homes. Hardly a week goes by without some publican in Bermondsey or Southwark or somewhere getting picked up for allowing clandestine Carlist meetings in his upper rooms. Those soccer hooligans who attacked the Germans reminded me, this is perhaps just the romantic in me speaking, of a regiment under Clive of India which fixed bayonets and charged a Franco-Indian force thirty times their number during the Seven Years' War . . ."

"Romantic? That little rant managed to be classist,

militaristic, atavistic, racist, anti-peace and male-assertive all at once!" She looked peeved, but not genuinely angry.

"It's true that I'm secretly rather pleased that a century of peace and brotherhood hasn't completely bred out the instinctively aggressive nature of the English people. What the German fans sang – it sounds worse in German you know – was really unforgivable."

"Why rise to them? Why not just sit back and enjoy the game?"

"Because everyone knows, deep down, that what they were singing was true. That's why it had to be punished. Most people in this country – God, I could never talk to anyone but a foreigner about this! – actually *do* know in their heart of hearts that Aachen was a terrible mistake and we should have stayed independent. So when Germans, who do after all pretty much run the Union today, point out that they have now succeeded by hard work and stealth in doing what we British twice stopped them doing by force last century, it's bound to make our blood boil. It shouldn't, because we're all part of one big happy Union now, but human beings aren't quite made like that yet. At least we aren't, thank God. It takes more than thirty years – thirty years today by the way – to erase a millennium of tribal allegiance."

"But all that Second Nat War stuff was over a century ago. Germany has been peaceful and democratic now for a hundred years."

"A century this Saturday. Quite a week for anniversaries."

"That's right. All they've done since is work harder and produce more and show more leadership than the rest of you in the Union. We Americans cannot understand why they shouldn't be allowed to enjoy the fruits of that, without you nats constantly still dragging up what happened a hundred years ago."

"Because, Gemma, they force you to. It wasn't our fans who were chanting and crowing about domination. It was theirs. You don't get the Portuguese strutting around Brussels demanding a high euro-dollar rate despite its effect on our exports, or interest rates which suit *their* industry, it's the Germans. Every time. You don't find the Spanish threatening a scorched earth policy in Estonia, or the Greeks sabre-rattling against the Ukraine, do you now?" He felt a rant coming on. "One hundred and ten million hard-working, as you say, and committed Germans bang in the centre of the Union – or Reich as I've heard them call it among themselves when they don't think anyone's listening. It's no good feeling sorry for them any longer, they've won, they've no reason to boast their famous inferiority complexes now. They're in control. What were their fans chanting? Nothing more than the unpalatable truth. We made a historic error in ever allowing the European trading scheme to get political."

"With all this talk, it sounds like you ought to be in the Resistance."

"Too much of a coward. Anyhow, I still think it can be done peacefully."

"By writing snide articles about Aachen in the newspapers?"

"Yes, partly. It all helps. What's getting at you?"

"Ah don't know. You just sound so cynical. Ah mean, my country has been a union of states since 1776. Now with A.F.T.A. it's an even bigger union, and it works." This was getting like those endless aimless late-night philosophical conversations about life, love and politics he'd had with fellow undergraduates at university. But anything was better than Gemma hearing the radio news.

"But you started off with a common language, religion, revolution, values, assumptions, aspirations, manifest destiny, legal system, flag and all the rest of it."

"Well, you've got most of those things now. History's being written to emphasise the European dimension of everything. Oliver's being taught about the positive aspects of the Roman, Charlemagne, Holy Roman and Austro-Hungarian empires as forerunners of the Union, and virtually nothing about the English monarchy. The only times wars are mentioned it's in order to admonish the kids about the horrors of nationhood. Teaching dates has been completely phased out. Oliver gets marked down if he mentions them, as they 'over-contextualise' history according to his teachers! You've had a common currency since 2006, and although you're probably right about the Germans dominating the economy, well, they're good at it aren't they? What's the big problem?"

"The problem is that it isn't working. Look at the waste, the inefficiency, the smuggling. And the corruption! Why did Italy split into three regions rather than stay as one? Corruption. Who's cornered the black market in tobacco, foreign booze and Hollywood videos? The various mafias. Maltese in Streatham, Sardinians in Bayswater and so on. Our poor old homegrown East End villains never stood a chance! What do you do if Brussels refuses you your oak subsidy on the minor technicality that you'd chopped down all your oaks last year for the timber subsidy? You find the guy responsible and bribe him. Then there's Euroflation, seven million unemployed . . ." Horatio was getting into his stride.

They debated hard but flirtatiously until the M3 turnoff.

She was certainly spirited, and brighter than he'd previously given her credit for. He wondered whether he was right to pick up the sparks of a sexual electricity somewhere there too?

"Why did France let Germany get away with it?" The locust mind had leapt again. There was now no danger of her listening to the radio until after she'd dropped him off.

"With what?"

"With controlling the Union."

Horatio had a pet theory about France which he would never put down on screen, but which was probably safe to air to a foreigner alone in an electric auto approaching Ausgang 6 on the M3 on a bright and cloudless May morning.

"The French" – he wanted to say "Frogs" but remembered at the last minute that Georgie Worcester had got three days in prison and seven Ethnic-offence penalty points on his I.D. for doing just that – "had their political and military self-confidence – not their linguistic, cultural or culinary self-confidence, nothing ever could touch those – blown away between February and December 1916 at the Battle of Verdun. They lost 1.3 million men in the First Nationalist War, almost twice as many as us. Everything that came after that: the mutinies of 1917, Fourth Republic instability, Appeasement, Munich, the June '40 collapse, Vichy, the de Gaulle/Adenauer axis, the Coal and Steel Community, Treaty of Rome, Maastricht, Schengen, the Fast Track Six, the soft-then-hard euro, the Single Currency, Aachen, the whole lot, they all came about as a result of that national loss of will. It was shot up and left hanging, haemorrhaging away on the barbed wire at Verdun. Afterwards, they conned themselves into thinking they could ride the tiger, be the Greeks to Germany's Rome and so on. Why do you suppose they raised that statue to Marshal Pétain in the Place de la Concorde five years ago?"

"It was the hundredth anniversary of his becoming President."

"Yes, but why did they feel the *need* to commemorate him? Because for five years, when everyone else in the world was fighting the Second Nationalist War and millions were dying, he made sure that most Frenchmen weren't. You can be sure that if Norway was in the Union today they'd have a statue up to Vidkun Quisling in Oslo."

Gemma just nodded through all of this. Had the lecture bored her? It seemed so, for the grasshopper leapt again.

"You know something, Horatio. You've got a very attractive mind. Ah like the way you seem to formulate whole sentences before you say them. Most people, me for instance, just start off and work out the rest of it halfway through while we're speaking. You seem to know what you're about to say about three sentences before."

"Thanks, it's nice to know something about me is attractive." He was fishing.

"You're fishing."

"No I'm not."

"Yes you are and Ah'm flattered you're bothering. Actually, Ah do find you very attractive. Except for . . ." He waited. And waited.

"For what? You can't stop there." It looked as though she had. "Come on, Gemma. You can't lead a horse to water like that. Except for what?"

"Oh . . . nothing. Let's just say that Ah find you attractive."

"No. Sorry. You can't leave it at that! You can't say 'except for . . .' and then stop there!"

What could it be? The dandruff? (Wasn't too bad, he was on top of the problem now.) Receding hairline? (He *was* twenty-nine.) Teeth like mossy old gravestones? (He'd never forgive his mother for calling them that. *They* were much better now too.) The flecky upper lip? (OK, perhaps that.) "Say what it is you don't like and I promise I'll have all the necessary surgery. Please. *Please!*"

"Well, you're clearly besotted with that Cleopatra woman whose husband chased us around the houses yesterday afternoon. It was goddam confusing for Oliver to be introduced to a new friend of his mom's only to have to help to push him through the restroom window to escape a jealous husband. No woman likes to be involved in a stupid old cliché love triangle, it's bad for the ego."

He thought for a short time. "I see. Yes. That's fair. Although I'm not besotted actually. Anyway, if the past is anything to go by, my love life is programmed on self-destruct mode anyhow."

He badly wanted to change the subject and was helped by the approach of Ausgang 6. "Come off here" – he pointed – "and at the roundabout follow signs for Basingstoke." She turned off. He watched carefully in the rear-view mirror to see who followed. One blue petrol, which overtook them, and a couple of electrics. One red, one black. He noted the plates on his pager, just in case.

"How do you feel about your son being taught all that Union Civics and Lifestyle Studies crap? I mean, that test yesterday was such blatant federationist propaganda put out by the Education Commissioner."

"It was bad, wasn't it?" They passed Basingstoke shuttle station. They had lost all three cars. He was quite certain now that they were not being followed.

"Whereabouts do you want to be dropped off?" she asked.

"Anywhere near here'll do. You'll want to head off south now, presumably."

"No, not really. Ah'll take you anywhere you like. Ah've got plenty of time on my hands. Mr Weaning said Ah didn't have to file till twenty hundred tomorrow." For a brief moment Horatio considered taking her to a hotel and discovering, after a bottle or two of lunch, exactly how attractive she really did find him. Then he thought of Cleo and remembered why he was there. There seemed no harm in getting her to take him to Ibworth. He didn't want to be recognised in Basingstoke trying to catch a taxi. Not after having come this far.

"It's a village three miles or so outside Basingstoke. If you go into town we'll see some signposts."

Gemma brought up the subject of Oliver's father. He was American, and by her account a thoroughgoing pig. They had divorced three years before and his publishing job in New York was part of the reason she wanted to pursue her career in London. Before Horatio had a chance to show sympathy, or even be genuinely sympathetic, they were at the Free Fox. He asked her to drive a short way up the high street, wanting to avoid the pub.

"Could you stop just along here? Thanks. And thanks for the ride. You were great to do that for me. Now, you just have to retrace your steps to get back to the motorway." He was damned if he was going to say *autobahn*.

"You never told me what you're doing here," she said. "Something cloak-and-dagger again?" He thought quickly. Europol would be bound to ask her later.

"A relative has just died and left me some property. I'm just going to look over it." Almost true.

"No one too close, Ah hope?"

"No, in fact I'd never even met him." True again. She smiled.

"Do Ah get a kiss goodbye?"

"You certainly do." She made it last easily long enough to raise the eyebrows of any Sexual Hygiene Inspectorate officer.

"Where will you be?" he asked.

"South Hampton today and Dover early tomorrow to cover the King coming over the Bridge. He's due at 08.00."

"Why so early?"

"Ah don't rightly know. The Commission didn't want any big demonstrations in his support Ah suppose."

"I've got your pager and watch-fone numbers, haven't I?" She nodded.

"Maybe dinner when you're back?"

"Ah'd love that." 'Love', not 'like', or 'that'd be fine'.

"Great, I'll call you."

She got nearer to him. Horatio thought of Cleo but yielded at the last moment.

"I can't help feeling we've done this before," he said, watching her reaction closely for any scintilla of recognition of the power-cut kiss. She just smiled and drew his head back towards hers by the lightest of touches behind his neck.

That next kiss would have had the S.H.I. officer rapping on the windscreen with his clipboard.

Eventually she drove off. Horatio stayed waving at her auto until it disappeared around the corner and he could no longer hear it. Being electric that was not long, but it seemed it. He then walked along the high street, away from the Rectory. It was only thirty or forty metres but he soon convinced himself he was being watched by everyone in the village.

From the honeysuckle and clematis outside it, Number 4, Ibworth High Street, looked like a city-dwellers' ideal of what a weekend country cottage should be. But Horatio was too much on his guard to judge anything by appearances any more.

As he walked around the side of the house he prayed his hay fever would not make him sneeze. The thumping of his heart could probably be heard in Basingstoke.

Why should creeping around people's houses have to be done by him, rather than some Hunky Regular hero? Before the class and sexism legislation there had been a popular fictional character called Bond. Now *he* would have known how to deal with situations like this. Someone conventionally macho like him would have fitted the bill far better.

Horatio peered in at the kitchen window by the back door. As he put his hand up to the pane he felt a sudden sharp jab in the small of his back.

"Hands up! If you make any sudden movements I'll put a bullet in you!"

His hands shot up.

"I'm a rambler," said Horatio, proud of the cover he'd concocted for himself, "and I'm exercising my Right to Roam." He was about to turn around and explain about the recent Private Property (Ramblers' Rights) Directive 77/107 when the voice – deep, husky, but he thought a woman's – added: "The slightest false move and you're dead."

16

11.33 Tuesday, 4th May

"Whatever you say."

"Are you armed?"

"No, certainly not." A hand started checking under his armpits, between his legs, right down to his socks. Having been frisked professionally hundreds of times, prior to entering practically any public buildings during the latest Tenth May bombing campaign, Horatio could tell she was an amateur.

"Get inside. Slowly and quietly." Horatio opened the door and took a few paces into the dingy kitchen, his hands on top of his head and the muzzle of the gun stuck firmly into his ribs. He wondered whether twenty-nine was old enough for an obese, terrified, unfit male to have a heart attack. "Now walk very slowly into the next room and sit on that settee under the light where I can see you." As he turned round to sit down, Horatio made out a large, ugly, rather hairy woman in her late fifties or early sixties. She was pointing, slightly gingerly, a heavy pulse gun at him. It looked old-fashioned, but no less lethal for that.

She sat down on the other end of the sofa.

"Who are you and what do you want?"

"Well, I'm not a rambler."

"I'd guessed that."

"My name's Horatio Lestoq. I was the man who found Admiral Ratcliffe's body on Sunday. I've since found that I was mentioned in his will, and after that I was charged with his murder. Right now I'm on the run from the police."

"I'd better call them, then." She made as if to press the "On" button of the vid-fone on a small table beside her. Horatio talked quickly.

"Please don't do that. Two reasons. Firstly, I'm completely innocent, and secondly I *have* to speak to you, Mrs Dodson. I believe we are both in the most terrible danger. And the police can't help us, either."

Naming her like that was a risk, but her age, familiarity with the house, unfamiliarity with the gun and general demeanour made him judge it one worth taking.

"How do you know who I am?" He exhaled.

"I didn't for sure, but it's you I must see."

"How am I to know that you really *are* Lestoq?"

"Look on the cable news channel. I'm there, complete with picture."

"Stay where you are." She crossed over to her modem on a table under the window and tapped into it, still covering him with the gun.

Sure enough there were several screen pages devoted to him. It was a different photo from Marty's on the 09.00 news. Horatio took a few seconds to recognise the video shot from the camera in Basingstoke police station, taken when Snell had told him to say cheese.

"No great likeness, but it's me."

"All right. It seems we're on the same side. But instead of you asking me questions, can I just tell you straight off what's happened here?" At last she put down the gun. He dropped his arms. They had started to ache.

"Yes. Yes, that's a better idea."

"Sir Michael was always very kind to me. He'd been . . . a sort of . . . business associate of my husband's and I came out to live here to take care of him, help bring up his granddaughter, cook for him sometimes, that sort of thing, after my husband died. I didn't need the money or anything. We just got on well."

"I'd like to talk about your husband's death, too."

"About Jake?"

"I've reason to suspect he was murdered." She gave a start like she'd been jabbed with a cattle prod on high voltage.

"Oh my God!" She put her hands up to her face: "I knew it!"

Horatio went over to sit by her on the sofa. "I'm sorry, I shouldn't have . . ."

"No, no . . . it's all right." Then the words flooded out, interrupted only by occasional gasps for breath. Jean Dodson had been waiting for a quarter of a century to find someone to tell this to, someone who didn't think her unhinged. Horatio just held her hand and listened.

"I sort of knew it, you see — but I couldn't get the police to make any enquiries about the man, Evans they said his name was, who was driving the truck — I knew it but I've never really been able to face it . . . I haven't let myself think about it much for fear I'd go bonkers but Jake told me before he went out that day, he said, like specially, 'Now Jean, when you go down the shops today, be sure to remember they're changing the roads round this morning. Mind you go and drive on the right,' and then I remember, clear as if it were today, he sang one of the jingles from the TV adverts: 'Right is right, stay right and you'll be all right!' — you won't remember them, you're too young. They were on every channel that Christmas and New Year. So what I could never understand is why" — she was sobbing now — "*why* would he forget his own advice directly after? It just didn't make sense."

"I believe he was murdered. Was he at all frightened?"

"He'd spent a fortune — we'd won the lottery a couple of years back you see — on security for protection for the house and us. He even used to carry around this stupid old gun." The words were being held up now by the sobs. Horatio didn't know what to say. He was about to make some sympathetic noises about making tea, but he knew that he had to get on.

"Jean, there's something else. I believe the people who killed your Jake also killed Ratcliffe."

"No, it was a woman who killed Sir Michael. The truck driver was a man called Evans. And he didn't work for Atgas either. I called them up about two years later I was so disturbed, and the man from Personnel told me they'd never had a man fitting that I.D. on the staff. Not in 2019. Not ever." But Horatio was not concentrating on Evans.

"A *woman* killed Ratcliffe?! How do you know?"

"I saw her." Horatio's mouth lolled open. "When the doorbell rang, Sir Michael said he expected it was you. He wanted me to be there to meet you to tell you what I just have about Jake's death. For your newspaper. But he wanted to get what he called a 'personal matter' out of the way first. So he asked me to wait outside till he called me in to meet you. 'Doctor Lestoq and I will only be a few minutes. Then I'll call you back in, if that's all right, Jean,' he said. He was always such a gent, in a non-sexist way of course. Anyway, I went out the French windows and waited on the lawn for a few minutes watching the doves. Then I thought I heard a call — well, more a sort of cry — and I walked over and looked in at the sitting room to check and I saw a woman standing over him holding one of the sofa cushions up against his face. She was big, and poor little Sir Michael was so small. He didn't stand a chance. He wasn't even struggling. His hands had fallen down by his sides. I was so frightened I didn't rush in or bang on the window or anything. I hope the Lord Jesus will forgive me for running away, I know I'll never be able to!" She broke down again and shivered with tears and remorse. Horatio did his best to comfort her, but he knew he was useless at that sort of thing.

"By the sound of it what you did was exactly right." Horatio comforted her, patting her gnarled, hairy-knuckled hands. "It was all over by then from the sound of it. You'd have just been next, otherwise. So what did you do?"

"I ran across the lawn as fast as I could and down the street and called the police. They arrived quite soon afterwards but too late to catch her."

"And just soon enough to catch me. Did you see her leave? What was she doing?"

"No, I was too scared. I didn't go out again."

"Do you think she saw you?"

"Don't know. Her back was to me. But she might have seen me running away."

"Why didn't you go into the Free Fox? It's much closer to the Rectory than this place."

"They hate me in there. I'm always getting the Environmental Health onto them."

"But this is a bit more serious than late-night drinking!"

"I know!" She rocked forward, her head in her hands, tears flowing freely. "I know!" Horatio wished he could ask her these questions less directly. But they had to be asked.

"Why on earth didn't you tell the police that it was a woman who had killed him, and not me?"

"I know I should have, but I was so flustered I didn't specify who it was. I just said Michael was being murdered and put the fone down. You know how the police sell everything to the papers these days. They might have leaked my name. I was scared, so I didn't say who I was or switch on the vid part of the fone. I made sure only to say my piece and hang up. I was scared. Anyhow I never got a look at her face, you see, because she had her back to me."

"Can you describe her at all?"

"Not really. That's why I'd be so useless to the police. I couldn't say if she was thirty or sixty. She was quite tall though. Darkish hair. She wore a dark blue dress. It was a bright day outside and quite dark inside. We'd had the French windows open, but hadn't put on lights in the room." She stopped, thought for a moment, and said, "Also . . ." Then she stopped again.

"Yes? What? . . . You really *must* tell me everything, Jean. For your own sake as well as mine."

"Well, Sir Michael gave me something to give to you and I didn't want the police coming round asking questions and maybe turning this place upside down like they did to the Rectory."

"The *police* did that?"

"I assume it was them. They came around about two hours after the first lot, the ones who took you away. Although they were in plain clothes they certainly looked like police, dressed alike, same age, short hair. Two autos full of them. They had guns too."

"But they weren't in uniform?"

"No. Except three of them wore the same long, dark green overcoats. They certainly weren't just vandals though. I mean, they arrived with sledgehammers and saws and jemmies and things. And there was no, sort of, whooping and yelling like you might expect a load of hooligans to make. I thought of calling Sergeant Wilkinson, our local man, but I was worried they might realise that I was the original witness if I did. I suppose I could have called anonymously again, but I was so scared. I'm sorry, Dr Lestoq."

"Horatio."

"Horatio. Lovely name by the way." He loved her for that. "I'm going to leave here tonight, my sister's coming round this evening to take me away."

"Now, Jean. The police are after me as you know. If I'm arrested again it's essential that you tell them about the woman, otherwise I could easily get convicted. You must tell them it was you who made the call. They'll protect you from the murderer until she's caught. Will you do that for me?" She thought for a moment and then nodded slowly. She really was fantastically ugly, he thought. "But there's something even more important than that. You must give me whatever it was Sir Michael gave you. Why did he give it to you, by the way? He could just as easily have handed it to me himself if he thought I was at the door."

"He said he didn't want to have it around in case you got violent about the 'personal matter'."

"Violent? Have you any idea what that might have been about?"

"No."

"So he gave you a package?"

"Yes."

"Where is it?" He prayed she wouldn't say that it was in the Rectory.

"Up in my bedroom, I'll get it for you. I'll be glad to be rid of it."

She stood up from the sofa and went into the hallway. Then

he heard her climb the stairs. Half a minute later she returned with a small brown envelope which she handed him.

"There you are. Now I've done what Michael asked I feel a whole lot better. Oh and Dr Lestoq, Horatio, please take that too." She pointed to the gun on the table by the sofa.

"No, you keep it."

"It's no use to me. I was terrified when I picked it up just now. I don't think it's even loaded. I was too scared to open it up to find out. I've got the bullets upstairs. Shall I get them?"

He nodded. She left again, this time for longer. She reappeared with three boxes of shells and two old stun cartridges. He managed to fit all but one ammo clip in his pockets. The last one he left on the sofa table.

"How did you get here?" she asked.

"A lift from a friend." Fear crossed her face.

"Don't worry, she went away long before I came here."

"How are you going to get back, then?"

"Don't know. I'll have to risk the shuttle, I suppose."

"But the police'll be watching the stations. You might get spotted."

"I've no other way."

"I'll drive you back."

"No. That could be dangerous."

"My sister's not coming for hours and I'm not doing anything here but waiting for her. Or the murderer. And I ought to do something for the person who's trying to avenge the only two men in my life who've ever mattered to me."

"You could wind up on a charge for aiding and abetting. Thanks, but no."

"Come on. Let's go." Jean had decided. "My auto's in the next street. It's a battered old green grade 7 methane. It's so old it doesn't even have a roof number! I'll go out and get it started. Once it's up and running I'll turn it round and drive it up outside the front door. A beep on the horn means there's trouble. Once I'm alongside you come out. Don't bother to lock up, just get in quickly and we'll be off." Horatio nodded.

Just after she'd left, Horatio realised that he should have warned her to look underneath the car before putting her I.D. in the ignition.

PART
III

17

12.05 Tuesday, 4th May

Once safely onto the M3, and fairly certain they were not being followed, Horatio opened the gun, found it to be unloaded and slotted a stun-cartridge and full clip of ammunition into the butt. It gave a satisfyingly loud click when he pushed it shut. The stun-voltage dial read normal. Fine. Next he took the Admiral's envelope from his pocket and opened it. There was a two-by-two-centimetre microtape and a letter written on Rectory paper. He started with the latter:

11.10 Saturday, 1st May 2045

My Dear Horatio,

I feel I can call you by your Christian, or "given" name as we are supposed to say nowadays, although we haven't met. I'm writing this in case you do not appear today, in which case I will ask Jean Dodson to deliver it to you in person. Please take care of her, she is an innocent in all of this and knows nothing about what her late husband and I did. I have recorded all that on a tape which should be enclosed with this letter.

You must do whatever you think right with the knowledge that I am giving you. As a nonagenarian, I have only escaped the various Health Commission euthanasia programmes because I am rich. I'm in no position to say how you should act. I do know, however, that if I was your age I would shout it from the rooftops, despite the fact that it will render me as one of the blackest villains ever left unhanged. Perhaps I am. It's certainly how I feel now. How I've felt for years.

As I hope to be able to tell you face to face this morning – but wish to take no chances over – you are my grandson. That is why I suppose I initially expected you to know who I was in our talk today. It was naive of me, really, as I had agreed with Heather – the woman you know as your mother – that I would not contact you.

But I judge now that you have the right to know.

The person you believe to be your father, Commander Robert Lestoq, was a brave and honourable man. He could have led the Insurrection, and later the country, had he lived. I was delighted when he married Heather, my daughter-in-law Flora's elder sister. My happiness was redoubled when Robert became shipmates with my own son James.

It was when they were away serving together, in the Second Submarine Flotilla stationed at Simons Town, that you were born. James and Flora's deaths four months later came as a horrific shock. They died, as you already know, with your "father" in the Atlantic Gas explosion in Ebury Street. That you and Heather survived was little short of a miracle. But what Heather came to tell me soon afterwards was almost as much of a shock as the news of the explosion itself.

It was the evening after the joint funerals. We had never really got on because Heather disapproved of my having scrutinised the Aachen Referendum for the Commission. But this was far more important than any of that. She told me that when she and Flora had been pregnant together in South Africa – Azania as they call it now – they had made a pact. It was the sort of pact which only sisters, and close and loving ones at that, could ever make. They had both ordered twins, Heather had asked for boys, Flora one of each.

They pledged that should anything go wrong, they would both leave the Nelsonia General Hospital with babies, whatever happened.

Flora had her twins on 2nd January. Five days later Heather produced two stillborn sons. So my daughter-in-law decided to keep the girl and let Heather keep the boy. You. They pledged never to tell the fathers, the children or anyone else. Ever.

It was just the sort of selfless, noble act of which Flora was so capable. She was young enough to have more children, whereas Heather was childless, seven years older, and had already miscarried twice. They knew it was her last chance. They vowed always to live near one another, so that Flora would always be able to be more than a normal aunt to you. I believe it could have worked.

It was only possible because the husbands were incommunicado under the Antarctic ice-cap and they themselves were far away from friends and relations in Nelsonia (or Jo'burg as I've called it most of my life). They had little trouble in bribing the right Azanian official to provide birth certificates dating yours a week or so later than Cleopatra's. As cousins, their close D.N.A. connection did not raise any eyebrows back home when they registered for Union citizenship. It worked perfectly.

It was only after James and Flora were killed with your father – or I should say Robert Lestoq, as of course my own son, James, was your true, biological father – that Heather told me the truth. She was in a very bad way, emotionally, mentally and financially, after the explosion.

I only learnt the truth from her on the condition that I never told you what had happened. Heather was very short of cash – Robert's life insurance counted for little and his service pension for less. It was also in the days before the Commission subsidised Extended Kinship Groups. I was, for reasons you'll discover from the enclosed tape, very well off at the time. So I gave your mother an allowance and settled enough on you for an education. Even after private schooling was abolished I never stopped the money, paying for your books, food, clothing and accommodation. I also made you a joint beneficiary of my will. All I asked was to be sent information about you so I could read about my grandson's progress through life.

Otherwise we have kept far apart. I have now decided to tell you, and therefore possibly the world, the truth. I believe you have a right to know who your father was, and that you have a sister called Cleopatra Tallboys whom I brought up here and who now works in the Political Intelligence Department of Europol. You must decide for yourself whether you wish to contact her or not.

You will discover from the accompanying tape – if you have not found out already, and your tone over the phone last night suggests you might have at least guessed – how my fortune was made. I have followed your career with pride, if at a distance, and have read your articles on the Aachen Referendum which Heather sent me from *The Times*.

Not a day has gone by without me loathing myself for my treachery. I was dreading the thirtieth anniversary of my betrayal on Wednesday morning, and now I will not have to see it. I've booked myself into the Health Service's 'Golden Sunset' Programme at Basingstoke General for 09.00 on Monday morning. I will pay for my crime that way.

Good luck, Horatio – a brave English name by the way, do honour to it – and if you do choose to publish, please do your best to protect poor Jean Dodson.
Your loving grandfather,

Michael.

18

12.25 Tuesday, 4th May

Reading in autos had always made Horatio feel nauseous, but never as much as this. He had been orphaned by letter. Posthumously. He felt utterly betrayed, alone, even vaguely suicidal. He doubted Robert Virgil could save him this time.

"Tell me about the tape, Horatio."

"It's the story of your Jake and Sir Michael; the secret of what they did and . . . of why they died."

"I've been thinking. I *do* want to hear it. I need to know what happened. You do understand?" He nodded. "It's best if you play it."

Horatio took his journalist's pad and pencil from his pocket in order to take down the Admiral's words in shorthand. As he did so, Cleo's *billet doux* fell out. His eyes fell on the third sentence:

"*Last night was wonderful.*"

It was a love note. From his own sister. His twin. His mouth went dry and very sour.

He slotted the tape into the auto stereo and heard the opening bars of Beethoven's Ninth. The Union anthem. He appreciated the Admiral's sense of irony. They listened on, but there was no sound of Ratcliffe. He fast-forwarded the tape.

Still only music.

With a sudden panic he wondered whether this was some hateful practical joke? Or had the Admiral, at ninety-one, got the tapes mixed up? His heart pounding hard against his ribcage, Horatio fast-forwarded to almost the end. Still only classical music.

Might it be on the other side? He jabbed the "Side Over" button and then "Play".

More bloody Beethoven. He fast-forwarded and then pushed "Play" again.

Yet more of that symphony he had heard night and noon throughout his life. It had even been piped into the dormitories at his prep school in an attempt to foster Euro-patriotism.

Just as he was about to press "Fast-Forward" again the music suddenly stopped:

"Testing, testing. This is Admiral Michael Ratcliffe speaking at eleven-thirty hours on Saturday, 1st May 2045. I am about to record my posthumous confession to a crime. Posthumous, because by the time you hear this I will have undergone the Health Commission's Voluntary Assisted Euthanasia Programme. My crime is so complete in its treachery and grievous in its consequences that I have not the strength of will to face the people whom I have wronged.

The year after my retirement as a senior naval officer I was offered the post of Chief Scrutineer for the South-Western Region for the Referendum which was about to be held to endorse and ratify the Aachen Treaty of Complete Union, which had been signed there by the Heads of Government of all the various E.U. countries on 1st April 2015.

Having served as Chief Communications Officer (Home Fleet) in my time, and about to take up two non-executive consultancy posts with electronics companies, I knew more about systems than the Commission had obviously bargained for. I imagine they expected some red-faced twit, a dim-witted sailor who looked good on cable but would not really know what was going on. Someone who would certainly not work out what they were up to.

Whilst reviewing the electronic systems on the Wednesday prior to Thursday's vote, I discovered what I assumed was a simple systems error. The binary electrode which counted the votes at the central terminal for the electoral headquarters of the Region, situated in Salisbury Town Hall, had been inverted, i.e. inserted back to front. This meant that each "Yes" vote when it came in would automatically have registered as a "No" on the Salisbury mainframe, and of course vice-versa. I thought at first it was merely a simple but devastating design fault.

I immediately informed the Chief Computer Engineer, Jacob Dodson, who had been seconded from his job as electronics division regional manager of Racal-Philips for the period of the Referendum. He expressed surprise and concern at the inverted chip and told me he would put the matter right immediately. He had no idea how it could have happened. As it was a straightforward case of switching it about face, the work could be done in a minute. I was quite satisfied.

During the actual voting, which took place, as every schoolboy knows, on Thursday 4th May 2015, I made it my business to check that Dodson had indeed made this easy but vital adjustment. I made my way to the communications room which had been set up in the Mayoral office, unlocked it with a special key of which I believed only Dodson and I had copies, and went inside.

I well remember entering the silent, panelled room and walking over to where the specially designed Referendum computer stood, behind the mayor's chair against the wall. The electrode had been returned to the correct position all right. But just as I was about to leave I noticed some wiring underneath that I did not remember having seen before. It didn't take me long to realise that someone had re-routed the charge to a *second* microchip, almost out of sight of the first, a chip which performed precisely the same function as the original one had, of inverting the votes.

The polls had opened at oh-seven hundred. It was nearly noon. I resolved then and there to declare the vote for the entire Region invalid and institute an urgent police inquiry. My first call was to the man who had appointed me as Scrutineer, David Mackintosh, the then Foreign Secretary and later the first Foreign Commissioner.

Mackintosh sounded shocked and jittery. He begged me to say nothing to anybody and to take no action until he had investigated the matter thoroughly himself. He also ordered me not to touch the electrode but to allow the false, inverted figures to be sent on to London that evening. When I pointed out that I could simply reverse the figures to give the correct result he categorically ordered me on no account to do so. He assured me it would be dealt with officially, immediately and at the highest level. He went on to say that he would be trying to find out whether the same thing had gone on in any other regions. He therefore did not want to prejudice the chances of a successful outcome of the investigation by going public with the news too early. I well recall him saying he wanted to ensure that those responsible for this titanic fraud on the British people would be brought. to book.

I suppose that even after a lifetime of obeying orders I should have questioned my superior officer in this, but I did not. Instead I went home that night with a heavy heart, having transmitted to London the as I knew it, inverted, 59 per cent "Yes" to 41 "No" result for the Region. Once received there it was added to the other regional figures and gave, as we all know, the final 52 per cent to 48 per cent national "Yes" vote.

The next morning's papers were full of the "historic decision". Denmark, Portugal, Greece and Sweden had all had equally close outcomes. I wondered then, as I often do today, whether the same organisation that fixed our result might also have been at work in those countries too. Certainly the Commission had disbursed vast amounts to set up identical mainframes and voting systems in all member states in time for the Referendum. They would therefore presumably only have required the same inverted electrodes in strategic areas to adjust those figures as well.

I'll never forget that morning, reading articles about how the Ulster Protestants would take to the United Irish Region, whether Wales would benefit from independence and whether the termination of the union with England would leave Scotland a net contributor to or beneficiary of the Union. I had served in the Falklands

Campaign in 1982, I'd had friends on the *Sheffield*. Great Britain, the nation my friends and I had fought for, was disintegrating before my eyes.

On a fraudulent vote.

But for that second electrode in Salisbury Town Hall, Aachen would almost have been thrown out. Had the same thing also gone on in Southern and South-West Central? I didn't know for sure, but I had my suspicions.

I decided to call Mackintosh again that next morning, to ask about arrangements for the re-vote. It was whilst I was actually on the fone trying to reach him that his "special advisor", a self-confident young man in his mid-twenties called Gregory Percival, arrived at my house with someone he introduced as Francis Evans. I thought at the time that this second chap, with his flat nose and cauliflower ears, looked as though he would have been more at home in one of those illegal backstreet boxing matches than the marble corridors of the Foreign Office. I soon found out what he was there for.

I imagined they had called to confer about how to catch the culprits, but I was soon proved very wrong. After a failed attempt to persuade me that the result was "all for the best", Percival argued that should the Referendum decision be overturned, mass unrest would follow. He also pointed out that the alteration in South-West England would not actually change the overall result, and went very quiet when I voiced my concerns about the two other regions. This was of course before I'd heard of the so-called suicide that morning of Jack Minter, the High Court judge who had scrutinised South-West Central.

I told Percival I knew my duty and would carry it out.

I'd leave the political implications to others better qualified. I was not interested in hearing the various arcane international relations arguments he was putting forward either. It also had not the slightest effect when he informed me that the Referendum machine had been deconstructed that morning, and therefore no physical evidence survived of my allegations. He said I'd either be dismissed as a crank or written off as an ultra-nationalist. He also informed me that Jacob Dodson would be denying all knowledge of even the first inverted electrode.

He had brought a Report, ostensibly written by me, which confirmed that the Referendum had been conducted freely and fairly in the Region, and he demanded I put my signature to it. He showed me where Dodson had already signed. When I refused, his accomplice took out a knife and placed it up against my neck. His mean little eyes glinted with excitement at the prospect of slitting my throat.

I'd faced physical danger enough in my naval career not to be overly afraid, and I told Percival (untruthfully) that I had already made several copies of my allegations which I had given to a friend to send to various national and international newsagencies should anything at all untoward happen to me over the next few months. Evans was told to put the knife away after that. I now realise that they must have thought that the coincidence of having two Chief Scrutineers dying within hours of the vote would have been too much for even our lapdog media to ignore.

Then Percival took something from his pocket. It was a wedding photograph of my son, James. God knows where he'd got it. He made the most obscene threats about what would happen to my boy and Flora if I continued to refuse to sign. The way the ape Evans grinned at me I was sure he was serious.

So I thought again.

Joan, my wife, had died some years earlier, and the prospect of a lonely old age because of my own obstinacy appalled me. It was to protect James and Flora. Would my sticking to principle deny me the chance to see grandchildren? That thought above all others made me change my mind. Even if I managed to persuade the police to arrest Percival – or even Mackintosh – I could guess the conspiracy was deeper than that. It included the thug Evans and whoever switched the electrode, for a start. How could I be sure some confederate of theirs would not carry out their threat?

I'd never thought myself a greedy man, but I made Percival pay heavily for my silence. I was selling my honour and resolved that it would not come cheap. We came to an arrangement whereby I would win the Euro-Lottery to the tune of five million euros. The condition was that I never left the Union or breathed a word to anyone ever. I agreed to have my passport visas deleted from my I.D. and I received the money at the end of the year.

After Flora and James died in an Atlantic Gas explosion in London in April 2016 I briefly considered telling the world what had happened. But I'd signed the report, taken the money and felt myself hopelessly compromised. I also now had a baby granddaughter, whom I was bringing up myself. Furthermore, it was in the middle of the Insurrection, as Britain slowly and painfully came to terms with what her loss of sovereignty really meant. It would probably cause even more bloodshed were I to spill the beans. I didn't want to be responsible for a civil war. So I stayed silent and always have.

Until now. Thirty years have passed. I'm about to die. It's time to speak.

When Jake Dodson became greedy and told me he was going to try to blackmail them into giving him as much as I had got, I warned him most strongly against it. I even offered to give him some of my own cash – whatever he felt he needed, within reason. He took no notice and died soon afterwards. The release of the name of the lorry-driver – Francis Evans – was, I was certain, a further warning to me. I invited Jake's widow to come and live in a cottage in the village.

The full implications of my iniquity and cowardice did not really come home to me until some time later. It was when Argentina invaded the Falkland Islands in April 2025 that I first really appreciated the full ghastly magnitude of what I had allowed to happen. When the Union voted not to oppose it, and the English Commissioners were outvoted on the motion to send a Task Force to liberate them, then I knew I had betrayed my country.

Brussels was ordaining that the islands could not be liberated because of the effect on the Union economy. The German, Belgian and French Commissioners refused to allow the euro to be exposed to the inflationary pressures resulting from the increased expenditure which the recapture of Port Stanley would inevitably involve. They said sovereignty over some-where so distant from the metropolitan continent was an absurd, outmoded concept, a hangover from the old days of British imperialism. According to them the islands were really only a troublesome historical quirk the Union was best rid of. They were, as it was put at the time, "of no strategic or economic interest" to the U.S.E., so the Commission decided to let the Argenti-nians keep them. Pro-federationist newsagencies crowed about how at last the five regions which used to make up Great Britain would now perhaps look inwards to their continental future and no longer backwards and outwards towards their oceanic past.

I knew for certain then that I was as much a traitor to my country as were the Macleans, Philbys and Blunts whom I'd despised so much in my youth.

I observed Percival's meteoric career, as he pro-gressed all the way to the job he now holds as one of the most powerful regional Commission Secretaries in the Union. I knew what he and his friends had done. They must have had – must still have, mind you – many well-placed confederates inside and outside the Commission. Examination of the Referendum results in the other two regions where there were large pro-Aachen majorities, Southern and South-West Central, has convinced me that the same electrode-switching probably went on there, too. Together, we three regions delivered the majority for the blasted Treaty. And that's only in Former Britain. God knows what went on in places like Denmark, Greece, Portugal and Sweden.

All I know for certain, though, is that as Official Chief Scrutineer for South-West Region I hereby declare –

albeit thirty years too late and posthumously – the result of the Aachen Referendum in my Region to be invalid.
Over and out."

19

12.45 Tuesday, 4th May

Horatio could not help marvelling at the depth of their cynicism. They had not attempted to manipulate the voting figures once they were collected – fiddling a million here, half a million there. They had automatically *assumed* that the majority of Britons would be against Complete Union and therefore transposed every "no" into a "yes" in certain key regions.

They had simply taken it for granted that the British people would not want to lose their thousand-year-old nation state, but they thought, with that invincible conceit of the Europhile, that the man in Brussels knew best. British sovereignty was betrayed through a nifty piece of electronic legerdemain. It was almost enough to turn Horatio into a rabid nat.

And what brinkmanship! Had the majority been much larger someone would surely have smelt a rat. But at 52–48 per cent it was close enough to convince. Equally tight results were recorded in at least four other regions. It would certainly be worth investigating some of the referendums there, too.

It must have helped enormously, Horatio surmised, that pre-vote opinion and exit polling had been banned a decade earlier, ostensibly for being "anti-choice" and "bad for democracy". They would have shown up the discrepancies.

Deconstructing all the referendum machines the very next morning was smart too. There wasn't even a museum piece in existence, as Horatio knew from his attempts to track one down for an illustration for the first of his *Times* articles.

Then the very simplicity. Whoever thought of using the binary nature of computers was a near-genius. And the audacity. Had it leaked out that the Referendum had been fixed there would have been a lynching. The revelation that elements in the Commission – right up to and including the Foreign Commissioner himself – were using the Lottery as a slush fund would be explosive enough. Horatio could not help but be impressed by what he was up against.

He looked across at Jean. Tears were coursing down her chubby, warty old cheeks. She was hyperventilating. Horatio had been so absorbed by the high politics of the situation that he selfishly hadn't bothered to think about what effect the tape would have on her.

"Jean? Jean, are you all right? Pull over here." She was in the slow lane in any case. She veered off right and came to a halt on the hard shoulder. She pulled her I.D. out of the ignition. Horatio leant across and wrapped his arms around her. Then she put her head on his ample breast and cried and cried. After a few minutes, sniffling, she asked for a handkerchief. He pulled out the silk one from his breast pocket to give her to dry her eyes.

"I can't blow my nose on that, it's silk."

"Go on, it doesn't matter, I don't mind," he said, despising himself because he did.

What did Jean dislike most about all of this, he wondered? The original crime? The political side? Jake's greed? The treachery?

"We don't know how they threatened your husband. They

probably told him they'd harm you if he spoke out. He really had no alternative. It just shows how much he loved you." He stroked her hairy forearm gently, desperately trying to think of something else soothing to say. Eventually she composed herself enough to speak.

"You must tell everyone, Horatio." A hardness had entered her voice for the first time since she had stuck the gun in his back. "It's your duty to Jake and Sir Michael. And really, as well, when you think of it, it's your duty to Britain too. You must let everyone know what these evil, evil people have done to all our lives." 'Britain', as opposed to North England, or Wales, or Scotregion, sounded unfamiliar to Horatio. Strange, romantic, and somehow right.

"I know. I will. *We* will." He judged she had turned the corner from despair to resolution. "But right now we badly need to get to London. If we stay here much longer we'll be stopped by the police, and then where'd we be?" The Nicotine Inspectorate roadblocks they sometimes had at Chiswick, and the cameras at the various tollbooths, were enough of a worry without their being photographed by the hard shoulder emergency services' cameras.

"I'm all right now," she said, blowing her nose again on his thirty-euro silk handkerchief. "Let's go." She pushed the I. D. card back into the ignition. "It was hearing Sir Michael's voice that set me off. Thinking that I'll never hear it again. He was the best friend I've ever had. I'm going to be so lonely." They set off again, with Jean driving at 70 kph, as fast as the speed governor on her auto would allow her.

One fat, selfish, hypochondriacal academic and one even fatter, ugly, moustachioed old widow. Trying to alter the course of history.

As they entered central London, Horatio devised a plan to

lose anyone who might be following. He asked Jean to pull into the auto battery recharging depot halfway down Piccadilly. He told her he would then get out, attach the recharger line and make as if to go into the depot office to pay in cash. Instead, he would nip out the back and onto Regent Street. It meant they could not say goodbye properly, or make any gesture to imply he was not coming back. She was just to wait for as long as she could, then get out, pay normally and drive back to Ibworth.

Jean, still looking distraught, nodded bravely. Could he leave her in such a state? Without even saying goodbye? He had to.

It worked. Three minutes later he was halfway down Regent Street. Safe. Alone, of course, but in control. He did not so much fear the cameras which were stationed at the beginning and end of most streets, it would be terrible luck if he was spotted from those. Much more dangerous were the "Have You Seen This Person?" photographs which he now saw on the front pages of the *Mail, Sun* and *European*.

There were other photos of him now, including a particularly unflattering one taken after his graduation ceremony, complete with mortarboard and an incredibly self-satisfied I've-just-taken-a-double-starred-first smirk.

Fortunately, the *Indy* had photographs of the ex-King's Mother, Princess Diana, celebrating her eighty-second birthday with her billionaire husband at their Malibu dream home, so he was off that front page at least.

Through a combination of trams, taxis, walking and endless doubling-back, Horatio reached Knightsbridge without – he was certain – being spotted. Walking down the Brompton Road, he saw the huge white Catholic church ahead of him. He had an idea. Stopping at a corner newsagent's, he bought some detox de-alcohol chewing gum.

Entering the Brompton Oratory he walked twelve pews up on the right, genuflected and entered. Then, with the 14.00 service about to begin, he knelt and pretended to pray. As he did so he slipped the tape from his inside pocket and, removing the gum from his mouth, attached the tape container securely to the underside of the seat in front. He feared for a moment that a priest walking towards him had spotted something, but she walked past oblivious. Then he made a second copy of his notes. Every minute spent on the streets increased his likelihood of capture. And he must not have the tape on him when that happened.

Sitting silently in the ornate baroque splendour of the Oratory, Horatio's thoughts turned to questions of the spirit. His mother was not his mother. His lover was his sister. He had every right to go mad. Why could he not just opt out altogether? Live abroad like Marty suggested? Forget what he had learnt? The glorious Italian altarpiece and high altar was, he remembered, originally from St Servatius Maestricht in Rome. That brought him back to the political aspect. How much of a nat Fifth Columnist was he? Really? He had secreted the tape, but what next? He felt like a whist-player whose only good card in his hand was the ace of trumps.

Leaving the church he turned right and then right again up Exhibition Road. He could see Hyde Park in the distance at the other end. He walked past the Victoria and Albert Friendship Museum on his right and Federation College of Science, Technology and Medicine on the other side of the road. Stopping at a fone booth halfway up he called Cleo, taking care to cut off the vid link. He attached his pager fone-scrambler to the receiver. He had forty seconds.

"Do you remember where you said you used to play as a child, and I said I did too? Meet me there. Now. Don't get followed." He hung up before giving her a chance to answer. She'd come.

He then walked up the rest of Exhibition Road, crossed Kensington Gore at the Euro-Geographic Society and set off towards the Albert Memorial. The morning's clear, light blue sky had clouded over since he'd left Jean. It was Major-grey now and threatening rain. On the north-east corner of the memorial, emerging from the permanent blue plastic awning, was a group of larger-than-life-sized statues representing Asia. A half-naked female pharaoh sat astride a haughty camel. She was flanked by a sphinx and a handmaiden on one side, and a fierce, turbanned bodyguard armed with a scimitar on the other. Horatio recalled that the sculptor, John Foley, had reputedly died of a cold caught from the wet clay he kept on his lap while lovingly sculpting young Asia's breasts. Cleopatra would know where to come.

His sister, he thought, a shudder at the reminder of what they had committed together replacing a kind thought at the last moment.

He resolved not to tell her. What possible good could come of filling her with the same sense of self-disgust that he felt? The Admiral was dead. Heather — his aunt — could be trusted to continue to keep her twenty-nine-year silence. He would do the manly thing for once and not unload his guilt onto someone else.

He saw her get out of a taxi at the entrance of Albert Hall across the road and step inside. He did not see her emerge but five minutes later she reappeared almost next to him. True tradecraft.

"Darling, what's happened to you?" She tried to kiss him on

the lips but he turned his head at the last moment so it landed ineffectually on his left earlobe. Anything more would have scalded him.

"Just about everything. What's happened to Marty?"

"He's off the scene altogether. Either suspended or sacked, I can't find out which. For freeing you. I'm putting my job on the line seeing you now. And sod all thanks it seems I'm getting for it!" She looked around, almost theatrically. "Who *knows* who may be watching us now with some ultra-lens. Or listening in. We've got gadgets that you just point at someone and you can hear what they're whispering half a kilometre away. It was such a stupid place to choose!"

She was starting to get emotional, drawing deeper and longer breaths. "I'm beginning to wish I'd never met you now. I'm sure grandfather would be alive if you hadn't pestered him. I'm beginning to think . . ." Big, pear-shaped tears started to well up in the corners of those transmarine eyes. The sexual element completely banished now by his special knowledge, Horatio was not about to buckle. She was rubbing her tears away with the back of her hand. The gentlemanly, brotherly thing to do would have been to comfort her, but Horatio needed to interrogate her further.

"Why did you leave this morning?"

"I had a watch-fone message calling me into work. To prepare for this rally on Saturday. I didn't want to wake you. When I got there I heard they'd tracked you back to your flat. They were about to send in a SWAT team. I warned you on your modem. Bugger all thanks I'm getting for that too!"

"Is it traceable?"

"I sent it via Marty's terminal, but it still might be."

"Who do you think killed your grandfather?" *Our* grandfather, thought Horatio for the first time.

"I don't know."

"Have you the slightest idea where Marty might be?"

"No. He's just disappeared. He's taken your file with him. We've searched his flat and put a watch on it."

"Why did he provide the police and E.B.C. with my photo?"

"Don't know that either. His job's on the line. One thing's for certain though, you mustn't trust him any more. Darling?" She looked down at him. He walked up two steps of the Memorial to return her gaze. "You do remember last night?" The thought repelled him now. He nodded.

"You trusted me then. Why can't you trust me now?"

"In what way?"

"Tell me what you went to see grandfather for. I might be able to help. I know you didn't kill him – though I've no evidence for it – but I believe you. You're no murderer, although I can't persuade P.I.D. of that any longer. Especially now you're on the run. They've got the Bridge and every port and airport covered in case you try to skip the region." She ostentatiously looked behind her. It reminded him of the Widow Twankey in pantomime. "But soon enough you will be arrested and this period will count heavily against you. Please just trust me. The clue is obviously in what he wanted to give you. What was it?"

Horatio thought for a moment. Then handed her one of his shorthand transcripts.

She read it, nodding and every so often looking up at him wide-eyed. Occasionally her pretty chin dropped in astonishment.

"What's this, a copy?"

"Yes."

"Do you think it's genuine?"

"It fits in with other evidence."

"Such as?"

"A note I've found relating to Percival bribing a scrutineer, analysis of the Referendum results, the repetition of a killer's name, the murder of a judge named Minter thirty years ago and so on." Actually there wasn't much in the way of "so on", and the rest was completely circumstantial. The Referendum machines were destroyed, Percival's note was ambiguous, the interview had been wiped and Minter had been declared as suicide. It really all hinged on the Admiral's tape.

On what he now thought of as the Aachen Memorandum.

"My God." She sat down on the steps as the full implications of the Admiral's revelations sank in. "It's enough to shake one's faith in the Union, isn't it?"

"Yes. It is. And you work for it. Imagine what effect it'll have on ordinary people. Let alone nats! Do you know Percival?"

"No. Well, I know of him of course. But I've only met him once myself. I saw something of him at school. I was there with his daughter."

"The one who works at the glistening bank?"

"That's right. She surveys their French Impressionists and Dutch Masters. She was at Marty's party the other night. Goes out with David Fraser." Was there nothing that hack would not stoop to? A father-in-law like that could fix him up as a M.U.P. in a nanosecond. Or, if he was interested in serious power, Percival would find Fraser something substantial in the Commission. What an operator.

Cleo set her jaw. She studied Horatio for a moment and said; "Together we could take the lid off this whole thing. This alone, in your handwriting, wouldn't stand up for a second. We need the original to initiate a prosecution. We can do it, though, I know we can!" He was proud of his sister's resolution.

"How?"

"For a start we could bring Percival in for questioning. You won't get anything better right away my darling. No newsagency would touch it with our libel laws. But with the original of this, Europol might be able to interest some serious people. Important people. Brussels people. A tough interrogation of Percival might bring something out."

"He'd outwit any interrogator you have. And as for Brussels! You do see the political implications of all of this, don't you?" He hoped he didn't sound too patronising. "It's not just Percival who'll go down if this gets out. The Memorandum calls into question the whole post-Aachen constitutional settlement, our place in the Union, everything political we've taken for granted all our lives!"

"First things first. The law's the law. My superiors will obviously need the original of the document. Where is it?"

"Somewhere safe."

"Don't you trust me?"

"Right now, I don't even trust my mother," said Horatio, with more truth than Cleo could possibly have imagined.

She held out her hands. He put his in them. She looked soulfully into his eyes, but the hypnotic effect was no longer there, not now that the sexual element had been eliminated.

"I love you and you must trust me," she whispered. "We can only hope to succeed in this if we work together. I know love is a big word for people who've only just met, but I really feel there's something between us." If only she knew what it was, he thought. "They're looking for you," she continued, "but I could get it easily. Now where is it?"

He shook himself free. He wasn't about to put his twin in

that kind of danger. Being in possession of the tape could be a death sentence for her. It was time to take responsibility. To do something a Hunky Regular Guy would do.

"It's safe. Don't worry. Tell them this is the deal. If you can get someone senior in your office – Bittersich or someone – to take a serious interest in prosecuting this I'll let you have it. Till then just use my notes. They're pretty rough but they explain the position well enough."

"Does anyone else know where it is?"

"No. No one." Alarm bells rang. He had to protect himself against P.I.D. Specifically against Alex Tallboys. What had the Admiral told Percival? "But tell your bosses that if anything were to happen to me, facsimiles of the original will start arriving on editors' and politicians' desks in Oslo, Washington, Beijing and Auckland before the end of the week. I've organised that at least." She thought for a moment.

"All right, I'll go back to Thames House now. Tonight I'll let you know what I've got. Oh, and darling." She moved so close to him their noses were almost touching. Her scent smelt expensive and smuggled. He recoiled.

"Yes?"

"Why do you shrink away from me? You didn't even let me kiss you. What have I done? What's happened? I'm on your side you know. We must both find out who killed my grandfather. And we must blow this conspiracy sky high. But we can't do it if we don't trust one another. I've just told you I'm falling in love with you, yet you haven't betrayed the slightest flicker of pleasure at hearing it. Have you forgotten all about last night?"

The memory of it sickened him. His *sister*.

"I'm sorry, Cleo, I'll explain everything later. When we have time. Of course I love and trust you."

"Is there someone else? Is that it?" Gemma's face filled his mind.

"No, of course not. Look, I'll explain everything soon." It sounded so contrived and pathetic.

"What's wrong with now?"

"Now we've got a continent to wreck!"

"Where are you staying tonight? Your flat's under twenty-four-hour surveillance."

"No idea."

"How about mine?"

"Far too risky."

"It's the ideal place. They'd never expect it. It'll be the only safe place." He could always sleep on the sofa. Where else was there? What other friend could he trust apart from the absent Marty? Could he even trust him? It was better than the streets. It made a mad sort of sense.

"Fine."

"The entry code is 0112006. Memorise it. Don't put it in your pager."

The first of January 2006 was the date the pound sterling was finally abolished. Easy to remember.

"I'll talk to Bittersich when I get back to the office. He'll probably have to clear any deal with 'E', who'll want to talk to Brussels. It might well help that I don't actually have the evidence itself on me now, you were right about that." She thought for a moment. "You know, with Percival as the quarry this will make both our names. We could wind up famous. But it's bound to get very rough first. That's why I keep saying you have to trust me. You do, don't you, darling?"

"Of course I do." In order to avoid having to kiss her on the lips he kissed his finger and touched her on the end of her beautiful, Lady Pamela Berry nose. Then he walked away, northwards across the Park towards Bayswater.

07.46 Wednesday, 5th May

Horatio woke to the sound of Cleo's modem bleeping the "Urgent" signal in the next room. He leapt up and looked around.

She hadn't returned that night. Fine. That at least saved him from explaining why he couldn't sleep with her. Where was she?

He ran over to her modem. The bleeping was loud and insistent. And getting even louder. He lowered himself into her workstation seat.

"*URGENT! URGENT! URGENT!*" the screen read. But unlike his modem yesterday it demanded her password.

He could hardly remember his own eleven digits. What would Cleo's be? There was no chance of cracking it. He'd just have to get out fast.

It was probably a warning about another SWAT team.

Then it came back. They'd talked about passwords at Marty's party. What had she said? She mixed her date of birth with her mother's maiden name, or something basic like that. They'd laughed that she didn't use something more original.

Presumably Flora's maiden name had been Ellis too. Assuming they were twins it would be his date of birth as well.

So that's ELLIS 7.1.2016. Five letters, six numbers. Eleven. They'd fit in between one another. It was a long shot.

He tapped in 7-E-1-L-2-L-0-I-1-S-6. Nothing. He tried it backwards. The bleeping got louder. Logic told him he had about as much chance of stumbling on the right answer as of winning the Euro-Lottery. She was probably just indulging in party talk and had really chosen something absurdly esoteric. Horatio's own codeword was 9-L-9-E-2-I-0-L-4-A-3, for the day they took his love away. Could a password be deemed subversive?

He feared this was a dangerous waste of time.

He tried it alphabetically, then in ascending numerical order, then both backwards.

The bleeping just got louder. Almost at a scream. He couldn't see any volume switch. Could the neighbours hear? Should he run?

After his fifteenth try he remembered what the Admiral had said in his letter. The births were registered a week or so apart, to fool the fathers. She was officially five or six days older. He tried 9-E-1-L-2-L-0-I-1-S-6. Nothing. He started the next combination with a 2.

Eureka!

The screen cleared and the message came up.

"*URGENT!* 08.00. 5/5/45. *LASER ON W.W. MOTORCADE. ENT BR. SEC* 7. ROUNDING UP USUAL E.R.M. & 10.5 SUSPECTS. LIAISE P.I.D. SP BR & B.-B.B. SIGINT. REPEAT URGENT! ERASE THIS. ENDS."

He looked at his watch. 07.50. Wednesday, 5th May.

This wasn't a warning. It was a plan.

It hadn't happened yet!

Who'd sent it? He pressed 1471 but the screen went blank.

He stared at his watch again. 07.51 flashed up as he did so. He had nine minutes. Where the hell was Cleo?

He ran over to his pager. Marty first. He'd know what to do. Horatio knew he'd be tracked whether he used his own pager or Cleo's vid-fone. It had better be his pager. They'd never believe he stumbled on her entry code and modem password and telling them to anyone would surely put suspicion onto her. Dressing frantically, he considered his options.

Then he remembered.

Gemma was due at Dover to cover the King's arrival! How many sections were there on that Bridge? Every schoolchild knew. With a sick thud located somewhere in his inner colon, Horatio remembered there were seven. The last was at Dover. This was not some terrorist outrage against the Bridge. This was assassination.

If P.I.D. knew about it before it happened, surely they'd stop it? What was that about "the usual suspects"? It sounded remarkably casual. Like something out of the final scene of that embargoed Humphrey Bogart movie.

He must act. Now.

Gemma had given him her direct number. Where was it? Page 1101 of the pager. He got through. Damn! It was her ansapage.

"Hi! This is Gemma. Ah'm afraid Ah'm busy right now, but please leave a message."

"Gemma!" he yelled into it. "Get away from the Bridge! Run now! Stay away from section seven! It's going to be hit any moment now! Get out of the area! Now!"

His next call was to Marty's flat again.

"Hi, Marty?"

"Hello, yes, who's speaking?" But it wasn't Marty. He recognised the voice. It was Tallboys.

"Listen, Alex, this is Horatio Lestoq . . ." Tallboys started to speak. "Shut up and listen. There's going to be a laser attack on the King's motorcade in Dover in about eight minutes' time. Stop it! Now!" He clicked off. What was Tallboys doing in Marty's flat?

Next he got through to the P.I.D. receptionist. Cleo wasn't there.

"I'm afraid Ms Tallboys is not in today. Would you like to speak to anyone else?"

"Michael Hibbert, please. It's an emergency." Another minute clicked up on his watch as he waited to be put through. 07.52.

"Hibbert speaking."

"It's Horatio Lestoq here."

"Horatio!" Surprise. So Hibbert was *au fait* with his case. Just as well. Doubtless he had already pressed the "Call Trace" button.

"Listen carefully. Any moment now there's going to be an assassination attempt on the King in Dover."

"King? What King?"

"Don't play games. This is an emergency."

"OK. Details please. You do know Europol gets about twenty of these calls a day."

"This is for real."

"They all say that, too."

"Laser attack. Channel Bridge section seven. At oh-eight hundred this morning."

"And what is it you want?" The tone had gone clipped. Nasty. Lean and hungry.

"Well, protect him of course. Change the route. Alter the

schedule. Cut the walkabout. Do whatever you people do to protect V.I.P.s."

"No, I mean what do *you* want, politically? What are your demands?"

"Demands?"

"Yes. Money, release of internees, flights to Oslo, that sort of thing. What's your organisation demanding, Dr Lestoq?" The cent dropped.

"Look, *I'm* not behind this. I'm just warning you about it!" He couldn't stay any longer. Thirty-two seconds were up. They'd be tracing his pager's whereabouts. He clicked off.

Next was Weaning.

"I'm sorry, you are not through-accessed to Mr Weaning." It just had to be Penelope.

"For God's sake!"

"He doesn't want to take your calls," she said, in a voice oozing satisfaction.

"Listen here, Aldritt. Tell him there is going to be an assassination attempt on the King in seven minutes' time and Gemma Reegan will die in it if she's not warned." Ten precious seconds later Weaning came on. He sounded aggressive.

"What's all this?"

"You must get Gemma out of the area. Tell her to get away. They're going to laser section seven of the Bridge in" — he checked his watch — "about seven minutes' time."

"You've cracked. Who are going to laser it? This time you've gone too . . ."

"I mean it, Weaning. They are going to kill the King and anyone else near the beam! You know what lasers can do. Remember Kuwait! Get her out of there!" He clicked off. Had his hysteria conveyed a sense of urgency, or just lunacy?

Then he called the New Zealand Embassy and was put through to a security officer named Cradock. Halfway through telling him, Horatio realised he'd have to get out. If Hibbert had managed to trace his call successfully he needed to leave Cleo's flat right now. A SWAT team could already be on its way already. No sirens this time. He dressed and got out in less than thirty seconds. He hoped the poor Kiwi had got the gist.

No signs of anything unusual on the street.

He'd done his best, he thought, as he walked towards Talgarth Road. But was it enough? Depressed, defeatist, deflated, there was only one person he could turn to now. Three minutes to go. There was a cash vid-fone in the Director's Court Metro station. He'd risk one more call.

"Hi. It's me. I need to talk to you."

"Where are you? I've been so worried." Heather looked it. "All those dreadful things they've been saying about you in the papers. Can I help you in any way?" This was the real, unconditional love and support he needed. The sort he so rarely got from her when he was young. Now he knew why.

"There's going to be an attack on the King any minute now."

"What?!"

"You know the King is coming over the Channel Bridge this morning."

"Yes."

"There's going to be an assassination attempt on him."

"What can we do about it? Have you called the police?"

"Yes. But I suspect it's them who are behind it."

"Horatio, you're obviously in danger. We must meet. You look terrible. Is there anything you need? We must meet today. Where? Speak in some sort of family code, as I'm sure the police will be bugging my phone now. Do you need anything?"

"Yes I need to know the truth about a few things."

"I'll come up straightaway."

"I need to talk. Watch out though. If you *are* being bugged, the house is probably being watched and you'll be followed. Take care."

"Don't worry about me." She smiled. "It'll be like old times. Right now, I'll get on to someone I know in Southampton."

Riley's thesis had detailed the various ways how, as Robert Lestoq's wife, she had bamboozled the police, MI5, Special Branch and the various Euro-spook agencies in support of her husband's campaign against the superstate. Until it had all ended suddenly and tragically on 6th April 2016. He thought of somewhere they could meet.

"How about the statue commemorating Rory's hero?" She thought for a second.

"Got you. Yes, I'll see you there in" – she checked the vid-fone clock – "ninety minutes." The fone clicked. Assuming Europol were bugging her, they would have been able to trace that call. Time to go.

She would have to move fast, assuming they didn't stop her leaving altogether. Horatio assumed they would prefer to follow her in order to catch him, and also that she would somehow evade them. Even the road cameras could not track every number plate as they came up the A3. She'd suddenly stop in autoparks, reverse down one-way streets, turn U-turns in tunnels and shake them off one way or another. They'd need a helicopter to follow her, and she'd spot that. He saw with satisfaction that rain was starting to spit down now and dark grey clouds filled the sky. That ruled out their tracking her car roof number by satellite, as in the recent Albanian mafia case in Ludlow.

He walked down onto the Talgarth Road and caught a tram into town, sitting in the front seat so nobody could see his face. He paid the driver in cash. Accessing his pager onto the news, Horatio mentally braced himself for the worst. It was 08.02. As he was reading the top news story, about preparations for celebrating the 120th anniversary of Founding Father Delors' birth on 20th July, it flashed up:

NEWS FLASH! NEWS FLASH! LASER ATTACK ON ENTENTE BRIDGE. Several Dead. Many Feared Wounded in Assassination Attempt on William Mountbatten-Windsor. New Zealand Monarch Escaped Unhurt . . . repeat . . . Laser Attack on Entente Bridge. Tenth May Group Blamed.

Horatio's stomach knotted up. He read on as the newsflash was updated every fifteen seconds.

News is coming in of a terrorist attack on the motorcade carrying the King of New Zealand, William Mountbatten-Windsor, at the Entente Bridge at 08.00 today. As it arrived at section seven at Dover, the motorcade was hit by what has been described by experts as three high-velocity, high-voltage laser beams. It ignited the fuel tanks of the first three grade 1 petrol autos of the motorcade, causing large explosions . . . MORE SOON . . .

Eight bodies have been recovered so far. The beam was extremely powerful, prompting speculation that it came from a military rather than an industrial or sporting laser. The explosions could be heard all over the city. The beam seems not to have been fired for long enough for its source to be immediately traceable . . . MORE SOON . . .

Horatio could hardly bear to wait for the new information. He was not particularly religious, but he prayed and prayed, making God all sorts of probably unkeepable promises if Gemma turned out to be all right. Perhaps she had been somewhere else, perhaps she had been late, perhaps she had got his message in time, perhaps, perhaps . . .

It appears the motorcade had stopped moments earlier in order for Mr Windsor to meet the people and take his first steps on English soil since he left 28 years ago, with his father the late ex-King Charles III . . . MORE SOON . . . The first beam hit the front auto as the chauffeur opened the door of the second limousine, cutting it in half and igniting the petrol tank. Immediately afterwards the next two autos were destroyed in the same way . . . MORE SOON . . . Nine people are now officially reported dead, there are reports of many more injured by flying glass and the metal bodies of the exploding autos . . . MORE SOON . . .

Europol has just announced that a warning was received a few minutes before the attack. Not enough time was allowed for police to act, however. It was given by the fugitive Dr Horatio Lestoq, the man wanted in connection with the murders of Admiral Michael Ratcliffe on Sunday and his neighbour Ms Jean Dodson today.

Jean? JEAN!

It seemed as though a hinge had been loosened on Horatio's world. It started to swirl around. Surely not Jean as well? This wasn't happening. He looked wildly around the tram. Was everyone watching him? Had they recognised him? Were they even then secretly paging the police, about to pull the emergency cord? Make a citizen's arrest? He got off at the next stop, outside the Anglo-German Friendship Museum on the Cromwell Road. He walked to the bench by the main entrance and sat down, trying hard to restrain tears. He must not draw attention. And he had to think logically. Now as never before.

If they'd got to Jean what had they found out from her? She'd heard the tape.

Keeping his face turned away from the cameras, he walked

back up Exhibition Road, reading the pager updates. What about Gemma?

It now appears that about a minute before reaching section seven, the motorcade had stopped and Mr Mountbatten-Windsor was moved to another of the autos further behind. The former Prince of Wales thus escaped the assassination attempt unscathed. The tour schedule has been suspended until he has visited the injured in Dover Central Hospital.

Horatio looked further down the page. A name jumped out at him.

. . . Jemima Reegan, an A.F.T.A. author, covering the visit for The Times. A few moments ago the deputy editor of that newsagency spoke to us. Mr Roderick Weaning described Ms Reegan as "an outstanding journalist and author who had made the Union her home. A kind, decent person who was popular with all who knew her."

"Made". "Was". Past tense. That was that. The worst.

And there was a kid. Oliver. He read on.

Mr Weaning has confirmed that Dr Lestoq called him just before the attack with accurate details about what was about to happen. Had Ms Reegan been close to the auto attempting to catch Mr Windsor's first words on South English soil, as was her expressed intention, she would have been killed outright. "She has paid a terrible price for her dedication and professionalism," Mr Weaning has said.

Horatio clicked off.

He walked past the Polish Hearth Club and the Goethe Institute and finally reached the top of Exhibition Road, beyond the last street camera. Could Jean have committed suicide? She was certainly distraught enough when he left her. Should he have stayed?

He felt a sudden constriction of the throat. Breath came hard. He felt like he had been punched in the solar plexus. He took a pull at the Salbutamol. Only after something approaching a minute of acute discomfort was he able to think again.

Despair pushed its way into his mind insistently, hungrily, like the first maggot was wriggling through an eye socket into a corpse's brain. He yearned for his Pluszac, however small a dose. Or should he just finish it there and then with Jean's gun? The world could think what it liked. He'd know why.

He must find out more about poor Jean whom, he remembered, the Admiral had admonished him to protect. Another terrible failure. He returned to the pager. He had his own EuroNet index mention now. For the first time since his Carlyle coup. *Lestoq, Dr Horatio. Pages 9661–9665 Y.*

Dr Horatio Lestoq, the twenty-nine-year-old Fellow of All Souls College, Oxford, is alleged to be responsible for the murder of Admiral Michael Ratcliffe – oh for the old system of *sub judice*, he thought – *and is now also wanted in connection with the Entente Bridge outrage. Europol recently named him as also being wanted for questioning over the death of Ms Jean Dodson, sixty-two, who was killed in Ibworth, Hampshire, this morning. She died when her auto exploded in the High Street. Dr Lestoq's fingerprints were found on a full clip of ammunition in the house.*

A man answering his description was seen walking towards Mrs Dodson's house at 11.30 yesterday morning. Ms Dodson is suspected of having been a witness to the murder of Admiral Ratcliffe.

They might as well have ended the news report with the words "*Open and shut case*", thought Horatio bitterly. He felt drained, nihilistic, wretched. He wanted to do something vicious. If not to his enemies, then to himself. A ruddy-bluish film was descending over his eyes. Sitting on the steps of the Albert Memorial he wondered how a supposedly clever person could be so bloody stupid so bloody often? There were another twenty minutes before his mother was due. But first he needed to know that she really *was* his mother. He needed to hear that the Admiral had got something wrong. Too many people had suffered because of his belated, lethal honesty. Horatio made his way slowly south-west across the Park towards the meeting place.

Jean was dead. Gemma was lying in some Dover morgue – what they'd been able to find of her. The photos of what military lasers had wrought in the Second Gulf War suggested there wouldn't be much. That massive concentration of light and energy simply evaporated everything in its beam.

The statue of William of Orange – his godfather, Rory MacAdam, had been a proud Ulsterman – stood outside Kensington Palace Modern History Museum. Rory had died during the Loyalists' brave but doomed march on Dublin. It was whilst he was standing in the drizzle under the trees in Kensington Park, keeping the statue in view from a distance, that Horatio realised he was being watched.

A man in a dark beret was loitering under the bandstand about a hundred metres away, pretending to take cover from the rain. But he glanced over in Horatio's direction just often enough.

Horatio's heart began to pound all over again. How many more were there? Would they start to move in on him. When? What could he do? He had Jean's gun in his pocket. Would he need to use it? He gripped it tight.

The first thing was to put as much distance between himself and the statue as possible. He mustn't get his mother – or aunt, or whoever she really was – involved in any of this. He started walking south towards High Street Ken, scanning the drizzling scene for any sign of confederates. The workmen on the rooftop of the Presidential Garden Hotel? The man selling *bratwurst* at the park gates? The jogger, perhaps? He walked quickly towards the road. Then, swinging around, he picked out the man following in his direction, hands thrust deep into a raincoat and seemingly oblivious of him.

As Horatio crossed the road, the rain falling more heavily now, he put his hand on Jean's gun for comfort. He had no idea whether the safety catch was on or not. He knew nothing about guns, and his cursory examination of this one on the M3 had not helped much. He decided to take De Vere Gardens and then double back down Canning Place, towards Victoria Road. Then, heading south past Douro Place and St Alban's Grove, he turned right into Cottesmore Gardens.

The man was still behind him. That settled it.

As he turned the corner into the quiet Kensington street, Horatio experienced another panic attack. He had always been slightly neurotic but this threat was all too real. What if it was not a policeman following him with a view to an arrest, but an officially-sanctioned assassin waiting for a suitable opportunity to rub him out? If these people could smash up houses, gag newsagencies, organise auto crashes, kill judges, asphyxiate people and then frame innocents for it, what would stop them just shooting him? Ever since the Met were armed, more and more people were being killed on the streets. Shootouts with the various ethnic organised crime syndicates were almost daily news fare. It would not be hard to explain away. His mother would know the truth, as would Cleo and Marty, but no one else would suspect anything. With the gun on him they'd just say he died "resisting arrest". Some cleaner would probably find the tape stuck under the Oratory pew months from now and doubtless throw it away. He took a deep pull on his inhaler.

Turning sharp left at the end of Cottesmore Gardens, past the last house with the blue plaque announcing that Sir Philip

Ziegler, historian and biographer, had lived there half a century ago, Horatio stepped smartly into the doorway of the first house in Stanford Road. He held the gun tight and resolved to be brave. If he didn't faint first.

After what seemed like a millennium, but was actually only about twenty seconds, the man in the hat and raincoat walked past. As he caught sight of Horatio he stopped and turned, looking surprised. Horatio froze.

"You gave me a shock!" the stranger said, with a smile.

In that same moment the man's hat, and then the left side of his head, flew off. The hat landed on its rim, rolled along the wet pavement and then flopped over. Skull, brain, blood and grey matter splattered far across the street. The body itself was knocked over by the power of the bullet. It toppled, what remained of its head first, and started bucketing blood onto the pavement. The gutter, which was already running with rainwater, ran dark pink to the nearby drain. To make the sight yet more macabre, the man's hands stayed stuck securely in the raincoat pockets.

Horatio stood stock still, taking it all in.

The next thing he saw was someone running down the street towards him. Horatio pulled out his revolver and took aim. The man wore gloves and a balaclava. He put his hands up but continued running. As he approached he shouted, "Quick! Horror! Come with me! Police'll be here any minute. Explain later!"

His nickname, yelled in a voice he recognised. Whose?

The man then walked over to the corpse and put his hand in the raincoat pockets. Taking out a gun from one and a two-way from the other, he thrust them into his own pockets and ran off down Stanford Road, shouting "Come on!" over his shoulder.

People were looking out of their windows. A middle-aged woman who had been unloading shopping from her grade 2 auto further down the street had seen everything. A large fragment of hairy, blood-soaked skull had landed a couple of metres away from her. She was holding her head in her hands and screaming hysterically in short, earsplitting bursts. And she was looking straight at Horatio.

Not knowing what else to do, he started off after the man in the balaclava. The police would come soon. The dead man *had* had a gun. Perhaps his life had been saved? Impossible to know. He couldn't stay there though.

He had gone too far, was in too deep, *not* to take risks now. At the end of Stanford Road the man darted left down Eldon Road and stopped by a small yellow electric. Horatio was followed.

"Get in!" Horatio did. As he sat down in the driver's seat, the man pulled off his balaclava.

Horatio then saw the face of his saviour.

Or his assassin.

09.10 Wednesday, 5th May

"Peter! For God's sake!" Horatio cried in between pulls on his inhaler. "Why are you following me? What's going on?"

Riley started the auto and drove away.

"I was sent to protect you. We believe you're in serious danger." They were driving north fast.

"Who's 'we'? And who was that man you killed?" They turned left when they reached Kensington High Street. As they drove alongside the park they saw three police autos, sirens screaming, driving straight towards them on the wrong side of the road.

"Shit!" muttered Riley. "They've got us." He pulled over and took out a gun. "We may have to shoot our way out of this, Horror. Just stick close to me." Horatio reluctantly pulled out Jean's gun.

But the police did not slow down. They sped straight past and swung off right into Victoria Road.

Horatio breathed out as Riley drove on.

"Listen to this two-way. That'll tell you who he was." Horatio put the receiver in his ear as Riley switched on the dead man's transmitter.

"Come in Spartacus! Come in Spartacus! This is Sigint. Do you read us? Where are you, Spartacus? Are you still trailing suspect? Let

us have your present position. Urgent! We heard a shot. What's going on? Police are on their way now! Respond! Respond!" Horatio switched it off and handed it back, not much the wiser. As he turned up Kensington Church Street, Riley threw the radio out of the window down onto the road.

"He was a Berlin-Brussels operative whom I saw on your track. When he had you cornered I had to take the decision about whether or not to fire. I'd been authorised to, so I did."

"By whom? Who the hell do you work for then?"

"I'll tell you when we're in the safe house."

"No! I'm not going anywhere unless you tell me now." Riley stopped the car halfway down Vicarage Gate. Without turning around to face Horatio, he said simply: "I work for the Tenth May Group."

"You – a terrorist! Jesus how absurd. You're a historian for Christ's sake!"

"And you're a logician. It hasn't stopped you getting mixed up in all this."

"How did you know where to find me? What do you want?"

"I was told you'd be in the Park. I was to watch you and get you out of any scrapes. If anyone tried to arrest or harm you I was to get you safely away. We're very rarely told we can shoot to kill – it was my first time. I thought a stunning would be enough but I had specific orders."

"Who gave you them?"

"My cell commander. Who'd have got them from Army Council London District. I can't tell you anything else about that."

Could he trust Riley? What choice had he? As they drove up Kensington Church Street and turned off right he asked what other operations he'd carried out for the Group. Riley seemed embarrassed.

"I'm only very junior, Horatio. This is the first time I've actually taken life."

"I see."

"So far it's jobs like I imagined this would be. Following, watching, protecting, that kind of thing. I was involved in blowing up the Santer statue in Commission Square."

Horatio remembered the incident. The statue of the arch-nationalist, Winston Churchill, had been taken down from its pedestal in Commission Square, ostensibly for cleaning. For a long while nothing happened, until one morning about five years ago a statue of former Commission President Jacques Santer was erected in its place. A week or so later, in the middle of the night, it was blown up, in what some papers called a terrorist outrage, but what had struck Horatio as little more than a jolly student jape. No one had been hurt and the statue was soon replaced.

"Pretty undergraduate stuff."

"And I was involved in springing Redwood." That was more like it. At seventy-two, John Redwood was the grand old man of antifederalism, having been one of the chief political opponents to Aachen. Yet even at that age he had been arrested on trumped-up charges of spying for the Americans. He'd been sprung from Pentonville by the Tenth May Group in a famously well-executed operation. Somehow they had managed to spirit him out of the Union altogether. He wound up overseeing the Free British Office in Oslo.

"You must have been all of about twelve."

"Eleven. My family went on a Swedish holiday with the old boy hidden in a false bottom in the camper van. We nipped over the frontier into Norway at an unguarded part of the northern frontier." The conversation had gone on long enough. He had to trust Riley.

"I'd like to meet one of your senior people. I've got information that they badly want. Can I give you the gist of it?"

"You could just as easily give it to them yourself. They'll send someone senior over straightaway, I imagine."

Riley restarted the auto and drove up Brunswick Gardens. The safe house was, he explained, known solely to his cell. Horatio was to let himself in and wait until he was met by whichever member of Army Council had been detailed to discuss the next stage.

"If you want a wash," he said, with a look which suggested that Horatio looked and smelled as if he did, "use the bathroom on the first floor. On no account open any curtains or windows. Here's the card. It's number nine." They stopped outside a large, double-fronted Kensington townhouse. "Be as inconspicuous as possible. Go."

Horatio stepped out of the car and, without saying goodbye or looking round, let himself in through the garden gate. As he walked up the short path he heard Riley drive off behind him. The card key worked smoothly, and once he had closed the large door behind him he let out a long, satisfied sigh.

Another followed five minutes later when he lowered himself into a hot bath. He'd explored the house and found it completely gutted. The only furniture, apart from a couple of futons in the upstairs bedrooms, was a mangy sofa on the ground floor. Horatio hated sleeping in anything but a proper bed. He dreaded the idea of a futon. There was a kettle, some U.S.E.-processed coffee and a good deal of unappetising-looking dehydrised food. Otherwise the place looked as though the builders were about to arrive. At least the cable managed to pick up most channels.

Was he right, he wondered, as he soaped around the vast white bloated belly of which he was so secretly and inordinately proud, to throw in his lot with a terrorist organisation? Especially one with such a monastic outlook on creature comforts? Would it not compromise his revelations, if and when at last he got a chance to make them? He had read the Commission propaganda about the Tenth May Group, of course. Their viciousness, implacability and so on. They took their name from the date in 1940 – Old Britain's *annus mirabilis* – when Winston Churchill became Prime Minister. For them it was the defining moment in British nationhood.

Like so many other English people, Horatio was in two minds about the English Resistance Movement. Not recognising the legitimacy of the Strasbourg parliament, the E.R.M. refused to contest seats for it. They also did not accept the Aachen decision and had finally resorted to violence to achieve their ultimate aim – an independent United Kingdom. Although the E.R.M. was outside the democratic process, many people in North and South England admired them and sympathised with their aspirations, especially when their military wing, the Tenth May Group, began specialising in daring hits on unpopular, "hard" targets. The kidnap of the Union Agriculture Commissioner from his own office in Brussels, for example, had been condemned by the media but applauded by the people, especially after the Commission obtained his release by rescinding a Directive which would have destroyed the English oak and lettuce industries.

They were supposed to be rigidly disciplined and ruthlessly efficient. Although they had started off amateurishly in the Twenties, the Group had been welded into an efficient unit, largely by the professionalism of the many ex-servicemen in their ranks. They had been fighting now for over twenty years, concentrating on taking out people they termed "Euro-quislings". They were now able to hit targets in North and

South England in a highly discriminating way. That was why people like David Fraser always looked under their autos every morning before driving to work. Gregory Percival had long been top of their hit list. Three times they had tried to assassinate him, each plot having gone awry at the last moment.

The English people might privately have applauded the E.R.M.'s ends, but most did not (at least publicly) condone their means. The blowing up of Commission buildings and personnel never commanded general public support. But this, Horatio reasoned, was largely because the Aachen referendum was thought to have legitimised the federal Union, however unpopular it might subsequently have become.

What would happen, he wondered, as he soaped around his athlete's foot, once it became public knowledge that Aachen had been fixed? Overnight these terrorists would become freedom fighters, their campaign proved morally justified all along. Instead of the psychopathic gang of fascist thugs continually portrayed in the media, Tenth May terrorists would become patriotic heroes overnight.

It was all down to him and the Aachen Memorandum.

What would they do to get hold of it? Was he ready to give it to them? What would he demand in return? Free Norway had no extradition treaty with the Union. A.F.T.A., perhaps? New Zealand might be an option worth exploring. He couldn't stay in the Union, but the thought of trying to live anywhere else depressed him.

The bathroom door swung open.

Standing in the doorway was the last person he would have suspected of being a senior field commander of Tenth May Army Group, London District.

The *very* last person in the world.

PART
IV

22

10.53 Wednesday, 5th May

Horatio's eyes popped and his mouth lolled open. He gawped like a halibut on a fishmonger's slab.

"Horatio." Heather Lestoq wasn't smiling. It was one of those businesslike, I've-just-read-your-school-report faces. He remembered it well. "I'm here to debrief you. I've been given full negotiating authority by Army Command." She was dressed in a bottle-green tweed two-piece. Her dark grey hair, usually impenetrably brittle and well-coiffed, looked a touch straggly.

"How long have you been working for the E.R.M.?" asked Horatio eventually. "And why didn't you trust me enough to tell me?" Lying there naked he didn't feel in a very strong position to argue his case. He got out of the bath and wrapped himself in the only towel. It didn't quite reach all the way around his waist. He looked and felt absurd.

"We're employed on a strictly need-to-know basis." Smarting slightly from that, Horatio asked how long she had been involved.

"Since before I even knew your father. I used to work in the European Foundation, a Eurosceptic organisation set up to campaign against ever-closer union back in the Nineties. We campaigned against Maastricht, the I.G.C. sell-out, the soft euro, the hard euro, then Aachen, and I stayed with it after it was forced underground."

"When did father get involved?"

"Oh, it was always me more than Robert. Those bastards" – he had hardly ever heard her swear before, it came as a shock – "killed the wrong person. They assumed that because he made the speeches and chaired the meetings, he was also writing the lines and organising the movement. But that was mostly me."

"*Killed?*" Horatio's mind was whirring.

"Robert was murdered. I've always been surprised a brainy boy like you never put two and two together. Atlantic Gas was perfectly safe in households by 2016. When I turned up at the flat, with you in my arms, there was no Atgas smell at all." She had never spoken to him about that day. Only to Riley, it seemed.

"You were there when it happened?"

"Yes. So were you. I remember every detail like it was last Monday. In fact far better than last Monday because last Monday didn't change my life for ever." Her voice had changed perceptibly. "Thursday the sixth of April 2016. I'd just come back from a Bruges General Staff meeting at Bonchurch Road. Everyone had been there except Ella Gurdon, the Group secretary, and Robert, who was being watched too closely. We were planning the next stage of the Insurrection. A mass rally at Trafalgar Square, as it was then called, I remember. Instead of going up in the lift to see Robert, I went down to talk to Evans, our new caretaker, about the power cuts. It was when electricity was being cut almost every day, during the first energy crisis, before they partitioned Saudi. Evans wasn't there, but after about the same amount of time that it would have taken me – us – to get up to the flat on the third floor, had we been going up in the lift rather than down to the basement, there was an explosion. It rocked the whole block. When I'd got halfway up the stairs it was obvious that the whole flat had been completely destroyed. Parts were still on fire and there was a chance of the whole building collapsing.

"The firepersons found Robert and Flora, at least most of them, in the drawing room. I'd had no idea she and James were going to be there. We were supposed to be going to meet them for dinner later, they'd probably turned up early and were having a drink before I was due to arrive." At last, she started to cry. Horatio was wondering when it would come. "Thank God they all died instantaneously. Jim, standing by the window, was blown about a hundred yards out into the street." She was speaking in a dead, matter-of-fact voice. "When it comes to terrorism, the B-B.B. have one or two things to teach us."

Horatio was reminded of a paragraph in a book he'd read at university, called *Paris After the Liberation*. The authors, whom he seemed to remember were the Beevor/Cooper husband-and-wife writing team, had postulated that gas explosions might have been used by the French Secret Service to eliminate political undesirables in Paris immediately after the Second Nationalist War.

"What makes you think it wasn't accidental?"

"You're so wonderfully naive." She looked tired. "When Evans returned he insisted he'd smelt something gassy, but I knew I hadn't. Yet the next day the papers – all of them without exception – carried the news that it had definitely been Atgas. And a couple of years later they did for Noel Malcolm in exactly the same way. Not very imaginative, the feds." Horatio recalled reading about the anti-federalist intellectual's demise in Riley's thesis. He'd hitherto assumed it to be one of history's ghastly but common coincidences.

"Why did you never tell me any of this? Or about your involvement in the E.R.M.?"

"I'm not E.R.M.; they're just politicians. Since Robert, Flora and James were murdered I've been strictly operational. Tenth May."

"But I could've helped." He put on his shirt and trousers.

"No, my love, you couldn't. I knew I could always trust you, it wasn't that. I remember when the Health Insurance Inspectorate tried to recruit kids to inform about how much their parents drank and smoked, you always misled them. While all your friends were busy sneaking on their mothers and fathers, I knew I could be proud of you. But I wanted something better for you than terrorism. I wanted Westminster, Brasenose, All Souls, well-deserved fame. I was so proud of you during all that Carlyle business, and over *The Seven Pillars*."

"You never let me know."

"I'm not one for molly-coddling."

"You molly-coddle Dick and Marcia."

"Do you want to hear my reasons or not?" He nodded for her to continue.

"I knew you had a formidable brain, one which the movement could have used. But when it comes to anything at all technical – and much of our work is *very* technical – you're a sweet incompetent. Can you change a bulb, Horace, or wire a plug? That's what terrorism is about, not writing essays." Horatio glared at his toes. He felt his cheeks redden. He put on his shoes and socks. "You're not like your father. You're simply not up to the physical and emotional stress of it all.

Your . . . you know, *trouble* would have hampered us. I didn't want to put you under any extra strains."

"There's another reason I'm not like him, isn't there?" spat Horatio. He was incensed at her characterisation of him as a bungling, unstable wimp.

"What do you mean?"

"I'm not his son. Am I? And you're not my mother. Are you?" Silence. He finished dressing.

"He told you that, did he?"

"Yes, he did."

"He wasn't your grandfather at all. And I *am* your mother."

"Do explain." He hoped it sounded sarcastic enough.

All Horatio's assumptions, everything on which he had based his life, were swirling in a maelstrom of conjecture and ambiguity. He again saw the man in the raincoat toppling over. Perhaps this would all end in a recurrence of the problem Dr Virgil had had to treat him for before his Finals. Or even a full-scale, four-funnelled, copper-bottomed nervous breakdown. His Pluszac was back in his flat. He hadn't taken any for nearly a week. He was entering injury time. If he wasn't there already.

"After your father's death I was short of cash. The movement couldn't help. It was before they got into computer fraud and all that sophisticated stuff. I'd always suspected what that spineless little shit had done for his so-called jackpot, but there was nothing I could do to prove it. I decided to string him a line about you really being Flora's son. For the money. It worked better than I expected. I showed him the birth certificates, claiming they'd been falsified. I also told him some mumbo-jumbo about D.N.A. which he swallowed. I didn't even need to rig a test. You see he *wanted* to believe it. He was generous, though, I'll give him that."

"Why are you telling me all this now?"

"Because you seem to have found out most of it and I want to put your mind at rest."

"There's something else, though, isn't there?"

She nodded. He suspected that the Ebury Street reminiscence had been told in such a graphic way so as to cede her the emotional high ground.

"The old bastard passed you something, didn't he? For years I'd suspected what he'd done. I once spoke to him about it, tangentially, but could never face him with it in case he tipped off the P.I.D. So far I've been impossibly lucky in escaping detection. They're suspicious of me, naturally, but nothing's ever been proven. I expect they think I'm too old now to be a threat. I went quiet after the explosion and they must have thought they'd seen the end of me. From the fone conversation you played me from that pub on Sunday it sounded like he was about to confess something to you. Was it about what he did during the Referendum? If it was, Horatio, I need it more than I've needed anything. Please give it to me. I know you think I was never much of a mother to you, so if not for me, then for your father's memory."

Horatio wasn't really listening. He'd anticipated all that part already. He was considering the wider implications of giving his mother the tape. He was thinking, in a way he never really had before, about his country.

The image that filled his mind was of the huge Union flag which flew over Attali House. The navy blue with its twelve gold stars had meant his country for him, all his life. He knew his father had been a nat, of course, but then he had no memories of Commander Lestoq. At school and Oxford he had been taught that the Union was a laudable institution, a force for peace. Uniglobers saw it as the first great step on the road to World Government. It had stripped Great Britain of its independence, of course, but wasn't that a historical necessity? Surely it *had* to be done, as the Information Commission kept pointing out, in order to resist the economies of scale wielded by the world's two other trading empires in the east and west. Didn't it?

The Union had its faults of course. Which country hasn't? It was sclerotic, corrupt, mafia-run in some regions. It was also protectionist, introverted and absurdly bureaucratic. But throughout his life it had been *his* country. Beethoven's Ninth was his anthem, however much it irritated him. His flag had twelve gold stars against a blue background. Well, more his logo. But a logo which people had fought and died for when the Baltic regions had tried to secede.

Now he'd discovered that it had all come into being not through the ideals that he had heard about at school, or the speeches of Schuman, Monnet, Pleven, Delors, Santer and Heath. Speeches which, as a child, he had been made to learn and recite along with his multiplication tables. He still had some of them by heart. He knew for certain that the Union had actually come into being through violence, bribery and fraud.

Wasn't all that in the past? How could raking it all up help the future? Weren't all nations born in blood as well as bravery? America would have fallen apart in the nineteenth century had Lincoln not been prepared to shed seas of American blood. The Asia-Pacific Economic Zone would never have been created if the Chinese hadn't finally buried Communism.

And what of British independence? He'd never known the Union Jack. He'd read of nat and Carlist groups waving it occasionally – especially in the anti-Commission riots of the last six months – but he'd never seen it fly over a public building. It was there in the history books of course, a rather ungainly collection of saints' flags interposed upon one another and often hung upside down. It seemed strange to think that anyone could have been particularly inspired by it, other than as an irrational psychological reaction.

But isn't that what he was taught nationalism and patriotism always were – irrational psychological reactions? Of course, he occasionally applauded when the Tenth May carried out some particularly daring mission, but did he really want nationalism back?

The Union Jack could only ever have appealed to the people of a few rainy, cold old islands a short way off the continental north-western littoral. It had none of the moral and spiritual – almost religious – significance of that golden halo of twelve stars. Neither did it hold out any special message or hope for Personkind. It was just a bald, territorial, tribal symbol. Yet his mother was standing there in front of him, arms folded, expecting him to betray the U.S.E. for it and the anachronism for which it stood. Viewed logically, which was how his academic background had trained him to view everything, the proposition seemed absurd.

But *was* it? Might not the British have thrived as an independent nation rather than as five regions out of the thirty-six? Might Westminster have been the right place for the British to be ruled from, rather than the regional bureaucracies of Edinburgh and Cardiff, or the endless corridors of Commission admin units in Brussels? The British had long been great inventors, merchants, soldiers, seafarers and traders. Why could they not have been another Free Norway, a Switzerland (before it was muscled in) or even a Singapore or Japan? They could have traded with A.F.T.A., A-P.E.Z., Azania, the Commonwealth, the Middle East. The Union, too, considering the trade deficits they used to run. That way they might have been able to retain their ancient rights and liberties into the bargain. They could have inaugurated a real New Elizabethan Age, rather than just the farce of one.

All these ideas flashed through Horatio's brain as the synapses telegraphed new, contradictory thoughts at a speed faster than the connection made by any microchip yet invented. What about truth? He was a logician and a journalist. He had a duty to it. (At least he did as a logician.) He had discovered a crucial historical fact – that the Referendum was fixed. That surely deserved to be known simply because it was true. What right had he to deprive the future of the knowledge that Britain – and possibly other countries too – had been conned into the continental superstate?

And Cleo? Not his sister, thank God. But his cousin. His desire for her had returned in a rush after what his mother had told him. He'd hardly dared spell out the implication – INCEST – to himself before, although it had been grinning at him like a gargoyle ever since he had read the Admiral's letter. But now that revolting notion had gone, he was swiftly returning to his original infatuated state.

She'd trusted him when he said, despite every appearance and a motive, that he'd not killed her grandfather. She'd offered to help him, at great risk to herself. She'd put her job on the line. What would happen to their relationship – to any chances of future love – if he passed the Memorandum on to a terrorist organisation which she was employed to combat? Yet she had been forewarned about the Entente attack. Why?

The logical thing to do would be to tell his mother that the Admiral had passed on information which was being processed by Europol for a possible prosecution, and that he would not give it to her to use for her own atavistic political ends. She had not trusted him with her secret affiliation all these years – why should he help her? What did either of them know about the stability of Atgas back in 2016; how could he prove that some shadowy group of Berlin-Brussels Bureau zealots had murdered his father twenty-nine years ago?

Because he did know. That was all.

Because they were still killing people a generation later. Because the Spartacus man following him earlier had carried a gun. (How had he known where to find him, by the way?) Because Jean was dead. Because you only had to listen to the Admiral's voice on the tape to know that the Aachen Memorandum was *bona fide*.

The swine had deprived him of the chance to grow up with a father.

"Tell me about the attack on the Entente Bridge." She looked blank. "Was it Tenth May?"

"Don't be absurd! King William's our figurehead, our totem. We want him to be Head of State of a Free Britain. We'd hardly want him dead."

"But the news . . ."

"Is directed, organised. There was a story planted earlier in the week about a plot to hit the Bridge." He remembered the *Sun* splash. "Pure black propaganda put out by the Information Commission so that people would blame us. They even claimed a fortnight ago that we'd stolen a heavy-duty military laser. All total rot."

"What happened then? I mean about the Bridge?"

"When you called me to tell me about the attack I contacted one of our operatives who's liaising with the Kiwis. They moved the King into a different car. You saved his life. How did you get the information by the way? Army Council would love to know." Could he betray Cleo? He ignored the question.

"I'll let you know in a second. Why didn't you stop the whole motorcade? I don't understand."

"That was a Kiwi decision. They believed the Europol Diplomatic Protection Unit when they said it was safe. Don't ask me why."

"I lost a friend in that attack." He paused. He thought of his last kiss with Gemma. His Adam's apple felt like a stone. "She might have become more than that one day."

Heather Lestoq walked over to him and enfolded him in her arms, like she had never done enough when he was small.

"You see what I've tried to protect you from?"

"Why can't you stop it, Mummy? Give it up. Just accept that the past is gone. The two Englands have been part of the Union for thirty years now. Killing people won't change that."

Instantly she took her arms from around him and stepped back. Her face hardened. He knew the phenomenon, the instantaneous withdrawal of affection, only too well.

"Terrorist movements always get what they go for if they stick it out." She counted them off on her fingers. "The P.L.O., E.O.K.A., Algerian F.L.N., E.T.A., Irgun, S.W.A.P.O., Mau Mau, Angolan M.P.L.A., Z.A.N.U., the A.N.C.: they were all victorious. You'll see, if HomoRage continue this terror campaign against hetero advertising, they'll win in the end too. Every time C.R.I.P.S. blows up a Metro station without wheelchair ramps and lifts, what happens? More funds start to get targetted on the disabled. In five years' time the Matterhorn will be wheel-accessible! It was the great lesson of the last century. Terrorism pays. How do you think the I.R.A. got to the negotiating table? Their seven per cent support at the polls? No, they bombed their way there and so will we.

"Especially when you give me this confession of Ratcliffe's. It's the greatest coup in a generation of the armed struggle. And this time it'll lead to something. This Royal visit gives us the best opportunity for a popular insurrection since the Twenties." Her excitement was tangible. He tried to imagine what it must be like to spend a lifetime working and waiting for something, and then find it about to happen after so many false dawns. Maybe falling in love with Cleo would feel something like this.

"If we can show the people they were betrayed we could get just the spark we need. Look at those riots in Halifax and Leeds last week. All directed against Commission targets. The Union Jack was everywhere. People were singing the tribal songs; they knew the words to "White Cliffs of Dover", "We'll Meet Again", even "There'll Always Be An England" It's coming south fast. Both Tenth May Army Council and the E.R.M. Steering Committee believe the time's come to act. A general strike will be called for Monday week if the rally goes well on Saturday. So you see, things *can* happen. That's why we need your information now."

Horatio made his mind up. He would bloody well *make* history rather than just write it. He thought of Jean's admonition to him. Faltering, but heartfelt:

"Really, as well, when you come to think of it, it's your duty to Britain."

"The Admiral gave me a memorandum in which he explained that he was bribed to keep quiet about how the Aachen Referendum was fixed to provide a 'Yes' vote." A flash of pure triumph crossed her face.

"Yes! I knew it! I knew it! I've always known it! Who else knows about this?"

"You. Me. Jean Dodson, the Admiral's housekeeper did, but she's dead. And Cleopatra Tallboys."

"My niece Cleopatra? How on earth did *she* find out?"

"I told her today."

"You told her! Horatio, what are you talking about?"

"She's promised to try to obtain a conviction against Gregory Percival. I was to call her" – he checked his watch – "to arrange a place to meet and hand over the Memorandum." Heather Lestoq gave a hollow, mirthless laugh.

"That bitch is the most dedicated Euro-fanatic in the entire P.I.D. She's their liaison officer with the B.-B.B. special ops and Signals Intelligence Unit, for God's sake. How could you not have known that? She'll be using you to get hold of the tape solely in order to destroy it." A tone of disdain, almost contempt, entered her voice. "And afterwards probably you, too. You must have been able to see that! Just because you've been to bed with her it doesn't mean that you have to go and do everything she says."

How did she know about that?

"My poor darling." She shot a sympathetic, motherly glance over to him. Once again his world started to reel. Then she walked over and hugged him. Horatio started to cry. "And did she tell you she loved you for your mind? And did she say she preferred you to the – what do you call them – Hunky Regulars? I expect she also said she'd broken up with that maniac husband of hers, didn't she?"

He nodded violently. He was starting to shake. "I hope you're all right. We've lost operatives to P.I.D. stooges with serum-resistant H.I.V. You were protected?" He nodded again, the tears flowing freely down both cheeks now. His massive bulk was shivering violently as the full extent of Cleo's treachery sank in.

She'd come over to him at the party. Accessed his pager. Kissed him in the power cut. Taken him to bed. Doubtless she'd been under orders from Percival or someone to find out what he'd got on Ratcliffe. She'd read Riley's thesis. *Of course* she was informed about the Entente attack – she was in on it. The scheming, manipulative bint knew she was irresistible. She'd doubtless been laughing at him all the time. Tallboys was probably being treated to another video to put beside his Leila collection.

After mother and son had had what both believed to be enough silent communion, Heather said, "Pull yourself together now darling, and listen carefully. For some time now Cleopatra Tallboys has been deputy head of the counter-terrorist desk at P.I.D. with specific responsibility for infiltrating Tenth May. She's dangerous, she's very clever and she uses her sexuality like her friends used that laser, though I need hardly tell you that. She's a fanatic. Now, you must tell me exactly what happened. Did you meet her, as if by accident, after the first of your *Times* articles came out?"

He was blubbing openly now, wiping his dripping nose on the handkerchief Jean had already ruined. He nodded his head violently, like a sulking child.

"Where?"

"Marty's May Day party."

"Marty? Your friend from school?"

"Yes, and Oxford. Marty Frobisher. He works with her."

"Where is he now?"

"Missing."

"This is even more serious than I thought. We believe him

246

to be JACOBITE, our spy in P.I.D. It'd be a disaster for the movement if Cleo's blown him."

"Cleo told me not to trust him or call him."

Heather was thinking hard. Horatio continued, "Her husband was round at his flat the other day. He answered Marty's phone."

Heather sighed. "I'd better report this now."

"What can I do?"

"How far will you go?" Apart from putting her in any danger, Horatio resolved to do anything for his mother.

"Just name it."

She did.

23

14.24 Wednesday, 5th May

H oratio got straight through to Cleo at the office.
"What's the story?"

"It's good news. They're interested. Very. But as we suspected, they can only really act when they have the original document." He smiled to himself. He could have scripted this. He particularly liked the "we". "What is it, a sort of signed confession?"

"Yes, it's a document with various supporting papers — quite bulky really." That ought to help throw her.

"Whereabouts?"

"I've told you, somewhere safe."

A short pause. "Good. Now, I've got you total immunity from any prosecution if you get it to me. Not to my bosses, though. To me. You've got it in writing, signed by 'E' himself. Big people are coming over from Brussels for this. They're laying great store on the possibility of nailing our man. The operation has to be conducted in the strictest secrecy."

"You sound very tied up in it, for someone who's off the case." He clicked off, just before the forty seconds were up. He called again. She didn't comment. If she was disappointed it didn't show.

"He was my grandfather, remember. The getaway car tried to get you too. Don't you feel tied up in it?"

For the only time in that conversation he told the truth. "Of course I do. Any more on the auto?"

"No, no. Apparently Marty had been looking into it already. They'd got some satellite shots of where it was stolen, but the Ibworth disc disappeared on the day he was sacked."

"Curiouser and curiouser." (Well done Marty.) "Where is he?"

"We don't know. Our people are trying to track him down."

I bet they are! Horatio wondered whether Marty had skipped the region altogether.

"What was the number plate again?" asked Cleo.

"I didn't get a chance to see it. It was a grey grade 2 petrol."

"I'll get Satellite and Traffic Location onto it again. Stay there." He was put on hold. Beethoven's Ninth. No way would he fall for that. He hung up, waited a minute, then rang back.

"What do we do now?"

"Meet me in the same place as before at twenty hundred. I'll bring the immunity certificate. You bring the Memorandum."

"No. I wound up being followed last time I met you there."

"Were you?" She sounded genuinely surprised. Either she was an accomplished actress or this was more complex than he thought. The next thing Cleo said was almost to herself: "Perhaps they're onto me as well now. What happened?"

"I'll tell you when I see you."

"Where and when?"

"I can't make today. Or tomorrow. There are things I need

to tie up. How about eleven-thirty Saturday? Somewhere outside London."

"I'll just check." She put him on hold. That bloody Beethoven again. He clicked off, waited another minute and called back.

"Ten hundred's better for me. Outside London's impossible though. There's the big nat rally taking place in Hyde Park at eleven and I need to be around the central video monitor to identify ringleaders and generally keep an eye on it." She was so plausible, he couldn't help being impressed.

"A rally? I thought the Commission banned that sort of thing years ago. Unless it was a spontaneous demonstration of the people's love for the European ideal."

She laughed that full, ready, trust-me-I'm-really-one-of-you laughs which he had fallen for so easily only days before. "William Windsor's making a speech commemorating the centenary of V-E Day: the end of the Second Nationalist War. You must have read about it. We're expecting pretty much every E.R.M. sympathiser to be there in person, or at least watching it on cable."

"You mean to say you can tell who's watching which channel?"

"The appliance of science, Horatio. Now, where should we meet? It needs to be somewhere central."

Damn. Their first plan – to keep her well away from the rally – had failed.

"Commission Square? By the Santer statue at ten-thirty?"

"Fine. Yes. I like the irony. Hello? Horatio? Traffic have come back. A grey grade 2 petrol, licence W55 DCCE, was stolen in the early hours of Sunday morning from Reigate in Surrey. Belonged to a dentist apparently. Not much to go on there I'm afraid. Satellite stuff takes longer, but we're onto it."

"Has the auto been found yet?"

"No."

"Interesting."

"Horatio?"

"Yes?"

"You do still mean the lovely things you said about me the other night? I couldn't bear it if you were feeling differently towards me now, because of all this. Especially when I'm doing so much to try to help you."

"Of course I do. I'm crazy about you. As I will show you in person very soon." He clicked off with a few seconds to spare and smiled.

Part one of Plan A was in place.

16.00 Friday, 7th May

The previous forty-eight hours had been wretched. Waiting in the house, unable so much as to open a window, Horatio had been in turns bored and scared. Dehydrised food for every meal hadn't helped. It might have been true what the Mayor of London had said about people in the North going hungry, but why should he have to come out in sympathy?

Riley had been round twice to check he was all right. They'd had a good talk, mostly about politics. He'd joined the movement through conviction, that much was clear. But even the freedom fighter had begun to get on Horatio's nerves by Thursday night, and he'd welcomed the power cut that had thrust the house into darkness. It gave Horatio an excuse for an early night, as well as Riley good cover to leave. The growing unrest in the capital had led to rumours of the 22.00 curfew being reinstated for the first time since the Nat Subversion era.

On his second visit Riley brought disturbing news. The operative they had sent to the F.R.O. to steal Percival's note in the Treasury file 444/56432 had now not been heard of for thirty-six hours. Neither had their attempts to track down Kylie-Terèse Masterman come to anything. EuroNet revealed that His Honour Justice Minter had been found hanged in his study at lunchtime on 5th May 2015, the day after the

Referendum. He had left no suicide note, just his Report declaring the previous night's vote to have been "free and fair". It would be worth subjecting that signature to some graphology tests one day, thought Horatio.

Neither had the E.R.M.'s attempts to track down Oliver Reegan on Horatio's behalf come to anything. No one at the A.F.T.A. Embassy knew anything about him and the school had not seen him since the day of the test. The poor child might not even have been told. Horatio was in anguish; he desperately wanted to do something, but couldn't see even how to start. Once again, he felt helpless and pathetic.

Riley hadn't had the foresight to bring Horatio anything to read, so he was left with the Siberian tundra of daytime cable. If this was infotainment, they could keep it. The E.B.C. news channels told him, as he'd been expecting, that the Information Commission had officially connected him with Leila. 'OXFORD DON IN ULTRA-NAT PLOT' yelled the *Nine O'Clock News*. Predictably, the authorities were trying to blacken his name in advance of any revelations he might be about to make concerning Ratcliffe. That, too, was only to be expected. The twin murders and the Entente outrage were being linked in the public mind with nat secessionism, however illogical that seemed.

No one on the news shows he watched asked the obvious question: why should the E.R.M. want to destroy their idol, their number one political pin-up? Of all times to try to attack the Bridge, why should they choose the one when their King was crossing? No one could rally Free Britain like her ancestral monarch. Yet the question wasn't asked.

The warnings he had given Hibbert and Weaning about the Entente Bridge, suitably edited by the E.B.C., certainly sounded damning. "*Tell him there's going to be an assassination attempt on the King in ten minutes' time*," he'd said to Hibbert. He should have used a another form of words, but he'd been panicky and it was an emergency.

For the hundredth time that week, Horatio thought how unsuited he was for this kind of thing. Perhaps his mother had been right. If he was still alive when this was over, and if he was able to resume his academic career, he would return to his books, manuscripts, All Souls set, reassuringly unthreatening documents and, best of all, Room 132 of his favourite library. He pined for the Bodleian.

He also pined for Cleo. The fact that the attraction had been as intellectual as it was physical – genuinely, not in the way he'd always told dim girls it was – made her treachery even harder to bear. Would he ever find someone like her? Yet she had probably been only laughing at his jokes and sleeping with him for information and to protect Percival. Their relationship didn't count. It was yet one more humiliation in his seemingly doomed quest for affection. He reddened at the memory of her flashing her breasts over the I.H.R. vid-fone at the Institute. The slut. Horatio willingly gave himself over to further bouts of coruscating, masochistic self-laceration.

This would harden him, he thought, for tomorrow morning. How unbelievably close he had come to telling Cleo where the 'tape was! What sixth sense had kept it back? Then he remembered that it was not any sense at all, just a resolve not to put her in unnecessary danger. The same resolve had led him to refuse his mother's pleas to pick up the tape. He had not even told her where it was. He would do it himself. It fitted in perfectly with his escape plan.

As well as the E.B.C. and NewsChannel 17, Horatio watched other cable channels to kill time. But if infotainment was bad, the edutainment channels were worse. Culture-Channel 66 particularly exasperated him. It wasn't so much the rot they talked – he took that for granted – so much as the accents and slang. The snob in him was revolted by the presenter's flat, nasal, monotonal Estuary-Grunge. Horatio had always thought of snobbery as a mild moral good. To take pleasure from someone else's lineage, wealth, status or intelligence was, he believed, the exact inverse of envy, which he considered by far the most disgusting (and vulgar) of the deadly sins. Horatio felt pure anger when the presenter came out with sentences like "grunge groupthink won't dis the splutterpunk genre", and the guests on the show would then nod learnedly at this great insight into modern literature. He switched over.

The programme on EcoChannel 104 consisted of a ten-minute rant against "the barbaric Christian custom of so-called 'decorating' the corpse of a tree, a beautiful plant which has been kidnapped and murdered for a so-called semi-religious rite. How about showing some peace and goodwill towards all living things this Christmas? Think Green." And it was only the beginning of May! He switched again.

Horatio had never taken any interest whatever in sport, but he found it fascinating to compare the records won by athletes in the Steroids Olympics in Beijing with the Drug-Free Games in Kabul on TrackChannel 10. The sprinter from Kirghizstan, for example, had been able to smash the 7.125-second record for the hundred metres on an amazing concoction of muscle-enhancers, leaving the poor old drug-free runner from KwaZulu almost ambling in at 7.962. It wouldn't be long, Horatio guessed, before the Kirghiz's shiny round face was adorning pill-packs all over the Union.

Horatio videoed both 100-metre dashes. While he was

watching the runner in slow motion he noticed something strange. He thought he saw a bluish flash hit the screen for a microsecond. He rewound and played the tape once more. It happened again. So he rewound a third time. At the slowest possible speed he replayed the tape, frame by individual frame. The sprinter would be taking a stride forward, centimetre by centimetre on the screen, then suddenly for one frame he vanished altogether. He was replaced by a navy blue screen with the twelve gold stars of the Union. On the very next frame, a millisecond later in real viewing time, the runner returned to the screen again.

S.S.A. was back!

Subliminal Suggestion Advertising had been banned by the Commission in a controversial test case a few years before when the company Brain Inducer had tried to market a programme to help people stop biting their fingernails. Companies had hitherto been allowed to sell subliminal aids to combat arthritis, smoking, headaches, impotence, warts, indigestion, and so on, but they'd suddenly been stopped after the Brain Inducer court decision. Horatio now knew why. Brussels had its own product to push. S.S.A. was suppressed on the grounds that it gave consumers no choice. Horatio realised that the hypocritical nargs in the Commission were now using it themselves to promote Euro-nationalism.

He fast-forwarded to the next flash. This one, once he'd isolated the individual frame again, had a message. "EURO-GREAT!, ANGLO-GUILTY!" it stated boldly, in gold letters against a navy background. After a few minutes' work with the clicker, Horatio was also able to read "ENVY IS GOOD", and later, "BERLIN. BRUSSELS. AACHEN". Every channel had the slogans, even the children's. "UNION IS HOME" read one on *Jackanory*.

Once he was watching out for them he noticed how the messages came up every fifteen seconds or so. At least four or five times a minute. They passed so quickly they were barely perceptible to the eye or consciousness. It certainly didn't affect viewing in any way, but the brain took in the message without any critical faculties being activated to question the crude political and social propaganda.

JobsChannel 88 amused him. It said much about where the Union was going. Since England had been emasculated as a global-trading nation by the trade wars of the last decade, the only real growth industry had been in regulation. No less than the first *forty* pages of the employment channel's ads were for jobs in the various bureaucracies.

Horatio watched Situation-Vacant ads for the Euro-Rivers Authority, the Health and Safety Inspectorate, the Commission Trading Standards Office, the Sexual Harassment Bureau, animal welfare, child welfare, minority welfare, immigrant welfare, illegal immigrant welfare, plant welfare, the Regional Relations Commissariat, the New Common Agricultural Policy police, the Citizens Charter Complaints Council, Nationalist Symbols Squad (Flags Division), the Directive Implementation Commission, the Family Policy Enforcement Agency, Customs & Excise, the Sexual Hygiene Inspectorate, the Milk Inspectorate, the Differently-Abled Entitlement Bureau, O.F.W.A.T., O.F.A.T.G.A.S. (that one made him spit) and of course O.F.S.E.X.

CourtroomChannel 44 were showing a repeat of *Snell of the Yard: His Finest Moments*, clips of the bewigged *flic* solving crime after crime and invariably employing his moronic catchphrase, "I'm thinking aloud here."

Horatio switched back to JobsChannel 88 and saw yet more ads, this time for the Common Language Commission, the

Five-Year Plan Office, the Sandhurst Military Academy Gay and Lesbian Awareness Course Instructor Unit, the Cholesterol Curtailment Commission, the Private Roads Ombudsman, the V.A.T. Inspectorate, the Welsh Relations Bureau, the Blood Sports Vigilance Unit, the Competitive Sports Abatement Department of the Education Commission, the Neighbourhood Watch Denouncement Scheme, and so on and so on and so on.

The next channel was entirely devoted to America's Death Row. Televised executions had proved so popular that the Cultural Defence Directive had had to be amended to permit the import from A.F.T.A. of these gruesome vids. Long interviews with the condemned men's families, then the victims' families, the pastor, the electricians and so on, were the stock in trade of SnuffChannel 666.

Switching over quickly, Horatio found it quite hard to understand how a show on one of the porntainment channels could have passed the rules prohibiting fornication before the 18.00 watershed. It featured powerful, semi-nude super-women wrestling with each other to the lascivious cheers of a huge crowd in the Birmingham Velodrome Centre's teeming stadium. The show combined blatant lechery with exquisite sadism. Horatio was both bemused and titillated. He assumed the programme-makers were bribing the censors to let it on so early. Then he realised he was watching the popular show *Gladiators 2045*. It had changed a lot since he was a boy.

AdsChannel 104 was a revelation, too. He particularly enjoyed the one for the Princess Diana Clinic in Palm Beach. If you could somehow wangle an A.F.T.A. visa and a flight to California you were promised, for a mere seventy-five thousand dollars per week, courses which included (in alphabetical order): Anger Release Therapy, Clairvoyancy,

Colonic Irrigation, Crystals, Hypnotherapy, Female Assertion, Kick-Boxing, Liposuction, Mind Irrigation, Reflexology,
Seances (ouija board supplied), Sexual Abstinence Therapy
(optional), Tarot Card Reading, Telephone Assertion (costs
extra), Thai Boxing and, the most popular, Zen Buddhism.
The complete twelve-volume Princess Di Workout and
Homeopathy Vid Collection was thrown in free.

At least the cable, however proley and ghastly it was, took
Horatio's mind off what was going to happen the next day. He
knew, though, that he was going to be tested as never in his life
before. He had gone over it again and again as he lay in the dark
at night and during the power cuts. He would show his mother
how wrong she had been about him. He would do this himself.
She'd opposed the plan point blank when he'd first suggested
it, but he'd insisted, called Cradock at the Embassy and
arranged the rendezvous. If his life was going to be on the line
he would organise things his way. He had refused to let Tenth
May collect the Memorandum for him. He had told them he
was going to pick it up himself on Saturday morning and put it
to its greatest possible use. It was the right, the only, thing to
do. But the knowledge still left him with a fetid, incontinent
fear.

25

09.40 Saturday, 8th May

As arranged, Horatio left Brunswick Gardens and made his way on foot, neurotic as ever that the cameras had picked him up or that he was being followed by someone other than Riley, towards the Brompton Oratory.

The 10.00 service had just started. As soon as he entered the church he saw that an old man was already occupying the seat in the twelfth pew. There was plenty of space around, so he could hardly ask him to budge along. Anyhow, the old boy was praying.

A priest standing at the altar was intoning the Vatican Three Liturgy: "Jesus the Significant One, who sits at the mighty hand of GOD, the Father-Mother," he said, in a voice which implied that he did not like the new language at all, "and who has a very real and significant status in our hearts . . ."

Horatio genuflected before the thirteenth pew, slid in and knelt directly in front of the man. He put his hands behind his back and felt around for the tape.

It wasn't there.

He felt again. Nothing.

Desperation mounting, Horatio dropped a two-euro piece on the marble floor and, ostensibly to retrieve it, crouched down and looked under the pew.

There it was, slightly to the left of where he had been groping. Detaching the chewing gum proved messy but not difficult. By the time he left the pew and genuflected again, the old man, disturbed from his devotions, was staring with a mixture of *hauteur* and quizzical interest. Entering an antique confessional in the ante-chapel on the right, Horatio checked it and slipped the tape over into his jacket pocket, still sticky with detox gum.

Before leaving the church Horatio said a short prayer along the lines of Sir Jacob Astley's before the Battle of Edgehill: "O Lord, thou knowest how busy I must be this day: if I forget thee, do not thou forget me." It felt appropriate. Pausing only to nod to the altar when he reached the door, he walked out.

Moving fast down the Brompton Road on the opposite side from the Harrods Ultra-Shopping Experience & Al-Fayed Mausoleum, Horatio saw an old lady bent double with shopping. She was trying to cross Montpelier Place, but the autos weren't stopping. The Youth Euro-Leaguer in him took over. Without thinking, he asked her whether he could be of any assistance. As soon as he spoke he regretted it. She flung back her head and screamed at the top of her (astonishingly loud) voice, "Proud to be a Golden-Ager! Ageism alert! Proud to be a Twilighter! Help! I'm being patronised! Help!" Passers-by started looking across at them.

Horatio dashed across the Brompton Road traffic, turned right at Harrods and didn't stop running until he reached Herbert Crescent, where he had to take several long pulls on his inhaler. He thanked his stars no communitarian-minded citizen had chased him. Instead, there had been a stream of foul-mouthed abuse. What an idiot he'd been! Had he been arrested, or even cautioned, under the Ageist or Minority Patronisation legislation he would have been recognised and the entire, minutely timed plan would have been hopelessly compromised.

The route he took to the Haymarket was convoluted. He assumed he was being followed as arranged, but he couldn't spot Riley. After five minutes he began to worry that he might have lost him, then that he'd been captured, then that he was really a P.I.D. informant and was only waiting for him to pick up the tape before destroying it. And him.

He went into a Boots *apothekari* in Sloane Street for another Salbutamol cartridge, pausing by the pill counter. Should he get something to help steady the nerves and keep his adrenalin under control? A little Minuszac perhaps?

No. Those days were over. He was on his own now.

When all this was behind him, he promised himself once more, he would go back to All Souls and study quietly for his biography of Henry Percy, the seventeenth-century "Wizard Earl" of Northumberland, and never even so much as venture forth into the High or the Broad.

It was 10.29 before, by a combination of tram, taxi and walking, including several visits to large department stores and back-door exits – once via the kitchens of the vast Trocadero Sauerkrautorium where the smell of onions had him salivating like one of Dr Pavlov's spaniels – Horatio finally reached a huge glass-fronted building on the corner of Haymarket and Pall Mall.

Just as he was about to push open the Embassy's vast doors a voice he recognised called to him from across the street.

"Horatio! Stop!"

Cleo was running towards him. She was waving and shouting. She was wearing black, and even at fifty metres she looked sexier than anyone he had ever seen before. She was gesticulating vigorously and yelling "Stop! Horatio! Stop!" at the top of her voice.

In the split second in which Horatio hesitated, a tall blond man stepped out from the shadow of the doorway of the Berliner Bank across the street. He raised a machine-pistol to eye level and fired.

A woman's scream from close by told Horatio that Tallboys had missed him but hit a passer-by. Her shriek of shock and terror galvanised even Horatio's torpid physical faculties.

A second later a tram came around the corner of Pall Mall. Its windows were strafed with bullets. Horatio pulled the Embassy door open. A series of shots smashed into it at head height. One slammed into the glass ten centimetres from his ear. Amazingly it didn't shatter, but ten-foot cracks forked down it like Mediterranean midsummer lightning.

Horatio flung himself inside, sprawling onto the marble floor. There was commotion in the lobby. Two armed guards who had seen what had happened had already cocked their N-series machine guns.

As he looked up, Horatio saw they were pointed at *him*.

Visible through the glass to everyone in the foyer was the mayhem in the street. The gurgling shopper lay on the pavement, blood coursing from her mouth. The tram had slammed to a halt outside, its passengers lying in broken glass on the floor, screaming.

Horatio saw Cleo standing by Tallboys. They were both shouting. Then they ran off towards Pall Mall.

No one in the foyer moved. Least of all Horatio, who was sitting on the floor with his hands on his head. Then an authoritative voice was shouting, "Make way! Get out of my way!" A burly, fair-haired man in his early thirties was pushing through the mob of frightened visa applicants, secretaries and attachés. He walked over to Horatio and asked, in a broad antipodean accent, "Password?"

"Monty." Horatio's idea.

"We've been expecting you. Follow me." The guards reluctantly raised their guns. Horatio got up and trotted off at the New Zealander's heels down a series of long corridors.

"Lyle Cradock, second i/c Security," the man called over his shoulder, striding forward at speed. "You're late. We waited as long as we could but H.M. had to leave." Horatio started to burble. "Don't bother explaining a thing, I know exactly what's going on."

"But I thought ten-thirty was the agreed time." Cradock checked his chunky diver's watch. A real H.R.G. at last, thought Horatio with relief.

"It's ten thirty-six. His Majesty couldn't wait any longer. For cable tie-in reasons he's got to begin his speech at eleven hundred sharp."

Horatio, skipping along at Cradock's heels, was already out of breath. He couldn't get out of his mind the sight of the shopper clutching at her neck, the blood spitting from between her fingers. From the bullet which was meant for him. At least he was safe now.

"Has he read the Memorandum?" Cradock stopped by some lift doors and pressed a button.

"Yes, and he's shocked. He's agreed to play it in his speech. *If* you can get the tape to him. He doesn't see there's any proof or point otherwise. Unsubstantiated allegations would do more harm than good in this political climate."

"But how can we do that?" Horatio assumed that he was not expected to leave the safety of the Embassy after everything that had just happened.

"By driving bloody fast."

"What? Where? To Hyde Park?"

"Yes, of course."

"Now?"

"When else?"

"I don't drive."

"I do."

"But there are two people outside – at least two, there may be more – who want to kill me. This wasn't mentioned in our agreement. You're supposed to get me to Auckland by diplomatic container. That was meant to be the end of it all."

"I know. But now we've no other course." The lift doors opened. They stepped inside. Horatio saw Cradock jab "G" with his forefinger. As they went down a pulse gun appeared from Cradock's shoulder holster. Horatio saw his thumb flick the switch on the butt from Stun to Kill. His resolution turned to water.

"Why am I needed? Must I come?"

As soon as he'd said it, Horatio realised how cowardly it sounded. How cowardly it was. Almost before the last word left his mouth he wanted to correct himself. But he didn't. His fear was talking. Loud and clear. But Cradock didn't seem to be listening.

The lift doors opened and they walked out into an underground garage. Cradock turned around. His innocent-abroad blue eyes stared straight into Horatio's conscience, ransacking it. He counted the reasons off on his fingers.

"One, only you can identify the enemy. Two, I can't get to Hyde Park on my own in the time. I don't know this city well enough yet. Three, someone has to find the right passage in the tape. You can do that on the stereo. Four, we need a bloke up in the control room to make sure the speech isn't simply switched off. Tenth May have got one of their people in there, but every extra counts. It was down to you that my boss Colonel Upham moved H.M. to safety during the Entente incident. Now we've got to finish the job." He looked at his watch. "It's gone 10.37. Let's move." Horatio moved nowhere.

"Who's their man? Do you have his real name? I'll need it once I'm there."

"James Longman." Wadham College, Horatio remembered.

"I know him." He was at the party on Friday night. The one Mike Hibbert said had lain doggo ever since getting married to a Spaniard.

"Well, he's one of us and he'll be in the control room." That, thought Horatio, was the very first piece of good news today. He skipped behind Cradock's fast stride into the underlit garage.

"We need surprise," said Cradock, "and speed. Half of Europol will be on their way here after that performance upstairs. I'm going to drive straight up that ramp onto Pall Mall. You direct me after that. We'll be going very fast."

Horatio nodded miserably. His conscience and courage, which should have been throbbing, healthy, full-blooded organs, were, he realised, just shrivelled, yellow little walnuts. He despised himself.

It was as they approached the auto that Horatio recognised the grey grade 2 petrol.

"Whose auto's this?" he demanded.

"What? Never mind that. Get in."

"I said, whose auto is this?"

"One of your operatives," answered Cradock. "Come on, for Chrissake, or we won't make it!" Horatio stayed stock still.

His mind was whirring. The right-side wing mirror even had a slight dent in the front.

"Who? Whose operative?"

"Tenth May, of course."

"Who in Tenth May? I need a name!" He was shouting, surprising himself with his ferocity.

"Code name JACOBITE. Don't know the real one. Come on!"

"No way. I'm not getting in. Someone driving this car has tried to kill me. For all I know it might have been you. I want some answers."

He slipped his hand into his pocket and his finger into the trigger ring of Jean's gun. Rivulets of sweat were running down all the way down from his armpit to the gun.

"It was brought here last Sunday. We were asked to take it on. It was hot. We were going to dismantle it and lose it in pieces around the city. As you can see, it's the only halfway fast auto here. Now get in." Not an entreaty, still less a threat. Just an order.

Horatio did. Fearful and suspicious, he took a look in the back. No clues.

Cradock pressed a switch to open the Embassy garage gates. Shoving his feet hard down both on the brake and the accelerator, he revved the engine hard and loud.

As the garage doors swung up, a man dashed in under them. Tallboys. He stared around the garage, machine pistol in hand. His eyes accustomed themselves to the dingy garage from the bright sunshine outside. Swinging around in the direction of the revving car engine he caught sight of Horatio in the front seat. He smiled.

Horatio realised he was locked with a stranger in an enemy's auto in a deserted basement garage carrying the

Memorandum, whilst a homicidal maniac was taking aim at him with a machine-pistol.

"That's him!" he shouted, pointing. Cradock let off the handbrake and screeched the ten metres straight at Tallboys, who had time only to fire a short burst before flinging himself against the garage wall. He shot out the lights, but the radiator and windscreen were unscathed.

Hitting the ramp at speed, the auto flew up and landed in Pall Mall. Missing two cars by their paintwork, Cradock flung the car into a sharp right and sped off fast.

He took Pall Mall at well over 100 k.p.h. overtaking on the inside, ignoring lights. Horatio turned in his seat to see Tallboys sprint out of the garage, leap into the passenger seat of a waiting auto and wing off after them.

"Left here!" he yelled, as they got to the St James' Museum. The auto behind had attached a magnetic siren and flashing light to its roof. The noise of the shot, the screeching tyres and now the banshee police siren nearly sent Horatio into a terror-trance.

"Whack on that tape!" yelled Cradock, punching him hard on the shoulder to rouse him.

"Sharp right here towards Attali House!" pointed Horatio. Ignoring the red light and oncoming traffic and blaring the horn, Cradock swung right as they reached St James' Park and shot off towards the Charlemagne statue in front of the Bank.

"Off right when you get there!" Horatio pointed towards Hyde Park Corner.

He looked behind him, praying that Tallboys hadn't managed to negotiate the oncoming traffic. But not only had the driver – who Horatio didn't need a second glance to see was Cleo – accelerated between two lorries, but Tallboys was now leaning out of the passenger window, gun in hand.

His first volley of shots smashed the back window, sending broken glass flying around the inside of the car.

"Get to work!" shouted Cradock. As they sped up Constitution Hill, Horatio, crouching low in his seat, turned up the volume and fast-forwarded the Admiral's tape past the Beethoven and the opening words "*Testing, Testing*." Then he clicked it out, put it in its case and shoved it back in his jacket pocket.

Tallboys' next burst of shots sent shards of rear-view mirror ripping into Cradock's cheek, neck and shoulder. Blood spattered across Horatio's face. It was like being sprayed with warm soup.

"Over the roundabout and up there!" Horatio yelled, pointing up Park Lane. The Lanesborough Hotel, Arafat Statue and Apsley Class-Harmony Centre each flew past in quick succession. Then up Park Lane.

They could no longer hear Cleo's siren. Horatio looked behind. Where were they?

Cradock stopped by the Dorchester. He was losing blood fast. There was no sign of Cleo's auto.

Retching, Horatio tried to remove a piece of mirror from Cradock's cheek. He didn't dare touch the neck.

"We'll get you into the hotel. They'll have someone who can see to you there." Cradock pushed him off.

"Forget that. No time. Take my pass." He gestured to the chain around his neck with its plastic I.D. Traces of blood were appearing on his lips from inside his mouth.

"This?"

"Yes. Password's 'Wavell'." Cradock coughed as blood filled his oesophagus. "Got that?"

"Wavell."

"Get out. Go to the V.I.P. tent. See Upham. Now!"

Horatio pulled the card over Cradock's head, leapt out, crossed the road and lost himself in the huge crowd strolling towards Speakers' Corner.

The electronic clock above the stage, five hundred metres away, read 10.44.

Not enough time.

26

10.44 Saturday, 8th May

Horatio pushed his way, agonisingly slowly, through the vast, happy crowd.

"Excuse me, excuse me," he said, as he picked his way between small children and picnic rugs. There must be two hundred thousand people here, he thought. Most of them, he guessed, making a mildly pro-nat statement, paying homage to their ancestral Pretender-King and having a sunny anti-Establishment Saturday morning into the bargain. Very few, he imagined, could really be motivated by commemorating a war which ended a century ago. The last veterans of it had died off in the Twenties, now none but centenarians could even remember the immediate post-war period. Yet English people of all ages were turning up in their tens of thousands.

Horatio fought his way, shoving and pushing, towards the V.I.P. area beside the vast stage. Cleo and Tallboys would guess where he was heading. The bitch seemed to know everything.

He was sweating and feeling his heart palpitations. He tried to wipe Cradock's blood off his face and clothes as he walked. Would Cradock be OK? Should he have left him? Would his own Salbutamol hold out? He had the refill cartridge in his jacket pocket but ...

It was 10.51 before he reached the tent. A security guard in a scarlet tunic carrying an R-201 machine gun stepped forward.

"Wavell! Wavell!" panted Horatio.

"Yer name's Wavell? Wavell who? Who do you want to see?"

"No, *my* name's not Wavell." He gasped for breath. "The password's Wavell."

"What password?"

"The sodding password to get past you to see the King," he gasped. His throat felt horribly constricted. It was starting to throb. He knew the symptoms. He pulled out the Salbutamol and sucked hard three times. It wasn't helping.

The guard shot a look to a younger colleague, who had come over to see what was going on. They'd already been warned of a terrorist incident outside the New Zealand Embassy, and news was coming in over the intercom of an auto, registered stolen, which had been abandoned on Park Lane. An unidentified man had been found dead inside and there were reports of a short, fat, non-ethnic male escaping the scene. Embassy Security were thus in no mood to indulge jokers or nutters.

By now Horatio was wheezing, in serious pain and close to tears. He pulled Cradock's card from his jacket pocket and showed them it. Both guards knew Cradock well. They saw the blood on Horatio's shirt and jacket. Then they recognised him.

"Hands up! Spreadeagle yer legs! Keep your hands apart and up where we can see 'em!" The first man jabbed the machine-gun muzzle into Horatio's stomach, winding him. The other one removed Jean's gun and ammo clips from his pockets.

"Jeez!" he whistled. Horatio was struggling for breath, but

he couldn't reach for his inhaler again in case they thought he
was going for a concealed weapon. Neither could he tell them
what was wrong. He just went purple in the face.

The first guard detached a crackling two-way from his
epaulette and spoke fast into it.

"Colonel Upham, sir. Assassination suspect at main V.I.P.!
I've recognised him, too. It's the terrorist, the Channel Bridge
one. Carrying a weapon! Bit antique, but it's loaded. He was
attempting to impersonate Lyle Cradock, sir. He wanted to
get to the King. There's blood all over him. Repeat: probable
assassination attempt! We've got him though. Gold Star Alert!
This is not, repeat *not* a practice. Over."

"We'll be there right away," replied a voice over the two-
way. "Watch out for any others. Good work. Over and out."

Horatio was choking and faint. His hands were up on the
canvas wall of the V.I.P. reception room. The winding had left
him nauseous, vulnerable and demoralised.

"I need my inhaler," he croaked.

"Frisk 'im, Joe," said the older of the men.

"Turn out yer pockets." Horatio did as he was told. "Right
out." He did, and his I.D., pen, inhaler, extra Salbutamol
cartridge and five two-euro pieces fell out onto the ground, to
be studied by the younger guard. He was given back the
inhaler which he clasped and sucked on hard. The older guard
switched on the pager.

"Yup, it's Lestoq all right. We're gonna be famous Joe."
Miraculously the tape, still sticky with gum, stayed attached to
his pocket lining, out of sight. After an eternity, in which
Horatio prayed the tape would continue to defy gravity, Joe
said, "OK. Keep facing the wall. You can stick 'em back now,
all except the pager." Horatio flicked his pocket linings back in

and bent down to pick everything else up off the floor. As he did so he heard people sprinting up behind him.

"Turn around." There were two of them.

Horatio blinked.

Could it be?

27

10.55 Saturday, 8th May

Affecting not to recognise him, Marty, gun in hand and without even a clandestine wink, barked, "Who are you?"

Should he play Marty's game? Could this be a second Get-Out-Of-Gaol-Free card?

"Horatio Lestoq," he said in as quiet and dignified a voice as possible. The breath was coming easier now.

"The man wanted by Europol?"

"Yes."

"In connection with the Entente Bridge outrage?"

"Amongst other things I'm innocent of, yes."

"What are you doing here?"

"I need to speak to the King. Now. Before he makes his speech."

"Why?"

"I need to give him something."

"What?"

It was his last hope.

"Wavell."

"What did you say?" It was the other man. A Kiwi by the sound of him. Horatio could not quite make out the badge on his lapel. "What did you say just then?"

"I said Wavell. It's the password. Only these gozos hadn't heard of it."

"No one but Cradock, His Majesty and I know it." He turned to Marty. "This puts a *very* different complexion on matters. I've got orders about what to do with anyone, and I was told *anyone*, who came here and gave that password." Marty walked over to the corner of the room and beckoned the New Zealander over.

They stood for about half a minute and from the looks Horatio was able to shoot over they were arguing hard. Then they returned. The New Zealander spoke first, asking Horatio, "Do you know this man?"

Marty had started this non-recognition ploy, whatever it was for. He'd better stick to it.

"No."

"OK Horror, it's all right," said Marty. "You can tell him the truth now." Horatio took a long look at Marty and shook his head.

"No. I don't think I've ever seen you before. What's your name?"

"For Christ's sake, Horror! You can snap out of it now." He sounded as if he meant it, but Horatio was not about to give away whatever Marty's game had been.

"No, honestly, I don't recognise you. I'm sorry."

"Right," said the New Zealander, "that settles it." He turned to Marty. "You must be mistaken. You're stressed. It's understandable." He turned to the guards. "Frisked him thoroughly?" They nodded. "Right, come with me." They took a few paces towards the corridor, Marty following. The Kiwi turned round. "You'd better stay here. We need maximum protection against any confederates who might attack here."

"I think I should come along too," said Marty. "In case he tries anything."

"It's quite all right, I can take care of him."

"He's a proven killer. Colonel, I insist."

"Thanks, but no. I can cope. Stay here. All right, Lestoq, you go first. Down there." Marty looked at the other guards and shrugged.

Horatio again felt an intense, bowel-loosening fear. He was going down a long corridor with another complete stranger who was armed and walking directly behind him. Marty had been left behind. What would stop the Kiwi just shooting him in the back there and then? They walked quickly and in silence until they reached a small, sparse, functional office. There was a desk, chair and a wall clock.

10.58.

The Kiwi closed the door behind him.

"The name's Upham, Bill Upham, I'm i/c Security, N.Z. Embassy. Give me the Memorandum, Dr Lestoq. I'll take it in to His Majesty. Then pick up Frobisher and go straight to the control tower in front of the stage. It's the tall building on stilts about fifty metres from here. You must protect it against any attempts to shut down His Majesty's speech. He's about to go on any minute." He held out his left hand for the tape, still holding the gun in the right.

"No."

"What?" Upham looked astonished.

"You heard. No. I don't trust anyone any longer."

"For God's sake!"

"I'll give it to the King himself. No one else does."

"This is absurd. There's no time left for this."

"Him and him alone."

There was a pause. Upham levelled a stare into Horatio's

eyes that would have shamed a pimp or a politician. Horatio returned it defiantly. Before it turned into a silence, Upham looked at the clock just as it clicked 10.59.

"Follow me." He led the way through two more doors and past three further sets of security guards.

Half a minute later they were standing in the presence of a tall, handsome, sandy-haired man. He was wearing old-fashioned naval uniform, complete with gold braid up to the elbow. Horatio was immediately reminded of the statue of Charles III at Madame Tussaud's, which he had once seen on a school trip just before it was removed under Democratisation Directive 56/789. The man was accompanied by four other people in suits. Upham stepped forward.

"Your Majesty, may I present Horatio Lestoq?"

Horatio bowed from the neck and wondered what to do next. What should he call him? "Sir", "Sire", "Your Royal Highness"? The Commission had directed that Mr Mountbatten-Windsor was to be the correct form of address during the visit, but that would hardly be appropriate.

"Ah yes, the famous Dr Lestoq. You have something for me, I believe?" The voice had that clipped, *pukkah*, regal timbre made famous by a score of broadcasts zealously picked up by the public every Christmas despite the Information Commission's annual jamming attempts.

"Your Majesty." Covered closely by Upham, Horatio detached the tape container from his jacket pocket lining and handed it over. The King then took a small recorder from his pocket. He took the tape from its case, inserted it, and pressed "Play" with his thumb. A detached, ethereal voice filled the hush: "*This is Admiral Michael Ratcliffe speaking at 18.00 . . .*" He switched it off, rewound for a half a second and pressed "Stop".

"Very good. Very good indeed. Well done."

The King, whom Horatio by now had time to notice was in his early sixties, about one metre ninety and as striking as his photos, was wearing the full dress uniform of a British Admiral of the Fleet *circa* 2015. The diamonds of the Garter star glistened on his breast.

"And the rest is exactly as it is in the transcript which was paged to Mr Upham on Thursday?"

"Yes, sir, precisely the same."

"And you believe the allegations made in it?"

"With all my heart."

"I see. Well, after this is all over, we will want to hear the full story of how you came by it. As you may know our intelligence people – specifically Messrs Upham and Cradock – have been working with people like your agent JACOBITE for some years now. They have been looking for just such . . . information as you have produced. At no small risk to yourself I understand." Horatio nodded in what he hoped looked like modesty. "Now at last this appalling deception which was perpetrated upon our people can be revealed. You're a very brave man, Lestoq. If we had any more time" – he looked at his watch – "which I see we haven't, I would be tempted to knight you here on the spot. On the field of battle, as it were!" He flashed the famous Mountbatten-Windsor smile. Horatio felt strangely light-headed. Small wonder, he thought, that the Commission feared this man's charisma; it was even working on a hard-hearted cynic like himself.

"Thank you sir. But I have to tell you that I believe Cradock might be dead now. From wounds sustained after an attack by two operatives of Europol's Political Intelligence Department." Horatio could sense the King's pain.

"Another of our finest. When this visit was arranged we

were promised complete protection for myself and my entourage. First came the attack on the Bridge. Now this."

"I don't believe you should go out there, sir. The people who tried to kill me are fanatics. They'll know, or at least they'll guess, that you have the tape now. They'll never let you play it."

The King twisted a cufflink with his fingers. It was a mannerism Horatio recognised as one of his father's trade-marks.

"My people have come to see me," he said, slowly and deliberately, turning to the others in the room, "and it would be an act of cowardice to disappoint them now. They would never understand it. Besides, we have waited twenty-eight years for today. I'll be speaking from inside a large transparent box which my security people have brought over from Auckland. I've seen it tested, it's quite remarkable. Both bomb- and bullet-proof." Then he added, with that engaging, Hugh Grant grin made famous by a million magazine covers, "Anyhow, I have to go sometime, and frankly I can't think of a much better way to do it than while revealing the facts of this appalling betrayal to my people and the world."

A clock struck 11.00. Good-natured chanting could be heard from outside, growing louder and louder.

"We want the King!"

11.02 Saturday, 8th May

Horatio and Bill Upham picked up Marty at the entrance and pushed their way out. The astonished security guards returned Horatio's pulse gun at the V.I.P. gate, and the three men shoved through the thick crowds towards the control tower.

"Tallboys was in your flat on Wednesday," Horatio shouted to Marty as they went.

"I know," Marty called back over his shoulder, "they've given it a right going-over. They stole my vid and photo albums and a lot of other stuff. From the look of the job it was the same lot who did over the Rectory."

"Did they get my file disc?" asked Horatio.

"How did you know about that?" They pushed harder through the mass of bodies in the crowd.

"Cleo said."

"Did she? The answer's no, I burnt it."

A great cheer went up from the crowd as the President of the V-E Centenary Committee appeared on stage, along with half a dozen other people who took their seats around the box from which the King was due to speak.

As they reached the bottom of the tower Horatio looked

up. He remembered seeing a documentary about its construction. Built by the Millennium Fund from Lottery money back in 2000, the eyesore had been described as "a hideous perspex shoe-box on stilts" by King William's father. Set on four steel legs thirty metres above the ground, it consisted of a single room about twelve metres square. All the film, vid-audio electronics, amplification, cable and recording equipment for the stage and Park was operated from a huge panel covered in switches and dials. Its darkened, one-way glasspex windows facing the stage rendered the room completely soundproof against all noise coming in or out.

Usually used to record pop concerts and Euro-Youth rallies, the tower transmitted what was happening on the stage to the outside world. All the cameras and sound systems from around the Park were subject to its overall editorial control. It was thus the only place where both the cable transmission and the microphones for the speech could be cut dead. Horatio appreciated immediately why the conspirators could not be allowed to take it.

As they approached the middle-aged security guard at the bottom of the sole lift, Horatio caught sight of Penelope Aldritt standing in the crowd. She was speaking into her pager. She must be one of those covering the rally for Weaning, he thought. Taking Gemma's place.

He ducked down behind Upham as he passed. It was definitely her, he couldn't have missed that nose. Had she seen *him* though? He didn't think so. There were three or four people between them. But the cow was easily clever enough not to let him realise if she had.

Marty gave a password to the uniformed guard, whose short hair, flat nose and boxer's ears rang a bell somewhere in Horatio's memory.

"Have a man and a woman been in here anytime in the last half-hour?" asked Marty. "She's tall, dark, greeny-blue eyes. He's taller, blond, blue eyes, well-built. Both late twenties/ early thirties. They could be posing as electricians or sound technicians. They'd both have full I.D. security clearance."

The guard, whom Horatio thought looked too old for the job, answered very definitely, "No one's come in during the last hour, sir. There are two electrical engineers up there at the minute, but they're both male and they've been here since 08.00." One would be James Longman, Horatio thought, relieved.

"Fine. If anyone answering those descriptions should try to come up, arrest them both and call me immediately. Shoot first if necessary."

"Fine." He smiled.

"I mean it. They're ruthless."

"Don't worry, sir," he said, tapping the N-series slung over his shoulder and winking, "so am I." The gesture should have made Horatio feel more comfortable, but somehow it didn't. The man's mouth had smiled all right, but his small eyes hadn't.

Marty, Upham and Horatio took the lift.

"There's one thing I don't understand," Upham asked Marty as they reached the control room, "why did you pretend not to recognise Dr Lestoq just now?"

"I'm glad you asked me that . . ." answered Marty, but before he could finish the sentence the lift doors opened and a shot punched straight between Upham's eyebrows. The bullet's entry hole was tiny and clean, but skull and grey matter were splattered all over the back of the lift as the body itself slumped to the floor.

Horatio flung himself to the ground, his hands over his head.

"You *bloody fool*" someone screamed. "I told you how to deal with it."

It was Cleo. Furious. Horatio tentatively looked up and saw Tallboys standing in front of the lift, pulse-gun in hand and a glint in his eyes as cool, hard and sparkling as the diamonds on the King's Garter star.

"Sorry." Tallboys did not look it. "I thought it was on Stun. I'd no idea . . ." Then he continued, illogically, "Plus I didn't know if Lestoq was armed." Cleo walked over, bent down and took Horatio's gun from his pocket. He got up, ignored.

"You're lying. You enjoy it. If you thought it was on Stun why did you hit him straight between the eyes? Professional pride? Give me that."

Tallboys handed over the gun. Cleo flicked the switch on the base of the butt and returned it. Horatio stood up.

"You are not — repeat *not* — to switch this onto 'Kill' without my permission." He nodded, crestfallen. She held out her hand. "Clean the lift. Get him out and use his jacket."

Tallboys hauled Upham's corpse out of the lift by the feet and then stripped off its check jacket. Horatio looked the other way, trying to concentrate on what was going on outside. Tallboys then steppèd inside the lift and the doors automatically closed behind him.

"Agent Frobisher. Come here." Cleo signalled Marty over with her gun. He walked towards her slowly. She kept it pointed at his heart. Even Horatio knew that a direct shot at the heart, even only a stun, could induce a coronary. "Closer," she said, "closer . . ." She took a swift look behind her to check the lift doors were shut, then a short step forward and, putting her gun hand behind his head, drew his face to hers.

They kissed. Passionately.

Horatio closed his eyes. Think logically. Fear, bewilderment, anger and frustration were all vying for the upper hand, but right now he just needed pure thought. He scanned the room. A lone soundman wearing headphones was flicking switches and busily organising the lighting and sound on the stage in front. Horatio could not tell if he was a conspirator too. Then the soundman turned round and locked eyes with Horatio. Hardly more than a boy, he was clearly petrified. From the scarcely comprehending look of terror on his face it was obvious he would do anything Cleo told him.

A man was lying sprawled on the floor in the corner. James Longman. Either stunned or dead, Horatio couldn't make out which. It didn't much matter. He had been Horatio's last hope.

"So tell me," Cleo asked Marty after they had at last disentangled. "What happened?"

"You wouldn't believe it. I'd been there for hours when Fatso arrived, but as soon as he did, Glory Boy there" – Marty gesticulated with his thumb towards Upham's corpse – "took him off me and in to see Rex. There was nothing I could do."

"So Rex has it?"

"I suppose so. Probably in micro form. I asked the guards. He had nothing on him."

"Shit!"

"I know."

"Couldn't you just have out-took Fatso and Glory Boy together?"

"There were two other guards there. I asked to go along with them so that I could try something like that in the corridor, but he ordered me to stay there on the lookout for you and Bonehead. How is he, by the way?" Cleo smiled and kissed Marty on the end of his nose. The lift doors were still closed.

"Jealous as ever."

"How did Fatso get here so quickly? I thought you were going to detain him in Commission Square."

"He went to the Embassy instead. By the time Bonehead,.as I wish you wouldn't call him as he *is* still my husband . . ."

"Not for much longer . . ."

". . . got Riley to tell him what was going on, I was still at the Santer Statue. Needless to say, Alex caused maximum mayhem in Haymarket and we had to follow Fatso and the junior Glory Boy, who were in the same auto that you delivered to the Kiwis on Sunday."

"So where's he?"

"After I stopped the chase to head off here, I sent Alex off in search but he couldn't find him. We've just heard from Sigint that he died in the auto." Marty whistled. Horatio felt nauseous again. Poor Lyle.

Marty, thought Horatio. Marty who had had the gloves and torches ready in his auto. Marty who wiped the Percival conversation from his pager. Marty at whose party he'd been picked up by Cleo. Marty who'd advised him to "drop it", or to flee to Norway. His best mate ever since his first day at school.

Cleo turned to Horatio.

"Come here, you." She frisked him, removing the Admiral's letter from his inside pocket. She continued frisking under his armpits. Then around his belly. When she got further down she grabbed his crotch and gave it a savage twist and then a tug. He yelped. She laughed exactly that happy, innocent laugh he'd loved hearing only a week ago. Then she took his inhaler from his pocket, held it up for a second between her thumb and forefinger and dropped it on the floor. She made as if to grind it beneath the heel of her knee-length black suede boot. Doom leered in Horatio's face. Just as her foot was about to descend, she asked, "Did you give the Memorandum to the King?"

"No."

"You're lying, of course." Her heel nudged the top of the inhaler. Even so much as a crack would render it useless. And him in mortal danger. "Because otherwise it'd be on you."

"It's being brought up here by someone, to be played over the sound-system when the King gives the signal."

"Who?"

Horatio thought quickly. Knowledge gave him a chance of survival. Ignorance none at all.

"JACOBITE."

A flash of recognition crossed her face. She nodded to Marty, "Tenth May code for the P.I.D. traitor who works for the nats. The one the Kiwis think is you." She turned back to Horatio.

"And who, if I may be the one to ask the bleeding obvious, is JACOBITE?"

"I don't know. I was also led to believe it was Marty."

"Who did you meet on Thursday at the safe house?"

"No one I knew." How could she know about that?

"I'd tell her if I were you," said Marty sardonically, "as there's a good chance she might hurt you otherwise."

"Oh no, I'm not going to hurt you my love." She paused, theatrically. "Alex has asked whether he can. I think this time I'll indulge him."

As if on cue, the lift doors opened and the cretin reappeared, grinning. Horatio again experienced the same brain-freezing terror he'd felt in the Embassy garage.

"Alex, the Memorandum might be being brought here. It's

probably in tape form. Go back down and tell Frank to let the person up, so long as he gives us plenty of warning like last time." Even through his terror Horatio could still feel Cleo's sexual allure. And her intelligence. She had outwitted him every single time.

"Cover Fatso will you?" she said to Marty as she opened the Admiral's letter.

"Why are you doing this?" Horatio wanted to end the sentence "Judas", but it was Marty who was holding the gun.

"Duty. Patriotism. We're trying to build a country here. You used to understand about those things before you started getting mixed up with nats and conspiring against the Union." No point arguing then.

"Why get me out of jail and take me to the Rectory if your boys had already searched the place?"

"Because we hadn't found anything, for all the fun we had. I needed you to trust me enough to give me the Memorandum once the Admiral had got it to you, by whichever means the crafty old bugger had thought up."

Cleo finished. She handed the letter to Marty.

"Interesting as a historical footnote I suppose, but it alters nothing. Except of course that we've committed incest, which sounds gloriously decadent, doesn't it? A new one that, even for me!" The giggle struck Horatio as satanic. Marty looked up, galled. She continued, "Of course, it *also* means I'm soon going to be committing fratricide if you don't tell me who you met on Thursday."

Both rooms filled with the opening remarks of the Chair of the V-E Day Centenary Commemoration Committee, spoken in a crisp, pre-Classlessness Queen's accent.

"*Ladies and gentlemen*" – a phrase not often heard – "*It is hugely gratifying to see so many of you here today. Europol, never very keen to exaggerate our numbers"* — the crowd laughed good-naturedly — *"estimates us at around a hundred and fifty thousand. You can therefore assume we really number at least a quarter of a million. Not bad for a rally which, courtesy of the Information Commission, has received virtually no coverage in the national media."*

There was a burst of applause, probably more at the sound of the severely discouraged word "national" than the President's predictable sentiments. This was clearly going to be as subversive a mass meeting as any of the recent ones in the North. There were Union Jacks flying in the middle of the crowd, which the authorities did not seem to be doing anything about, beyond photographing the culprits from the Europol choppers hovering overhead. Some helium-filled Union Jack balloons had been released and were floating merrily above the crowd, a standing rebuke to the police who could do nothing about them. The number of people was simply too great for the Interior Commission to want to cause *ad hoc* trouble, as opposed to the premeditated, *agent provocateur* kind which might reasonably be expected after the rally. The massed blue and gold ranks of armed riot police at strategic spots around the Park added to the atmosphere of expectancy, excitement and incipient danger.

"What do we do now?" Tallboys was looking rattled. "You heard him say 'national'? The old bugger's reneging on the deal already. Do we cut it or what?"

"We obey our original orders." She spoke with such contempt. "Allow the King to speak and only cut it if he looks like making a reference to the Referendum or Ratcliffe. Then we cut his mike and the cable transmission. If Sigint Control gives the order we might also cut him, too. We've gone over all this twenty times, please don't get jumpy on me now."

"Surely there'd be a riot."

"The Commission have enough police here to contain a revolution. Now get back to the control panel." Cleo turned to Horatio and pointed the gun at his nose.

"Who's coming here with the tape? We need to know your contact."

"I don't know. He only spoke to me over the fone."

"We've already gone over this," she said resignedly, jabbing the muzzle into his cheek. "Alex got out of Riley that you met someone high up in Tenth May. Sadly either Riley didn't know who, or he was being very brave. All Alex got was a rough description. My idiot husband" — Alex was busy talking to the soundman but Horatio doubted she'd have been any more flattering had he been listening — "let him die too early to be able to fill us in any further. He's a rabies statistic now and unless you tell me, you'll soon be joining him. For one last time," her voice suddenly rose in pitch, "WHO IS JACO-BITE?"

"He was an old guy. I'd never met him before. He didn't tell me his real name."

"Let's see if your description matches Riley's then. It'll go hard on you if it doesn't." Not as hard as if it did, he thought. The only thing keeping him alive now was this information. Marty was listening intently.

"*We are immensely fortunate to have with us today, on his first visit to this country since his family were forced into exile, His Majesty King William the First of New Zealand. . .*" Long and loud applause greeted the announcement, but through it was easily audible the flagrantly illegal punchline, "*and Fifth of Great Britain.*"

"You're right," Cleo called over to Alex. "We might have to close this down. I'll let you know once I've spoken to the boss.

If so, we'll have to get out of here fast. Can you help Alex set it up?" Cleo asked Marty, who nodded and walked over to the control panel. Horatio heard Marty ask Tallboys who'd shot Longman.

"My wife did the housecleaning while I tried to find Fatso and the junior Kiwi. Recognise him?" Tallboys booted Longman in the ribs. "His name's James Longman. Remember him from Oxford? Sound boffin. He's on a four-hour stun. So far. Apparently he didn't see her, so she hasn't decided whether to let him live." Tallboys' emphasis on the first two words of his answer left Horatio in no doubt that he suspected Marty and Cleo.

Unmistakably Etonian vowels filled the Park.

"*My fellow Britons*" — a collective intake of breath from the audience at the use of the severely discouraged and now almost obsolete word by the King, who was standing in the transparent security box on the podium. On either side of the stage, on ten-metre-square screens, his somehow still-youthful smile was projected to the multitude. Cleo ordered the soundman to get her an outside line, "No vid link though." Horatio watched her fingers tap out the numbers. The five twos in a row gave the exchange away. Brussels.

"*One hundred years ago this morning my great-grandfather, King George the Sixth, the King-Emperor, along with his daughter, my beloved grandmother Queen Elizabeth the Second, and Sir Winston Churchill, acknowledged a crowd of a quarter of a million people from the balcony of Buckingham Palace. They were celebrating the Allied victory over Nazi Germany in the Second World War.*"

Horatio counted about six completely politically incorrect statements in that sentence alone. From the look on her face, so had Cleo.

She got straight through. A direct line then. As she did so,

Horatio noticed her press the Record button next to the Scramble switch on the panel next to the fone extension.

"Hi. You're watching it . . . Yes . . . As I said, we're in place to cut sound and vid links. Soon we'll be in a position to cut Rex too if you want. Don't worry, this line's safe, you're on Scramble . . . How about 'Britons'? . . . Yes . . . all right, and same for 'national'? . . . Yes . . . OK, let me know what you want. Everything else's going fine . . . yes. Hang on, here's some more . . ."

"Our great-grandparents were right to celebrate V-E Day in the way they did, having gone through six terrible years of sacrifice and slaughter to preserve world liberty. They had saved these islands from the incursion of foreign institutions and systems of government after nine hundred years of British sovereign independence."

"He's going to try something on. Fatso says he's going to be sending someone here with the tape. We should intercept him easily enough, assuming F.E.'s on the ball. I can't understand why they're not here already though . . . What do you mean? . . . Yes, she told us when he'd be leaving the safe house. We followed him . . . Yes . . . Well, Alex saw Riley and grabbed him. I lost Fatso in the commotion . . . He must have picked it up and made his way to the Embassy . . . I went to Commission Square as arranged . . . Well if she bloody well knew he wasn't going there, she didn't tell me! . . . As it was, Alex only foned to say he'd got Fatso's destination out of Riley in time for me to sprint to the Embassy and find Alex strafing traffic and generally acting as though it was the Gunfight at the bloody OK Corral . . . All right . . . Yes . . . Let me know what you think. Bye."

She turned to Horatio and pointed to a heavy-looking metal box on the floor. "Take that over to Marty. Now."

Horatio walked to the corner of the room and bent down to

pick up the long, silver-coloured container by its handle. It was almost too heavy for him. He averted his eyes from Upham, who was lying just beyond it. Lugging the case to the control panel, he set it down, wheezing.

"Catch!" Cleo tossed him his inhaler. "We don't want you croaking out on us before all the fun starts." Once he had got his breathing back to near normal she threw over a key and pointed to the box, signalling him to open it.

"Our forefathers felt a justifiable pride in the way that they had stood against Nazi Germany. It had been Germany which ravaged the continent from September 1939 until the glorious moment arrived in May 1945 when the British, American, New Zealander, Australian, Canadian, Free French and Russian forces finally liberated all the many and various nations and peoples of Europe."

Disparaging Grossdeutsch Region like that, let alone mentioning A.F.T.A. and A-P.E.Z. countries in such a favourable way in a public speech, represented an enormous risk, thought Horatio, as he clicked the case open. And as for "all the many and various nations and peoples of Europe"! Yet it seemed to be paying off. The crowd was spellbound. It was the first time most people had ever heard so completely different a version of history from the established one. In schools it had long been taught that the pro-federationist Germans, Austrians, Cossacks, Belgians, Italians, Romanians and Vichy French had attempted to create a New European Order but were eventually prevented by a nationalist Anglo-Saxon/Slavic/Communist cabal which had employed a combination of immoral bombing atrocities, starvation and the nuclear threat to win victory. The outside world had combined to stop the unification of Europe. That was the moral of the 1939-45 period taught in schools across the

Union. The King was preaching historical heresy, but there was no protest audible from the crowd.

"Take them out and hand them to Marty." Horatio was looking at a series of long aluminium tubes. He handed them across one by one. The larger ones had U.S.E. Army markings and geiger-voltage warnings stencilled on their sides. Marty slotted each piece expertly into the next.

"It's a laser," said Horatio.

"Clever boy," said Cleo. "Indeed it's *the* laser. And if your Pretender makes trouble, rather than just giving us a paint-dryingly boring history lesson it might become the most famous laser in history."

"But it's far too powerful for that!" protested Horatio. "It won't just destroy the stage and everyone on it. It'd also kill scores of people in the crowd." The King's protective box would be useless.

"Correct. You see we need it to look like a slightly amateurish but altogether vicious job. Indeed *your* job. Check the sights Marty, but under no circumstances fire till I say. We don't want a rerun of the bloody Bridge fiasco."

"What?" ejaculated Marty testily. "I thought I'd got him. How was I to know he'd been moved? That was Sigint's fault."

"Your orders were to take out the entire motorcade. All twelve vehicles."

"I only had three beams. Any more and they'd have traced me."

"And as for passing Bittersich's message onto my home modem . . .!"

Horatio butted in.

"You're setting *me* up for this? It won't wash. Why should an academic be able to use a laser?" Cleo turned to him.

"Oh, it won't wash?" Sarcasm seeped from every pore.

"Well, try this for size. The notorious terrorist murderer Dr Lestoq was identified by nice old Mr Evans downstairs as he went up in the lift. He was with a loyal Kiwi security man who was later found dead on the floor. Another Kiwi is discovered in the car you were seen running away from earlier this morning. Plus there's a dead sound boffin" – talking through his headphones and adjusting the noise levels of the various loudspeakers around the park, the boy could not hear his fate – "and another stunned one who remembers nothing when he awakes except the word 'Lestoq' said as the lift door opened. The fingerprints on the case and every part of the laser match those of the said doctor of philosophy after he, as they tend to put it in these voluntary-death cases, 'turned the weapon upon himself'." Horatio noticed for the first time that Cleo, Tallboys and Marty were all wearing gloves.

"Then there's always Plan B, which is to blow up both of these rooms immediately we've left. Frank's wiring them up now. No pathologist will be able to tell if you, Longman over there and the technician here were stunned or fully conscious at the moment of death. 'Bizarre Terrorist Suicide Pact' – I could almost write the headlines myself. Either way, Plan A or B, if I were a choreographer, I think I'd be in line for an award."

"You'll be seen escaping," answered Horatio lamely. Pathetic. He was flailing around for arguments. He knew he'd have to do far better than that to stay alive.

"Hardly, in all the commotion. People will be on the ground, screaming, dying, panicking and frying. The Department will call in every camcorder for evidence, and we'll accidentally damage, erase or lose any vids featuring us. It'd hardly be necessary, because the 'mad-dog' killer will be obvious for all to see. Well, not *so* obvious, as presumably much of your head will be obliterated by your auto-euthanasia shot." She paused theatrically to let the ghastly plausibility of the plan sink in.

"The disc Marty brought us, which he'll be returning to file this very afternoon, shows that you needed psychiatric treatment at Oxford. You're still on some pretty stiff medication according to the I.D. which Marty borrowed off the Basingstoke police. You see, we know everything about you."

"That was depression, not madness. Not aggressive at all. In fact quite, quite the opposite."

"We're already onto your shrink. He'll call it what we want him to."

Poor Robert Virgil, thought Horatio, yes, he probably would.

"But if anything happens to me . . ."

"All the editors in A.F.T.A. and A-P.E.Z. blah, blah, blah – yes, I know all that and it's bullshit. You didn't have time to set that up when I saw you and we know you haven't had the Memorandum on you since. Anyhow, what editor would print an unsubstantiable, treacherous rant from a proven assassin and mass-murderer? Can't see it making many front pages. This is 2045, the era of responsible journalism, remember, not the 1990s." She paused again.

"Now, you can of course avoid all this nastiness, and instead we can set up Mr Joseph Jacomb here" – she jabbed her thumb at the oblivious soundman – "if only you will tell me one little thing. WHO IS JACOBITE?"

"You are," came a voice from the lift. "Nobody move."

11.12 Saturday, 8th May

The room froze. It reminded Horatio of the moment in the school play when the curtain falls a few seconds late, leaving all the actors posing rigidly after the last line.

His mother was standing in the lift doorway, pulse gun in hand. What had happened to the guard?

Like the moron he was, Tallboys moved. He swung round at her, gun in hand.

Heather shot him. The force of the stun flung Tallboys straight back against the soundman's swivel chair. The terrified occupant was swirled round as Tallboys hit the floor, his gun falling between Horatio's feet.

Cleo and Marty were still armed. His mother was in danger.

For the first time in his life, Horatio did something consciously brave. In a single swift movement he crouched down, scooped up Tallboys' gun and shot Marty full in the stomach. At that range even he couldn't miss. His own decisiveness surprised him, and from the look on his face when he took the stun and was blown back three metres against the wall, it had surprised Marty too.

"Drop it!" Heather ordered, pointing her gun almost in Horatio's eye. His jaw fell. So did his gun.

"*The Second World War is sometimes presented in schools today, in the media generally and by Euro-revisionist historians, as a tragically unnecessary civil war between morally equivalent groups of competing nationalists. Hitler the National-Socialist, Churchill the Tory Nationalist, Roosevelt the American Nationalist and Stalin the Communist-Nationalist. Some nationalists wanting a federated Europe, others against it.*" The King was getting into his stride and the crowd was listening intently.

"*Well, I have to tell you a very different tale. It is one rooted in the foundations of our island story and our ancient, honourable policy of always preventing any one country from dominating the continent. It is the story of decent patriotism and of responsible, respectable nationalism. It is the story of British liberty.*"

Heather walked over to Cleo and, covering her carefully, took Upham's gun from her belt. She stuck it in her own.

"Get him online." She ordered her. "Now!"

"Who?"

"You know bloody well who. I'm not playing your game, you're playing mine now. Just do it."

Cleo walked over to the control panel a few feet away and pressed Redial. Heather picked up the receiver and waved Cleo back against the wall with her gun.

Horatio at last allowed himself to consider a scenario so diabolical that, for all its intrinsic logic, his mind had hitherto shrunk from exploring it.

"It's me . . . never mind that, we've got a problem here. I've just worked out who JACOBITE is. From something Lestoq told me when I tried to get the Memorandum off him. . . Yes . . . I knew this stupid policy of trying to confuse him by all pretending to be against one another would backfire. Never a runner. The Ratcliffe girl just used it to warn him against Marty . . . yes, Cleo Tallboys, who d'you think?

. . . Yes . . . I only twigged about twenty minutes ago. I got here right away when I realised she'd . . . that's right. Tell me, have you spoken to her about our plans for Rex today? . . . DAMN! I thought so . . . did you give her orders? . . . She'll have recorded them . . . Can't do that, what will forensics say afterwards? . . . No, it *has* to be a conspiracy, no one'll believe he did all this on his own . . . He couldn't blow his own nose till he was ten. It'll be like the Thatcher thing all over again otherwise. Grassy knoll theorists till kingdom come! No, it's got to be clean and massive . . . Maybe he can be with the other guy here and I can out-take her now . . . fine, leave it with me. I've got no back-up though. Can you send someone reliable fast? I've only got F.E. downstairs. Plus we've got to lug Marty, and I suppose Tallboys, out beforehand . . . The idiot pulled on me just now so I had to stun him. She'd obviously debriefed him too . . . OK. Yes . . . Yes. I know. God, I'm going to *want* you when all this is over." She replaced the receiver. She was thinking.

So was Horatio. She'd been quite specific about the dates. She'd "remembered it like it was last Monday". She'd returned from a General Staff meeting on the day of the Atgas explosion, 6th April 2016. Yet Riley's thesis had categorically stated that the Bonchurch Road arrests had taken place on 3rd April – *three days before*.

There *was* no Bonchurch meeting for her to come back from on 6th April. She'd been at Ebury Street all along. Something else, too. Cradock had told him Upham had moved the King just before the Entente attack. But his mother had also claimed credit for it. She'd been lying. And she had his pager number; she must have given it to Frobisher before the party.

"I have to tell you, my countrymen, that this was no pointless, unnecessary European civil war we are commemorating today, but

victory over the most evil tyranny ever to have besmirched this planet, Nazi Germany."

Hearing Germany, the Union's *primus inter pares* as it was described in the quality media, described in this way sent a thrill of excitement through the vast throng. They were conscious that they were privileged to be present at an unmistakably historic occasion, one of those watersheds which only happen a couple of times a century, a myth-inspiring moment. When they found the cure for Alzheimer's in 2022 a generation of octogenarians suddenly woke up one morning with their lost memories back. This was like that. The more historically literate in the crowd thought of the Armada, Trafalgar, the Battle of Britain. The catharsis was tangible.

"You recorded him giving you orders, didn't you?" Heather hissed at Cleo.

"I don't know what you're . . ." Heather hit her hard in the mouth with the butt of her Smith and Hutchings 400. Cleo went down but not out. She looked up from the floor, holding her jaw, blood flowing freely from a split lip and broken teeth. Heather gesticulated contemptuously at the prone figures of Marty and Tallboys.

"You might have fooled those *dummkopf* but not me. Now! Where is it?" By a supreme effort of will Horatio managed not to look over to the Record button which Cleo had pressed before speaking to Percival.

"Mummy . . ." he pleaded. She swirled round.

"Don't call me that! *Surely* you must have twigged by now. Call yourself a logician! I'm not your mother, thank God. I adopted you after my miscarriage to keep the bloody marriage going. Don't think I wanted to either. I kept you on after Ebury Street solely for cover. Believe me, there was no pleasure involved. Since then you've been useful occasionally, such as when I nailed that Estonian bitch of yours. She clicked it was me, by the way. That was why you had to be kept away from court." Her eyes flashed again with a snarling cruelty. "And why she never made it to Finland."

That hit him harder than the butt-punch had hit Cleo.

"I will now play you a tape made recently by one of the regional Chief Scrutineers of the Aachen Referendum of May 2015. Last week he was murdered by agents of the Berlin-Brussels Bureau. It will astound you, as it proves beyond any doubt that this great country was tricked, conned, cheated into joining a Union which has been disastrous for her economy, her world standing, her true interests and her God-given independence. . . ."

The fone rang. Heather picked it up, nodded twice and said to Horatio, "Right, that's it. Get against the wall beside her." As Horatio shuffled over he saw her flick the butt switch from left to right. From Stun to Kill.

"Get that over here," Heather ordered the soundman, pointing at the laser. He did as he was told. "You might like to know by the way, Cleopatra, that when I held that cushion over your granddaddy's face he didn't even struggle. It was like flicking over from a boring cable movie."

"Why did you?"

"Because the old fool warned me he was about to spill the beans to the Boy Wonder here. I'd told Sigint we should have out-taken him years ago but no one listened."

"I need to know one thing," said Horatio, as he lined up beside Cleo, his back to the wall.

"What?"

"I can understand about Robert Lestoq, but you also killed James and Flora in Ebury Street. Your own sister and brother-in-law. Why?"

301

"Bad intelligence. We didn't know they were there. It's something I've got to live with." She raised the gun. "At least you won't have that problem."

"I've heard different." Horatio's nerves were whirring. Use logic. Buy time, *any* more time. "And before you kill us you ought to hear it. She's Flora's daughter, after all."

"What?" Heather hesitated. "No, I'm not falling for that." She had raised the gun and was pointing it straight at Cleo, who was leaning against the wall with her hands on her head, blood dripping from her lip. Her eyes were shut. She was muttering to herself. It seemed like she was praying. Had she cracked?

"I've got evidence that Gregory Percival ordered Evans – or whatever his real name is – not to tell you that he knew your sister and her husband had entered the building just before you. He said he wanted your total, unquestioning devotion and judged he'd get it if you killed your own sister for the cause." Horatio was flying blind, but he had to gain altitude, gain time. "He said he didn't love you, that his affair with you didn't matter two cents to him. He cared nothing for you and only tolerates you now because you saved his life so often. He despises you."

"What's your evidence?"

"It's in a letter to Frank Evans downstairs. Cleo took it off me earlier."

"Where?"

She turned to Cleo, who shouted, "Do it now! Fire! Go on! What's keeping you?!"

Horatio could not believe his ears. Was she suicidal?

There was a sudden movement on the floor in the corner of the room and Heather was hit in the small of her back by a force which sent her lurching forward a couple of paces, her arms splayed wide. She collapsed in a heap at Cleo's feet. Just behind where she had been standing, Longman was lying on the ground holding a pulse gun, a sweaty look of triumph on his face.

"Christ, you left that a long time!" yelled a terrified Cleo. "What the hell was keeping you? A moment later and we'd all be out-takes! There's lying doggo and there's bloody well opting out!"

"Sorry, Cleo. I'm a perfectionist. We've got everything we need now."

Horatio was still gawping as his brain rewound. Cleo had got to the control room before Tallboys, who had been sent off to chase around for Cradock. She hadn't stunned Longman at all, just told him to play possum.

He was safe. He was going to live.

"Let's get you away," said Cleo to Horatio. She was in pain, nursing her jaw. She tapped the soundman on the shoulder. He'd heard the shot despite his headphones and was in a state of tormented funk. Cleo asked him whether he wanted to leave and let Longman take over. He nodded, unable to speak. Horatio hoped he would make a reliable witness when the time came.

"Then go now. When you get to the bottom give Frank the security guy the password, 'Auk', and tell him to take the lift up now. After that, just run. Go direct to the police. The regulars, not the politicals. Tell them there's been a terrorist attack here." The soundboy nodded vigorously, still too petrified to speak. She turned to Horatio. "You'd better get lost too, it'd only complicate matters having you here. Steer clear of the authorities till we've cleared your name. We've got the laser, Percival's taped orders to kill the King, Heather's confession and, best of all, these three." She pointed at the unconscious bodies of Marty, Tallboys and Heather.

303

"Jim and I should be able to deal with everything now." She looked at Longman. "You know what to do." Longman looked down at the laser, and then crouched down beside it.

Horatio could see no more because Cleo was hugging his head to her breast.

"I'll never be able to forgive myself for letting that psycho kill Riley and those poor New Zealanders. It was never supposed to be like that. If only I'd driven slower, or swerved more, or . . ." She looked across at Upham's corpse lying by the lift door. "I *told* that bastard Alex to leave it on Stun."

Horatio sucked hard on his inhaler. He was barely taking it all in. Cleo looked deep into his eyes as she pressed "Lift Call".

"You were magnificent. Taking out Marty was crucial. I honestly didn't think you had it in you."

"Neither did I." Modesty came more easily now. Now they had won.

"Try to stay hidden for at least a day." She kissed him on the lips.

"There are so many loose ends, Cleo, so many . . ."

She kissed him again.

"Just like in the power cut at Marty's party? Do you remember?" He smiled. Was this what they said love felt like?

The Admiral's aggrieved, compelling, self-denunciatory voice rose in pitch as it filled the Park.

"I well remember him saying he wanted to ensure that those responsible for this titanic fraud on the British people were brought to book. I suppose that after a lifetime . . ."

Longman, headphones on, was staring out towards the stage towards the King and speaking softly into a mike.

The lift was on its way. Cleo, Horatio and the soundman stood by it. Just as it arrived, Horatio kissed Cleo goodbye.

The doors opened and all three found themselves staring into the barrel of a gun.

A gun held by . . .

A ghost.

30

11.22 Saturday, 8th May

"Hands up all of you! Drop it!"

Cleo let her gun fall to the ground. As Longman looked around to see what was going on, Gemma shot him in the left shoulder. He swirled right round in his chair and hit the control panel, face first, before falling off and onto the floor.

"You!" Gemma pointed to the soundman. "Get to the controls. *Schnell!*"

It was definitely Gemma, but with an accent as German as the Central Bank.

"*I wondered then, as I often do today, whether the same organisation might have been at work in those countries too.*" The Admiral's voice blared over the loudspeakers and to the watching millions at home.

"Everything must be just like normal," Gemma told the technician as she jabbed a number on her watch-fone. Horatio recognised the telltale digits. "Ja, I've cleared up here. Just in time, it looks like. They were just getting out. Frobisher, Ms Lestoq and Tallboys are all stunned. There's a dead man here too. From N.Z. Security . . . ja . . . I've also stunned one of the electricians. What should we do? . . . Nein . . . Ach, it's *far* too late to cut it now. The political damage is done. We have to up the stakes. I've seen the laser. It's fitted. . . . Jawohl!" She replaced the receiver and smiled.

Covering Cleo and Horatio with the gun in her left hand, Gemma heaved the laser, which the soundman had carried over for Heather, up onto the control panel with her other hand.

"Open the window." The technician did as he was told. She pointed the barrel out towards the stage. Straight at the King.

He was standing holding the tape recorder up to the microphone, his image amplified fifty times on the two huge tele-screens on either side of the stage. The crowd, which covered the whole of the northern end of the Park, seemed to have undergone a Damascene conversion. The solid, commonsensical, undemonstrative English had at first been curious about what the King was like and what he was going to say. But the steady, clear, self-critical tone of the Admiral's voice left no room for doubt as to the tape's authenticity. Now they were in a state of restrained but profound fury. There were no cheers or applause, just an angry people listening, thinking, evaluating. Deciding.

Most of the riot policemen stationed around the Park had taken off their helmets so that they, too, could hear it. Many hung their heads. Horatio saw one fellow in tears and another, close to the stage, rip off his blue and gold riot jacket and fling it to the ground. A cheated nation was in the act of rediscovering itself. And its honour.

"Great Britain, the country my friends and I had fought for, was disintegrating before my eyes. On a fraudulent result."

"Thank you for directing me to Frau Dodson, Herr Doktor," Gemma taunted Horatio. "And you are quite right, you know, we *do* call it the Reich when we think no one's listening." As she grinned her gums showed, hyena-like. "I much enjoyed our little journey. We have you on tape now, you see, saying how proud you are of your football hooligans, and talking about the historic error you British made ever allowing the European trading system to get political. We knew you'd confide in a flirtatious Yankee if you were left alone in a car with her for long enough. Suitably edited, it will make excellent copy for the newsagencies tonight."

How could he have fallen for the absurd Southern accent? Oliver had called her "Mutti", she'd known all the verses of "Workers of Europe" at the party and the Union Anthem at the class, she called it "maths", said sixteen-thirty not half past four; she'd never heard of the Indy 500. They hadn't heard of Oliver at the embassy. *Of course* she wasn't American.

Horatio heard himself say, "You'll never get away with it." He wondered why such highly charged moments produced clichés. Perhaps because everyone reverts to type, to instinct, during crises.

"Me? Oh I'm not here. You lasered me at the Entente Bridge, remember? Gemma Reegan's dead. It's you who are not going to get away. You see, Herr Doktor, posing as JACOBITE, Frobisher left the stolen car at the New Zealand Embassy. It was a fine day last Sunday. The roof number was clearly visible. Heather parked at the Rectory and made sure to speed away back to London after killing the Admiral, as you discovered almost to your cost. The Europol satellite pictures therefore connect the car to Ratcliffe's death which, especially since your crazy little journey here earlier, safely connects the New Zealand security apparatus to the King's death. The Asian-Pacific Zone will believe the Information Commission tomorrow when they show the pictures and say it was an inside job."

"Why haven't you killed us?" asked Cleo.

"I'm obeying orders," said Gemma regretfully, seemingly unconscious of the phrase's historical echoes. "Once Herr Evans has blown this place, after we've put Lestoq, Frobisher and Tallboys in the lift, it'll look very strange if they find bodies with bullets in them. One or two, of course, to explain what ruthless terrorists you both were, but you two must not have *predeceased* the explosion. No one will be able to tell if you were stunned or conscious at the moment of death however," said Gemma, raising her pulse gun at Cleo, "so, as you English say, night-night."

Cleo tried to rush her, but took the full punch of the stun on her chest. It stopped her dead. For a moment she balanced on her heels, but then she toppled back, unconscious.

Was it that shot, or had Horatio heard a tremendous crash from behind him? Gemma certainly looked surprised. She seemed undecided as to whether she should deal with the intrusion, turn to the laser, or shoot Horatio. Like Fraser at parties, she seemed to be looking over his shoulder for more important people.

To his horror, she ignored him, turned to the laser, took aim at the King, and squeezed the trigger.

THE TIMES Monday, 10th May 2045
9 pm update

T he SWAT team which stormed the Hyde Park Millennium Tower and shot Ms Inga Hagendorf had been alerted by Ms Penelope Aldritt of this newsagency. She had seen Dr Lestoq, the Oxford don who at the time was believed to be a terrorist suspect, entering the tower with two other men just before His Majesty the King was about to speak. It is largely down to her sharp-sightedness and quick thinking that the entire assassination conspiracy was uncovered in this dramatic way.

Ms Hagendorf, better known as the American popular historian Gemma Reegan, had already attempted to fire a laser beam at the King. Had Mr James Longman not decommissioned it moments before, on the orders of Ms Cleopatra Tallboys, there can be no doubt that His Majesty and very many others would have perished.

The only person left conscious after the SWAT team attacked the transmission control tower, apart from the Park's junior sound technician, Mr Joseph Jacomb, was Lestoq himself. Together they were able to explain to the authorities the sequence of events over the previous three hours. We understand that a tape recording made by Ms Tallboys of all the conspirators' regicidal discussions with Commission Secretary Percival is also being treated as Grade One evidence.

As well as out-taking Ms Hagendorf, the team arrested two

members of the (now-disbanded) Political Intelligence Department. Mr Alexander Tallboys, 30, and Mr Martin Frobisher, 29, were read the multiple murder charges when they came round from their four-hour stuns in the hospital wing of Paddington Green Anti-Terrorist Centre.

Mr Francis Evans, 52, was also taken into custody to be charged with the murder of Judge Jonathan Minter in May 2015 and of Mr Jacob Dodson four years later. It is understood he will also stand trial for the forgery of the Judge's signature on the Chief Regional Scrutineer's Report of the Aachen Referendum, and for conspiracy to endanger lives with an explosive device he was attaching to one of the Tower's stilts when the SWAT team arrived.

Arrested at the same time was Ms Heather Lestoq, 65, who has been charged with the murder of the late Admiral Michael Ratcliffe at his Hampshire home on Sunday, 2nd May. It is believed she will also be charged later today with the murder in April 2016 of her late husband Commander Robert Lestoq, as well as those of her sister and brother-in-law. The killing of Ms Jean Dodson has been attributed to Ms Hagendorf, according to information supplied by Dr Sir Horatio Lestoq, who is at present recuperating in Oxford, nursed by his fiancée, Ms Tallboys. On the expiry of her forty-eight-hour divorce tomorrow she will revert to her maiden name of Ratcliffe.

She is currently considering a proposal by the E.R.M. Provisional Government to act as one of the negotiators presently being so warmly welcomed in Edinburgh, Cardiff, York and Belfast, prior to their discussions on the reunification of the United Kingdom.

It is understood that investigations into the validity of the Aachen result are now under way in the Greek, Danish, Swedish and Portuguese regions of the U.S.E. Should fraud be discovered there also, it is widely believed that the same expression of "People Power" which brought half a million protestors out onto the streets in London on

Saturday and Sunday, might topple the Commission governments in Athens, Copenhagen, Stockholm and Lisbon, just as it did in London.

A warrant for the arrest of Commission Secretary Gregory Percival has been issued. He was last sighted boarding a Europair flight to Urgench, the capital of Uzbekistan.

Sir Horatio, the first Englishman to be created a baronet this century, has accepted the Deputy Editorship of The Times newsagency at a reported starting salary of fifty thousand New Pounds Sterling. The post was recently vacated by Mr Roderick Weaning, whose failure to warn a colleague of the impending attack on the Entente Bridge led to his summary dismissal.

Sir Horatio, as he can now be called after the repeal of the Classlessness Directive announced yesterday, is understood to be in negotiation with publishers for a book about his experiences of the last ten days. Its working title is rumoured to be 'The Aachen Memorandum'.

THE END